LATE

CHECKOUT

Alex Walters

LATE CHECKOUT

WEEKEND

CHAPTER ONE

Even up here, the thump of the disco was inescapable. She paused on the stairs, feeling weary, wondering whether she'd get any sleep tonight. It was nearly ten, and they'd said the music would stop at midnight. But her room was directly over the function suite, and in the mild autumn night the guests had spilled into the small garden at the rear of the hotel, smoking, chatting, drinking. When she'd left the party, the rest had been showing no signs of calling it a night.

She wasn't even sure why she'd come. She'd known hardly anyone other than the bride and groom, and they'd been too busy to offer much beyond an over-enthusiastic hug and cry of apparent joy when she'd first arrived at the reception. They'd had a brief chat about the old days later, but then the couple had disappeared into the crowd of well-wishers and that had pretty much been that.

She'd hoped some of the old crowd would be there, but—apart from a Sergeant who'd briefly been her boss back in Cheetham and whom she'd disliked even at the time—there'd been no-one she recognised. During the dinner, she found herself seated between two aged great-aunts of the bride, who both seemed, understandably enough, to be more interested in chatting to their own relatives than to her. Later, she'd made the effort to track down the Sarge, just to say hello for form's sake, but he'd no real idea who she was, so she'd quickly left him at the table with his wife and teenage son. And that, until the last fifteen minutes or so, had been the sum total of her social interaction across the evening.

Maybe she'd hoped to meet someone. It shouldn't have been impossible, after all. She was only in her thirties, not unattractive. At home, the problem was that, other than traipsing to and fro to work, she hardly ever got out of her flat. There'd been the odd night out with the girls, but those were fewer and further between as her friends became entrenched in their own marriages, relationships and families. She'd considered internet dating but lacked the courage to give it a shot. So the days dragged on. She didn't feel lonely exactly, and in some respects she was quite content with her solitary existence, but she did sometimes feel that life should have something more to offer.

Somewhere in the back of her mind, she'd harboured the vague fantasy that someone here tonight might take an interest in her, chat her up, maybe want to see her again. She hadn't seriously expected it would happen, but—well, you never knew, did you?

Except, of course, that you did, really. It *had* almost happened tonight, or at least for a short while she'd allowed herself to think it might. She'd been standing at the bar, risking one more glass of the bland red wine they'd been serving all evening when she'd heard the voice behind her. 'Let me get that.'

It wasn't much of an offer given that the bar was free for the evening, but she'd supposed it was intended as a gesture. She turned and found herself facing a good-looking man, a year or two older than herself. He seemed vaguely familiar but she couldn't think from where. 'Thanks.'

He ordered himself a lager, and, leading them away from the bar, turned his attention properly on her. The effect was electrifying. This was a man who knew how to impress a woman. It wasn't just that he was decent-looking—though he was and he knew it. It was more that he focused entirely on her. Even though they'd met only seconds before he made her feel as if, in that instant, she was the only thing that mattered to him. She didn't know if it was natural or some form of practised trick, but its impact was undeniable.

'Bride or groom?' he said. 'Or both?'

'What?' The bar was in an ante-room outside the function suite where the disco was in full swing but the noise was still substantial.

'Who do you know? Bride or groom?'

'Oh. The bride, really. I used to work with her years ago. We were best mates in those days, which I suppose is why she invited me. But we haven't seen each other properly for years. What about you?'

'Groom, really. We were workmates, too. Until a few years ago.'

She looked him up and down. Now she thought about it, he looked like a copper. Not too obviously and one of the newer breed, but the signs were there. CID, she guessed, rather than uniform. 'In the force?'

He smiled and tapped his nose theatrically. 'Sort of. But if I told you, I'd have to kill you.' His tone suggested that he was perhaps not entirely joking.

Maybe Special Branch, she thought. Not a line to pursue, anyway. 'Fair enough,' she said. 'I won't ask, then.'

'What about you?' he said, sipping his beer. 'Police, too?'

'Police staff,' she said. 'Intelligence officer. Out in Bolton now.'

His eyes widened slightly. 'Right. Heading back tonight?'

She wondered whether she could sense the way his mind was working. 'Staying over. Didn't want to be racing for the last train.'

'Staying with friends?' The question was asked casually but it partially confirmed her suspicions.

'No, staying here.' There was no point in lying, she told herself. She realised she didn't know quite what response she was hoping for.

He nodded slowly, as if considering his options. 'Well, that's nice,' he said, finally. 'Very nice.'

She wasn't entirely sure what he was referring to. 'It's not a bad old place,' she said. 'And it was too much trouble to head off anywhere else.' She knew she was rambling, waiting for him to make whatever pitch he was planning.

Instead he looked up and past her. It was as if he'd flicked a switch and turned off the full-beam charm he'd been directing towards her. 'Well, it's been good to meet you,' he said, but she felt he was already talking to someone else.

She followed his gaze and saw an attractive dark-haired woman standing at the door to the function suite. The woman, who looked to be barely in her twenties, was gazing round the room, looking for someone. It wasn't hard to guess who that someone might be.

'And you,' she said, allowing a trace of acid into her tone. 'Don't let me delay you.'

He turned back towards her and for a moment she felt a residual trace of that extraordinary personal charm. 'Look, sorry. That's the trouble with things like this. Always too many people you have to talk to.'

That hadn't exactly been her experience, but she made no response.

He hesitated a second longer, and then fished in his jacket pocket for his wallet. As he turned away, he discreetly slipped a business card into her hand. 'Would be good to meet properly some time. I'm London-based at the moment, but I spend a lot of time up here. Give me a call on the mobile.' His tone suggested he had little doubt she'd take him up on the offer.

She watched him make his way through the crowded bar, not directly towards the young woman but as if he'd been approaching from another direction. A practised two-timer, then.

Her first reaction was to tear up the business card and drop it into the empty beer glass he'd left on the table beside her. But she paused a second too long and turned it over. Not Special Branch, but the National Crime Agency. The logo. A PO Box address. A mobile and a landline number. And his name. Jack Brennan. Along the bottom of the card it said: 'Not to be taken as proof of identity.' Well, no, she thought, that was the point of business cards. You gave them to other people.

She knew she'd never call him. Even so, she'd taken her purse from the pocket of the smart jacket she'd bought especially for tonight and slid the card inside.

She hadn't wanted to stay after that. Nothing else was going to happen, however long she stayed. She'd left the bar and made her way up the wide stairs to the first floor. Up here, she could no longer discern the song playing in the disco, but could still feel the repetitive pulse of the bass pounding through the building.

At the top of the stairs, as she turned down the corridor towards her room, she felt a sudden unease. She never liked staying in hotels by herself. As a solitary woman, she felt vulnerable, conscious that hotel staff and others might have access to duplicate keys or the keycard system. And there were moments like this, walking down a deserted corridor at night, not knowing who might be behind each of these doors she passed.

She turned the corner and for a moment her heart almost stopped. A figure was standing in the middle of the corridor, blocking her way.

It took her a panicked moment to register that the figure was another woman. A dark-haired woman, shorter and slighter than herself. And, she realised, somewhat the worse for wear.

The woman looked around, apparently baffled. 'Trying to find my room,' she slurred. ' 'S gone...' She looked back and laughed. 'They've moved it, the bastards. While I was having a drink...'

'What's the number?' There was no choice but to help. The woman looked as if she wouldn't be able to make it downstairs again.

'This—' The woman held up her key. The hotel was old-fashioned enough not yet to have adopted an electronic system.

'That's down the other corridor. At the far end. You've come the wrong way. Do you want me to walk you down there?'

The drunken woman looked affronted. 'Can find my way, now I know where the bastards have moved it to.' Then she paused. 'Well, maybe jus' to the end of the corridor...'

'No problem.' She stood back and allowed the woman to stumble past her, following cautiously as the woman stumbled across the landing, at one point veering dangerously close to the head of the stairs. She stood at the end of the corridor, watching as the woman weaved unsteadily away from her. As she reached the corner of the corridor, the woman turned to wave goodnight, but then lost balance and tumbled sideways, disappearing from sight.

'Shit.' She knew she couldn't just leave the woman without checking she was all right. It wouldn't take a minute, and the worse that could happen was that she'd be told to bugger off. Taking a breath, she began to walk along the corridor. 'Shit,' she muttered again. 'A perfect end to a perfect sodding night.'

That was the point at which he *knew*.

He hadn't even been sure why they were there. A city break, his wife had called it. Kenny Murrain lived and worked in a city, all day and every day. He had no idea why he might want to visit another one, even for a weekend. Not even an overseas city, where some things might be different, where they might have pastries for breakfast or dine late into the evening. Just another rainy part of the same rainy country, full of the same desperate-looking stag and hen parties. Young people pretending to enjoy themselves. Why would he want that?

That was what he'd told his wife, only at greater length. As always Eloise had laughed and made the arrangements anyway.

It had turned out all right, though Murrain wasn't about to say so. The city had been sufficiently different to pique his interest. A cathedral. Walls and ruins that pre-dated the modern urban sprawl. Some winding streets with a scattering of independent shops selling over-priced gifts only bought by people visiting on city breaks. A decent secondhand bookshop where Murrain had wasted an hour while Eloise enjoyed a coffee and cake without his company. She'd coped comfortably with his absence, but, then, she'd had plenty of practice.

He'd been right about the stags and hens but they'd been no problem, other than cluttering up the hotel bar with their early evening pre-loading. He and Eloise had eaten in a pleasant little bistro and an upmarket Chinese place on their two nights, and retired to bed replete with food and wine, ready to enjoy a sound sleep and, in due course, a full English from the breakfast buffet. There'd been pastries too, if Murrain had wanted them, but that had been only a debating point, as Eloise had known only too well after all these years.

Murrain was an early riser, his body clock disrupted beyond repair by years of unsocial shifts. He woke both mornings at the stroke of six, no alarm needed. The first morning he'd lain awake, enjoying the peace and silence and the knowledge that, for once, he had no commitments for the day ahead other than to spend time with Eloise, who snored softly beside him.

The second morning was the same, except this time he woke with a vague, but nonetheless definite, sense that he'd been disturbed by something other than his own internal timepiece.

He lay on his back, listening, wondering what might have disturbed his sleep on this grey Sunday morning. His pre-ordered copy of the Observer being tossed against the hotel-room door? The rippling peal of the cathedral bells?

Screaming.

Distant, faint. But unmistakeable. The sound of a woman screaming.

He climbed silently out of bed in his pyjamas, trying to work out the source of the sound. He pressed his ear against the door, but the screams were no louder. He pulled back the curtains and peered out into the dull, misty morning. The room looked out over a rear garden, the metallic strip of the river beyond. There was no sign of anything or anyone moving out there.

He gazed back into the room. It was a modern hotel, a concrete edifice at the edge of the city centre. The room was a haze of pastel shades, instantly forgettable pictures, a duvet-cover in the chain's corporate colours. There was a flat-screen TV, several unused cupboards, a kettle, a bowl of teabags and coffee sachets, a satirically expensive minibar.

Finally, Murrain realised that the noise was emanating from the heating unit. He pressed his ear against the vent and the sound grew louder. The unit must be part of some hotel-wide central heating system. The sounds were being conveyed along the piping from some other part of the hotel.

He stepped over to shake Eloise's shoulder. 'El?'

She was a light sleeper herself. She turned over and blinked at him, dazzled by the morning light. 'Uh?' She hoisted herself up on her elbow and peered at her watch. 'You know it's six o'clock in the morning? I thought we had a deal. In perpetuity. I put it in the wedding vows. Love. Honour. Let me sodding sleep. Are you looking for a divorce?' This was, after all, only their fifteenth year of marriage.

'Can you hear that, El?' He waved his hand towards the heating unit.

'You woke me to say the heating's noisy? Thanks.' She began to roll back over in bed. 'I'll be consulting a solicitor as soon as I wake up.

Which, for the avoidance of doubt, won't be for at least a couple of hours.'

'No, listen.'

She realised he was serious, and sat up in bed. 'What?'

'Listen.'

She listened, craning her head towards the unit. 'It's a baby crying.'

'No, it isn't. It's a woman screaming. I'm sure of it.'

'It's a baby, Ken. They cry. It's not something you'll have experienced.' That was a familiar jibe, only half-serious like everything she said. She'd long forgiven his extended absences during Joe's babyhood, but she wasn't ever going to let him forget it.

He pressed his head to the unit again. 'It's a woman. It's a woman screaming.' He looked back up at her, his eyes showing the odd, childlike bewilderment that was one of the things she loved about him. Here he was, this big bulky *thug* of a man, twenty-five years a copper, his face permanently less than half an hour away from six o'clock shadow, his whole clumsy frame looking as if it might crush you without even realising. At moments like this he looked like a lost toddler.

'What can you do?' she said. 'Even if you're right. Which you're not. It's a big hotel. The sound could be coming from anywhere.'

'I could report it at reception,' he said.

'Report what? That somewhere, in some room, some woman might be screaming. For some reason. If it's not just a baby. Which it is.'

He was still crouched by the wall, straining his ears. But the sound had ceased. He hadn't even registered its stopping. Now there was nothing but silence.

And that was when he *knew*.

That he had been right. That it was real. That it had happened.

But not here.

MONDAY

CHAPTER TWO

'Excuse me—'

By now, she knew they'd forgotten about her. The interview had been scheduled for forty minutes ago, and they'd just left her here kicking her heels. There was no telephone and, without a security pass, no way back into the heart of the building. No-one had emerged to offer an apology, let alone a cup of coffee. Until now, other than the receptionist who'd shown her in, she'd seen no sign of human life.

'Excuse me—'

She'd caught sight of his head bobbing past the door of the meeting room where the receptionist had left her. She hurried out into the stairwell in time to see the secured door slam shut behind the man. With mounting irritation, she rapped sharply on the door's glass panel but the man continued walking away from her, oblivious to her presence.

Well, bugger them, then.

She hadn't even been sure she wanted to be here in the first place. She'd only come as a favour to her boss who was keen to keep on the right side of the local force. Let's show willing, he'd said. You never know when we might want them to scratch our backs in return.

The truth, of course, was that he wanted rid of her. Not because he didn't rate her abilities—though she'd no real idea whether he did or not—but simply because she was a supernumerary who was draining his staffing budget. He'd been landed with her after last year's game of organisational pass-the-parcel, and now he was looking for a gentle way to off-load her.

For her part, she was equally keen to move on, but only in the right direction. She'd been messed about enough over the last year. According to her file, she was an exemplary officer with a strong track-record and a commendation for her last major assignment. But that hadn't translated into the career progression she might once have expected. She wasn't surprised. Whistleblowers are always praised at the time and then treated as an embarrassment afterward. Your colleagues don't quite trust you and the top brass resent you exposing their failings.

Since her return from the field, she'd been moved from non-job to non-job, and had been left standing when the music finally stopped. So she wanted out, and soon. But probably not to a place where they couldn't be bothered even to acknowledge her presence.

Deciding to cut her losses, she picked up her coat and handbag and walked back out into the stairwell. She just wanted to leave now but even that option seemed denied her. She could make her way down these back-stairs in the hope of finding an exit but the stairway was marked 'Emergency Exit Only' so the chances were that she'd find another secured door down there. The thought of setting off an alarm as she exited was tempting, but perhaps only as a last resort.

She fumbled in her bag for the copy of the e-mail. The note included the name of the officer she was supposed to meet but no contact number. She waited a moment longer, staring through the door panel down the deserted corridor, and then pulled out her mobile and dialled Greater Manchester Police's public non-emergency number.

'Police. How can I help you?'

'Please could you connect me to DCI Murrain.' She gave the name of the building in which she was standing.

'Can I ask what it's in connection with?'

'It's a confidential matter. But it is rather urgent.'

'And can I say who's calling?'

She bit back her irritation. 'My name's Marie Donovan. He should recognise it.' But probably won't, she added silently.

'Please hold—'

There was a burst of anonymous music and then, much quicker than she'd expected, a voice said: 'Murrain's phone.'

'Is he available, please?'

'I'm afraid he's out at the moment. Can I take a message?'

Out. 'I was due to see him for an interview at eleven. Marie Donovan.'

'Ah. Right. Well, don't worry if you've been delayed. Kenny—DCI Murrain—is actually out of the office at the moment—'

'I haven't been delayed. I'm here. I've been here since ten forty-five.'

There was silence at the other end of the line. 'Oh. I see. And where's here exactly?'

'I'm not sure *exactly*,' she said. 'I'm in a meeting room off a back stairwell on the fourth floor. I was shown in here by the receptionist when I arrived. I've not seen anyone since and I can't get out of here because the doors back into the building are secured.'

She could hear a noise at the other end of the phone. The sound, she guessed, of someone scrabbling through papers on a desk. Distantly, she heard a voice say: 'Christ, bloody typical—' Then, speaking into the phone, the voice continued: 'Look, I'm really sorry. I'll come and find you. Don't move.'

As if I could, she thought. Through the door panel, she saw movement at the far end of the corridor. Then there was a tall, slightly gangling figure hurrying towards her. Finally, the door opened. 'Marie?'

She resisted looking around, as if there might be a crowd of visitors behind her. 'Yes, that's me.'

He held out a hand, with the air of a puppy demonstrating a newly-learned trick. 'DI Milton. Joe. Look, Christ, I'm sorry about all this—'

'I'm just relieved I've managed to escape,' she said. 'Thought I'd be stuck here all night.'

'Yes, I know. Bloody stupid, these meeting rooms, aren't they? It's always a pain when we have external visitors. They can't even visit the loo unaccompanied.' He stopped, embarrassed.

'Luckily, I hadn't reached that stage,' she said.

'Let me take you back through,' Milton said, after an awkward pause. 'I can at least get you a coffee.'

She followed him down the corridor and across another stairwell, then into a large open-plan office. There were five desks, all apparently in use, but the room was deserted except for the two of them.

'You were lucky, actually,' Milton said. 'Five minutes later and all you'd have got in here would have been voicemail.'

Donovan looked around the untidy office. 'Busy morning?'

'We've just had a call-out,' Milton said. 'I was delayed in another meeting. That's why I was still here.' He was in the corner of the office, where there was a small sink, a kettle and a compact fridge. 'Coffee?'

'If you've time,' she said. 'I don't want to keep you.'

'They won't miss me for fifteen minutes. Every other bugger's out there. It's a big one, this.' He filled the kettle and put it on to boil. 'You're from the Agency, is that right?' For a moment, she wondered if he thought she was a temp but then he went on: 'Looking to get back to real police work, eh?'

'Well—'

'Only joking. We've had good relationships with you lot, on the whole. But why would you want a secondment to a dump like this?'

She was beginning to find his enthusiasm mildly contagious. He seemed likeable enough, with his slightly ungainly manner, brimming with energy. 'It's been suggested that it might be a good development opportunity,' she said.

'Ah. Got up someone's nose, have you?'

'Something like that.'

He looked at her more closely. His face was slightly too narrow, she thought, as if it had been gently compressed from both sides. 'Marie Donovan,' he said, after a moment. 'I hadn't made the link. Oh, yes, you must have got up quite a few people's noses.'

'I think it depends who you talk to.'

'I'm sure.' He was spooning coffee into two mugs and pouring on the hot water. 'Don't get me wrong,' he said. 'I'm with you all the way. And I'm sure everyone knows you did the right thing. But it doesn't always win you friends.'

'Glad to know my reputation goes before me,' she said.

'Look, sorry, I didn't mean—'

'That's OK. I know you didn't.' She nodded as he offered milk, and then took the mug from him gratefully. It felt as if she'd been stuck in the meeting room for much longer than an hour. 'I'm used to it, anyway. It's better when people say something. Most of my current colleagues just avoid the subject. And me, if they can.'

'So what do you think about being seconded over here?' He spoke as if it was a done deal. Maybe he knew something she didn't.

'I'm open to offers,' she said. 'If the price is right.'

He laughed and sat down opposite her. 'I wouldn't get your hopes up here, then.' He took a sip of his coffee, then said: 'Sorry about this morning. It's not my place to apologise on Kenny's behalf. But he'll be mortified he forgot your appointment. He's got a brain like a sieve for things like that, but his heart's in the right place.'

'Is it?' She didn't feel quite ready to forgive DCI Murrain just yet.

He considered that. 'Well, mostly. Though his amnesia can be usefully selective as well.'

'You think he forgot my interview on purpose?'

'No, I'm sure he didn't. Well, almost sure. But stuff like that doesn't figure high on his agenda. In fairness, whoever was on reception should have done more than just left him a voicemail. Kenny's not great at checking his messages at the best of times. And this morning must have been frantic.'

'What's the call-out?' she said. 'Must be a big deal if it's emptied the office.'

'The biggest,' Milton said. 'Body found in a hotel in Stockport. Young woman, apparently. Particularly nasty killing.'

'Definitely a killing?'

'Looks like it. It would take some dedication to do that much damage to yourself, whatever your state of mind.' He looked pointedly at his watch. 'Are you in a hurry to get back?'

'Not particularly. Think they're glad to see the back of me for a few hours. Why?' She wondered, an uncomfortable second too late, whether he was about to invite her to lunch.

'It's just that I've really got to get over there. To the hotel. Wondered if you felt like coming. Give you a chance to see us in action.'

Not exactly lunch, then, she thought. 'Won't I be in the way?'

'We'll probably all be in the way at this stage,' he said. 'Tripping over each other till Kenny sorts us out. But it's not like you're just a member of the public, is it?'

'I still have my warrant card, actually.'

'There you go, then. I'm sure Kenny will be delighted to see you.'

I'm sure, she thought. The woman whose appointment he forgot. Just the way to get on the right side of your new boss.

It struck her, with a slight start of surprise, that she was already coming to accept the idea of transferring over here. She hadn't even met Murrain yet, and he'd hardly given her the best first impression. She'd met none of the team except Milton. Even so, she was somehow feeling more at home here than she had for a long while.

'OK,' she said. 'Let's go and meet DCI Murrain. If you're sure he'll be delighted to see me.'

'I can't think of anything he'd want more,' Milton said, swallowing the last of his coffee. 'Well, apart from a recently murdered corpse. And he's already got that.'

Even before he walked through the doors, Murrain knew this was the one. There was something about the atmosphere, the *feel* of the place. He stood for a moment in the car-park, ignoring the uniforms, the members of his own team, the scurrying SOCOs, and stared up at the louring building, the blank windows. Something about the place, or about what had happened here, but of course he had no idea what.

'Kenny.' Neil Ferbrache, one of the Senior SOCOs, was stowing some part of his box of tricks back into his white van. 'You're the lucky bugger who pulled this one, then? Congratulations.'

'Lovely morning for it.' It was a fine early autumn morning, with a cloudless sky but the year's first chill in the air.

'Never a good day for something like this,' Ferbrache said, darkly. 'Lads are just finishing off upstairs, then it's all yours.'

'No rush,' Murrain said, knowing it wasn't true. 'I'll just enjoy the fresh air.'

'Make the most of it. Not much fresh in there.' Ferbrache was notorious for his lugubrious manner. It went with the territory, Murrain reckoned, and in Ferbrache's case it was accompanied by a deadpan wit, demonstrated to best effect after a few pints. 'I'll talk you through it once I've finished packing up.'

Murrain stood back to allow Ferbrache to continue stacking equipment in the back of the van. Ferbrache was a stickler for good order—something else that went with the territory—and there was no point in interrupting until he was satisfied that everything was in its place.

It was a sound approach, Murrain thought, gazing round. The spacious car-park was thronged with badly-parked vehicles—a couple of squad cars presumably driven by the uniforms who'd been first on the scene, an ambulance with its blues silently pulsing, the SOCO van, and a scattering of other cars. Murrain himself had driven past the cluster of vehicles abandoned outside the main entrance and parked neatly alongside a row of cars that most likely belonged to hotel residents or staff. He was never irritated by others' disorganisation, but he preferred to maintain his own sense of order. Apart from anything else, it deflected attention from the more eccentric aspects of his character.

He returned his attention to the hotel itself. His initial frisson had long passed, and he felt more able to observe it objectively. He knew the hotel by reputation. It was a respectable enough place, if a little past its best. The sort of place that was frequented in the week by business travellers looking for somewhere inexpensive and reliable at this end of Stockport, and at the weekend by young couples or groups up here for the football or concerts in Manchester, with a scattering of wedding receptions over the summer. As far as Murrain was aware, unlike some of its counterparts on the Manchester side of town, this place normally held no particular interest for the police.

Ferbrache slammed shut the rear doors of the van. 'That's me sorted. I'll go and chivvy up the others.'

'What's the story, Neil? Only got the bare minimum from the control room. Stabbing?'

'Young woman. Late twenties or early thirties, I'd guess. Multiple stab wounds. A pretty frenzied attack. Attacked from the rear, as best I can judge before we've done any proper analysis. Taken by surprise, I'd say. Likely she was sitting down. Wearing only a dressing gown.'

'Someone staying with her, then?'

'Seems likely. Or one of them was visiting, if you get my drift.' He paused. 'No other clothes in the room, including anything else of hers. Looks like everything was cleared out.'

Murrain raised an eyebrow. 'Room booking will be interesting, then. Anything else?'

'Lots of blood. Lots and lots.'

'All the victim's?'

'I'd say so, but that's just an educated guess for now.'

'Prints? DNA?'

'Thousand and one prints,' Ferbrache said. 'Strikes me the cleaners aren't as thorough as they might be. We took any decent ones we could find. DNA? Christ knows. We'll see what we can get from the dressing gown and the body, along with the bedding, and we've taken samples wherever seemed sensible. We'll let you know.'

'Thanks, Neil. I'm sure you've done everything possible.' Murrain sighed. 'OK, let's go and see the damage.' He gestured to the members of the team clustered by the entrance. 'Let's get the show on the road, people. We'll see what's going on, then decide who does what.'

He followed Ferbrache into the hotel lobby. The building was probably Edwardian, maybe once an upmarket family villa. There would have been gardens at the back that had been sold off over the years, allowing other housing gradually to encroach.

He paused for a moment in the spacious lobby and looked around, trying to recapture the feeling he'd had when he'd first driven into the car park. But it was gone, and there was no point in chasing it. This was nothing more than an attractive, well-proportioned room, with a substantial dark-wood reception desk to his left, a comfortable-looking sofa and armchairs to the right, and a thickly carpeted flight of stairs ascending ahead of him. Cosy, he thought.

A worried-looking young man was sitting behind the reception desk, peering balefully at the comings and goings. The manager, presumably. Murrain nodded to him and smiled. 'We'll need to talk to you,' he called. The man nodded, not obviously reassured by this prospect.

The room was on the first floor, at the end of a corridor now sealed with Incident tape. Ferbrache led them to the door and, gently pushing it open, peered inside. 'How we doing, lads? Got the amateurs here now.' He was, as Murrain knew well, only half-joking. 'Easiest if you stay out here for the moment, unless you want to get suited up,' he said to Murrain. 'They've still got stuff to bag up.'

Murrain peered past him into the room, where the white suited SOCOs were still actively finishing off—taking photographs, collecting samples, sorting items into evidence bags. The room might politely be described as compact, he thought—little more than a rectangular box with odd proportions, suggesting that a large original room had at some point been sub-divided. There was a double bed, a small dressing table topped with a kettle and hospitality tray, a couple of bedside cabinets, and, on the wall opposite the door, a built-in wardrobe. A door on the left presumably led into an en-suite bath or shower room, and a too-large window on the right gave a view out over adjacent houses.

The body was visible from the door, lying on the floor in front of the dressing table, face down with the legs collapsed at an odd angle. The dressing table stool was on its side, a couple of feet to the left. Ferbrache's team would confirm, but it looked as if the woman, having been stabbed from the rear, had tried to turn on the stool and then fallen. There was indeed a lot of blood, a wide brown stain covering the top half of the dressing gown, an even broader pool that had seeped out into the patterned carpet. Designed not to show the dirt, Murrain thought. Good luck with that.

He could see the police doctor crouched over the body.

'Any guesses on the cause of death, Pete?'

Pete Warwick didn't look up. 'Funny boy. But, to answer your unasked question, yes, she was alive and conscious when she was stabbed.'

'Time of death?'

'Twenty four hours, at least. I'd guess sometime Sunday morning.'

'That long?'

Warwick finally raised his head. 'Stick your head further in here, Kenny, and you'll be less surprised. We opened the window as soon as we could, but there's no mistaking the fragrant scent of death.'

Murrain had recognised the truth of that as soon as Ferbrache had opened the door. There was a breeze wafting through the open window, but the smell it carried from the room was an unmistakeable mix of blood and putrefaction. Of course he hadn't really been surprised. But he felt no comfort in having his expectations confirmed. He turned to Ferbrache. 'Why wasn't the body found earlier?'

'Do Not Disturb notice on the door so cleaning staff left the room yesterday, apparently.'

'So she—and anyone she was with—weren't due to check out till today?'

Ferbrache shrugged. 'You'll have to ask our friend downstairs, but presumably.'

Murrain knew from experience that Ferbrache could rarely be tempted into speculation outside his remit. It was one of the qualities that made him an effective SOCO, if a limited conversationalist. 'Any other clues on identity so far? From the room, I mean.'

'Not a sausage. There are no personal items in there. No handbag. No purse. No phone. No clothing except the dressing gown, and that's one of Primark's finest.'

'All been cleared out, then.'

'That's the thing.' Ferbrache frowned. 'If you want my opinion—'

Murrain looked up. It was unusual for Ferbrache to offer any opinion that wasn't based on thorough analysis. 'Go on.'

'Well, it looks like a professional job to me. Not the killing. That looks anything but. From the number and position of the wounds, that looks like the work of someone who lost it. Frenzied. But the clear up afterwards. It looks like someone's gone to a lot of trouble to remove anything that might provide any clues to the killer's or the victim's identities.'

'You said there were prints, though?'

'Lots of them, yes. And maybe we'll strike lucky with those. But there're several places that have been carefully wiped down. The top of the dressing table. The bedside cabinets. The places where we might have been most likely to find the prints of whoever did this.'

'Doesn't seem to square, though, does it?' Murrain peered back into the room. 'An attack as uncontrolled as that. And then a methodical clear up?'

'No,' Ferbrache agreed. 'But that's how it strikes me. Your job to explain it.'

'Thanks for that, Neil.' Murrain smiled. The last thing he wanted was to discourage Ferbrache from offering the benefits of his undoubted wisdom. 'But, no, I'm really grateful. You've spent more time up to your oxters in murder scenes than any of us. If that's how it strikes you, I'll wager money you're right.'

Murrain was delighted to see that Ferbrache actually appeared to be blushing. Another first. 'Well, it was just a thought.'

'And a good one,' Murrain said, judging it was time to move things on. 'How long do you reckon your boys are going to be?'

'Fifteen, twenty minutes. Then we'll get the body shifted. And it's all yours.'

'Something to look forward to.'

Murrain made his way back downstairs and surveyed the small cluster of officers waiting in the lobby. 'Anyone know where Joe is?'

One of the DCs, a very solidly built young man called—inappropriately, Murrain had always felt—Will Sparrow, said: 'Phoned to say he's on his way. Was stuck in some Resources meeting so got held up.' He glanced across at his colleagues in a way that suggested some subtext to this information, but for the moment Murrain had no inclination to pursue it.

'OK. We've got a major enquiry on our hands here. Looks like a Category A. Once Joe gets here, I'll get him to start putting all the gubbins together.' Administration was one of Joe Milton's strengths, whereas it definitely wasn't one of Murrain's, which was why Milton had ended up attending that morning's Resources meeting in the first place. 'In the meantime, we need to start talking to the hotel staff and any other guests. I'm assuming no-one's been allowed to leave since the body was found?'

Sparrow shook his head. 'Uniforms have done as good a job as they could. But a lot of the guests had already checked out or left for the day. The body wasn't found till the cleaner went in mid-morning.'

'OK. I'll go and have a chat with our friend over there. See what information we can get. You lot can start taking statements from the guests who are still here. Especially anyone who stayed overnight Saturday. Anything they saw, heard. Especially any of them who were in the rooms close to the crime scene. What about the cleaner who found the body? Where's she?'

'He,' Sparrow corrected, then looked embarrassed. 'Apparently. Young Polish lad, according to the uniforms. He's downstairs.'

'You go and get a statement from him, Will,' Murrain said, 'as you're clearly less prone to gender preconceptions than I am. Obviously need to refresh my diversity training. Find out if he was on duty yesterday as well, or if not who was responsible for that room. Again, anything he saw or heard. You know the drill.'

He watched as the officers dispersed into the dining room and lounge where the guests and staff had been asked to wait. This was the supposed 'golden hour' when you were most likely to gather valuable evidence, while the details were still fresh in people's minds, when witnesses were still relatively accessible. But most serious crimes, and especially most killings, were easy enough to resolve. The perpetrator was generally obvious—the spouse, the parent, the young thug caught on CCTV with the bloody knife still in his hand. Most were in no state to deny what they'd done, even where the evidence wasn't already damning.

But this had a different feel. It was likely to be a Category A because the perpetrator was, at least for the moment, unknown and because, given the nature of the killing, there could be a continuing threat to public safety. It might be, of course, that they'd have some immediate breakthrough in identifying the victim or the other occupant of the hotel room. But Ferbrache's comments had given little reason for optimism.

Murrain's instincts were already telling him that there was going to be nothing simple about this one. And Murrain, as his colleagues knew all too well, was always one to trust his instincts.

CHAPTER THREE

The nervous young man sitting behind the hotel reception looked up as Murrain approached. He was smartly-dressed in a dark grey suit. To Murrain's eyes, he looked more like an aspiring management consultant than a hotel manager.

'DCI Murrain. Senior Investigating Officer. You're the manager?'

'Owner,' the young man said. 'Well, co-owner. With my mother.'

'Family business? It's a big place.'

'My mother and father bought the place and did it up about twenty years ago. I took it over when dad died, a couple of years back.'

'Hard work, I imagine,' Murrain said.

'Been a tough few years, but things are picking up now. There's not a lot of competition round here, so we do all right.'

'Good to hear. Is there somewhere private we can chat, Mr—?'

'Callaghan. Tim Callaghan.' The young man was looking even more nervous than before. 'I don't know if there's much—'

'It's just some background questions,' Murrain said. 'Imagine you'll know the place better than anyone.'

Callaghan nodded. 'Come though into my office.'

Murrain followed him into a surprisingly capacious room behind the reception desk. It was a well-ordered place, with a couple of largely empty desks topped with PCs, shelves neatly lined with box files, a row of filing cabinets, and, in the far corner, a hefty-looking safe, presumably for guests' valuables.

Callaghan gestured for Murrain to sit. 'Would you like some coffee?' He began to reach for the phone but Murrain shook his head. 'Don't worry. My people will have started interviewing your staff. Just routine stuff, you understand. Whether they saw or heard anything.'

'So how can I help you?'

'Not good for business, something like this, I imagine?' Murrain said.

'You tell me. I've never had an experience like this before. We've had the odd guest drop dead on us, but only from natural causes. It's an unpleasant business, this.'

'Very,' Murrain agreed. 'I'm assuming you didn't know the young woman? The victim, I mean.'

'Why would I?'

'I meant, she wasn't a regular guest?'

'No. I didn't actually see her when she checked in on Saturday but the name wasn't familiar.'

'So what information do you have about her? And about who she was with?'

'Well, actually, not much about her. We ask guests to fill out a registration form, but it looks as if it was completed by—well, the man who was with her.'

'Do you have the card?'

Callaghan reached for one of the box files on the shelf behind him. 'We ask for details like address and e-mail, mainly so we can use them for marketing purposes. We go through them every few days and transfer the details into the database if they're not there already. Of course, these days a lot of guests book on-line or through internet agencies anyway so we've often got most of the data anyway.'

'And in this case?'

The relevant card was on top of the stack. Callaghan had clearly already been looking at it. 'The room was booked over the phone. It tends to be the older guests who do that these days.'

'Do you ask for a credit card number to confirm the reservation?'

'We don't normally bother if it's a telephone booking. People occasionally let us down but it doesn't happen often. We're not usually so busy we're turning people away.'

'A phone number?'

'Yes, we usually ask for a contact number. Hang on.' Callaghan turned to the PC on his desk and tapped on the keyboard. 'Should be in the booking system.' He scribbled a number down on a pad next to the PC. 'There.'

It was a mobile number. Murrain pulled out his own phone and dialled. As he'd expected the number was unobtainable. 'Probably a fake,' he said, 'but we'll get it checked out.' He tore off the top sheet of the pad and slipped it into his pocket. 'What about the names?'

'Mr and Mrs James,' Callaghan said. He looked down at the card in the folder. 'He's written Mr P G James on the card. No mention of his wife, but then there often wouldn't be.'

'Address?'

Callaghan slid the card across the desk towards Murrain. They'd have to get it checked out for prints and DNA, but Murrain had little hope they'd find anything. The address given was in south west London, an SW19 postcode which Murrain knew from the tennis to be Wimbledon. 'Does your PC have an internet connection?'

'You want me to search on the address?'

'See if it's real,' Murrain agreed.

Callaghan tapped the details into the PC and swivelled the screen around so that Murrain could see. The postcode was unrecognised, and the street address was not found anywhere in the Wimbledon area. The only equivalent London street name was in Ealing. 'Presumably another fake, then,' Murrain said. It would probably be worth checking the Ealing address in case it had some significance to the killer, but that was clutching at straws. There was no other useful detail on the card—no e-mail or car registration.

'No great surprise, but at least we're finding out what we don't know. What about at check-in? You must ask for card details then?'

'We do normally, yes. But not this time. For some reason, they paid cash, up front.'

Murrain sat back in his chair. 'That must be unusual?'

'Very. Obviously, we don't have a problem if people want to do that.' He smiled. 'I've occasionally had people asking for discounts for cash.'

'Who was on duty when they checked in? Who'd have been on reception?' It was the first slender lead, Murrain thought. The receptionist was more likely to remember someone who behaved abnormally.

29

Callaghan returned to his PC. 'Ivana,' he said. 'She does weekends and evenings for us, usually. She was on last Saturday.' He looked apologetic. 'I'm afraid she won't be here at the moment. She has a day job, as well. Cleaning.'

'But you've got contact details?'

Callaghan nodded, and set a document off to print. 'Address, phone numbers, all that. It'll all be there.' He took the sheet off the printer and pushed it over to Murrain. An address somewhere in Heaton Mersey.

'Any CCTV in Reception?' Murrain asked.

'We've got one covering the room. And a couple of cameras outside. I'll get the weekend stuff downloaded for you. It's all electronic.'

'OK. Have you got the check-in time?'

'Just after four, according the system. It would have been a busy time. We had a wedding reception on Saturday. Bride and groom turned up at about 3.30 so we'd have been fully engaged with that.'

Murrain sighed inwardly. Possibly deliberate, he wondered. Turning up at a busy time so the hotel staff's attention would have been elsewhere. The car-park would have been heaving with arriving guests so the chances of catching anyone on the CCTV would be reduced. On the other hand, looking on the positive side, it potentially gave them a stack more witnesses. 'We may need to interview those who were here on Saturday, where we can. You've presumably got contact details for the wedding party? At least for those who stayed over?'

'Is that really necessary? I mean, the bride and groom will be in the Maldives by now.'

'Sadly, I don't have the budget to follow them out there,' Murrain said. 'And I imagine their minds will have been elsewhere on Saturday. But it'll probably be worth talking to anyone who's local. Depending on what progress we make from talking to people here.'

'I'm sure we can let you have those details.'

'If we can have names and addresses of anyone who was staying here Saturday night or last night. I assume most of them will already have checked out, except for those we're interviewing at the moment?'

Callaghan nodded. 'We were fairly full Saturday night—mix of the wedding guests and people up for the weekend. All but a handful of those would have checked out Sunday morning. We're always quiet on a Sunday night but a few people stay on because we do a cheap deal. We had a couple of business types who were staying over before meetings who'd have checked out early this morning. Both regulars.'

'Don't imagine they'll have much to tell us if they only came last night but add them to the list. Do you have any longer-term guests?'

'No. It's mostly just weekenders and people traveling for work and the like.'

'And we'll need a complete list of staff, with contact details. Helpful if you could indicate who was on duty on Saturday or Sunday. Any staff live in?'

'A few. We've got some staff accommodation at the back. We get people coming to work here over the summer. Anything else?'

'Not for the moment. We'll probably need to talk to you again in more detail.' Murrain had been jotting items down on his notepad. 'But, for the moment, list of guests. List of staff. Any other contact details you can give us on the wedding party. CCTV footage from the weekend. Any other thoughts that you might have? Any other possible sources of information we've not talked about?'

'Well, there was one thing—' Callaghan was fiddling with the PC again.

'Go on.'

'I noticed when I checked the booking record this morning. Looks like that room ordered breakfast in the room on Sunday morning.'

'Breakfast?'

Callaghan's eyes were fixed on the computer screen. 'Guests can put an order out on their door before eleven. You know, to get breakfast in bed.'

'You're saying our Mr James did that?'

'Looks like it. We charge extra so he shouldn't really have done it given he'd paid cash, but I don't suppose anybody bothered to check.'

'And the breakfast was delivered?'

31

'Presumably. Cereal. Full English. Coffee. Eight o'clock.'

Murrain blinked, trying to process this information in his head. They'd got no definite fix on the time of death yet and the pathologist was unlikely to commit himself to anything so definite. In his own mind, though, Murrain had no doubts.

'Breakfast for two?' he asked, quietly, already knowing what the answer would be.

'No,' Callaghan said. 'That's the thing. It was breakfast for one.'

CHAPTER FOUR

Murrain emerged from Callaghan's office with the air of an animal blinking back into the light. The hotel reception was almost empty except for a couple of uniforms standing guard in the entrance. Murrain eased his way past them and stepped out into the car-park, feeling the need for cool autumn air.

What sort of killer takes breakfast immediately after committing the act?

A pretty cool one, that was for sure. And one with a strong stomach.

Murrain had assumed initially that the breakfast had been left untouched. That the killer, or perhaps even the victim, had ordered it the previous night, not realising that by the time it was delivered it would be superfluous to requirements.

But that hadn't been the case. Callaghan had called down to the kitchen and spoken to the young Slovakian waiter who'd delivered the breakfast. There had been a 'Do Not Disturb' notice on the bedroom door but he'd knocked and a voice from within—a male voice, as far as he'd been able to judge—had told him to leave the tray outside. He'd returned an hour or so later to collect the tray. The food had been eaten, the coffee largely drunk, and the tray replaced in the corridor. The 'Do Not Disturb' sign was still in place.

That was an interesting point, Murrain reflected. The young Polish cleaner had entered the room this morning presumably as part of his usual routine. That suggested the 'Do Not Disturb' sign had been removed at some point after the collection of the breakfast tray. If the killer had intended the body to remain undiscovered for as long as possible surely the best tactic would have been to leave the notice in place. The hotel would eventually have realised that the guests hadn't checked out but that probably wouldn't have been until later in the day.

A very cool killer, then. Not too worried about how quickly the body would be found once he'd had time to organise his own exit.

Murrain made a note to check whether the 'Do Not Disturb' notice and the room key had been found. The likelihood was that both had been simply left in the room. He wondered about the possibility of finding prints or DNA on the breakfast tray, but the waiter had confirmed that all the cutlery and crockery would by now have been through the hotel's industrial dishwasher and that the cloth napkin had already been laundered. Murrain had been left in the unusual position of cursing the hotel's efficiency.

Another question was when the killer had left the building. Murrain would normally have assumed that no-one would want to spend longer than necessary in the same room as a badly mutilated dead body. But then he'd have assumed no-one would want to eat breakfast in those circumstances either.

Even so, it was unlikely that the killer would have remained in the room longer than necessary. He'd obviously stayed long enough not only to enjoy his full English, but also to conduct the thorough clear-out that Ferbrache had described. That would presumably have taken an hour or so. It was hard to see why he might have stayed longer, increasing the risk that he might be discovered at the crime scene. Something else to check with whoever was on reception at that point, and also on the CCTV footage. They'd also have to check out whatever CCTV might cover the surrounding area, particularly the busy A6. It might be feasible to link recordings of cars parked in the hotel with those entering or leaving the area at the appropriate times. More likely to be successful for the Sunday when the traffic would have been quieter.

It was at this point in any major investigation that Murrain felt most conscious of the multitude of possibilities opening up before them. Most often, of course, you never reached this stage. Generally, the answers were right there in front of you and it was simply a matter of showing your working as clearly and rigorously as possible.

But in this kind of case, where there were no immediate answers, all he had was an unimaginable vista of questions. A vast array of data to be gathered and analysed and cross-checked in the hope that something, some clue or connection, would emerge to help them focus their attentions. No doubt it would, and soon. But for the moment, it felt little short of hopeless.

He'd known from the start this was a strange one. He'd known from the moment he'd woken on Sunday morning to hear the screaming. He'd known it was real, that it was happening, and that it was happening *now*. He just hadn't known where or how. Or, more to the point, *why* he knew. Why *he* knew. Then this morning he'd felt that same old tingling, that same sense of something falling into place. Some connection being formed.

He felt the same sense now. Suddenly, unexpectedly, the same frisson.

He watched as another car pulled into the car-park, the driver slowing briefly to wave his warrant card at the uniform at the gate and proceeding to pull in alongside Murrain's own car.

Joe Milton. Finally. The man who could help inject some organisation into this chaos.

Still troubled by the unexpected sensation he'd felt a moment before, Murrain walked over to greet his colleague. He stopped as the passenger door of the car opened.

Milton emerged from the driver's side, smiling in a manner that told Murrain unequivocally that something awkward was coming. 'Sorry I'm late, boss. Resources meeting. And then—well, I was playing host.'

Murrain looked quizzically at the woman now standing by Milton's car. She looked as uncomfortable as Murrain felt.

'Marie Donovan,' she said, holding out her hand.

Murrain took the hand and shook it while his brain went into overdrive. After a moment, he said: 'Shit. I mean, good morning. I mean, Christ, I'm sorry—'

She was smiling now. 'It's OK. I can see you're busy.' She gestured towards the hotel. 'Joe's looked after me very well.'

'Oh, but, I mean, it's inexcusable of me—' Murrain looked towards Milton in the hope that the younger man would dig him out of this but Milton was showing no inclination to intervene. 'What time was I supposed to see you?'

'Eleven. But, like I say—'

Murrain was looking at his watch. 'God, I'm sorry. I'm hopeless for things like that. Joe will have told you. It's really nothing personal.'

'I didn't take it personally,' she said. 'I didn't know whether you'd really only agreed to see me under sufferance. I thought we were maybe just wasting each other's time.'

'No, no. Not at all,' Murrain said, though he knew he'd had to be talked into going ahead with the interview. Yes, they were short-staffed, like every other bloody part of the force. But he was always suspicious of being landed with other people's cast-offs. 'No, I was really keen to meet you.'

That wasn't quite the truth but he realised now that he was glad she was here. He couldn't pin it down but it was something to do with the sensation he'd experienced just a few moments before. That inner sense that something else was falling into place.

'Look,' he said, 'we need to talk properly.' He was racking his brain to remember the details of her background. She was with the National Crime Agency, he knew that, and she'd been working as an undercover officer. Before that, she'd been a DC with the Met, with good experience of doing analytical work. Well-regarded, he knew. Then she'd got herself mixed up in all that recent mess that had left the Agency reeling. Not her fault—and in fact she'd emerged with a commendation—but he could imagine she might be looking for a change of scene. 'Are you OK to hang around for a while?'

'Nobody seems too eager to have me back,' she said.

'It'll give you a flavour of how we work,' Murrain said. 'For good or ill. Though I can't say there's anything typical about this case from what we've seen so far.' He was smiling now, more relaxed. 'And first I'm going to demonstrate Rule 1 in the Kenny Murrain Manual of Management. Which is to delegate everything to DI Joseph Milton at the earliest possible opportunity.'

Milton had clearly known this was coming, and seemed untroubled by the prospect. 'OK, boss,' he said, with only a touch of weariness. 'Fill me in.'

Fifteen minutes later, Milton was camped on his mobile phone in the corner of the hotel lounge, leaving messages, calling in favours, setting activities in motion. It was clear he was in his element.

'Good job he finally deigned to turn up,' Murrain said. 'I was getting worried I might have to start doing some of that myself.' Murrain had settled himself in another corner of the lounge with Donovan sitting opposite. 'It'll take Joe a quarter of the time it would me.'

'He seems very organised,' Donovan said.

'Much more than I am,' Murrain conceded. 'Hence my diary cock up this morning. Joe's a natural administrator. But it's not just that. He knows how to sweet-talk people as well. You might not think it to look at me but that's not one of my strengths either.'

Donovan took a sip of the coffee Murrain had summoned up. Actually, when she did look at him, she doubted that was true. He didn't have Milton's easy-going charm, but she could imagine he usually got his way. There was something about him that commanded respect. He was a tall, slightly shambling figure, with tightly-waved grey hair cropped close to his head. She could imagine that, in his younger day, he might have been one to throw his weight around but there was no sign of that now. He spoke softly, with a faint trace of a Lancashire accent.

'So why do you think you might want to join us?'

She was about to reply that, actually, she wasn't sure that she did. But she knew by now that wasn't true. She'd already been won over by Milton but had reserved judgement on Murrain until she'd spent some time in his company. Already, though, she found herself warming to him. He seemed straightforward, open. She also had the sense that, for all his self-deprecation, he knew what was he was about. 'I just get the feeling that the Agency's a bit of a dead end. For me, at least,' she said, after a pause.

'You've ruffled a few feathers?'

'Not deliberately. I just found myself in a situation.'

'And you handled it impeccably, from what I understand.'

'I wouldn't go that far,' she said. 'But I hope I did the right thing.'

37

'Exposed a corrupt cop,' Murrain said. 'Has to be the right thing.'

'Not everybody shares your view, unfortunately. I mean, they don't say it openly. But some think the boat was better left unrocked.'

'That's one reason why the police still have a lousy reputation. There are too many—including some at the top—who'd rather brush things under the carpet than risk embarrassment. They can't see we have to apply the highest standards to ourselves.'

'They gave me a commendation. Told me they'd look after me. It's never happened. It was partly my fault, maybe. I made the decision to move up here. I'd had enough of London.' She stopped. 'Long story, but there were too many memories. I wanted a new start. They told me that was fine. Plenty of opportunities. But I've just been moved from pillar to post. Never given a substantive job. Just 'special projects'.' She'd already said more than she intended and she was conscious that some bitterness had crept into her voice.

Murrain was watching her with interest. 'I've been there,' he said. 'Or somewhere similar. What is it you really want to do?'

'That's the question. At first, I thought I wanted to go back into undercover work. I think I'm good at it, and I actually enjoyed doing it. Well, 'enjoy' probably isn't the word, given what happened. But I found it stimulating. Challenging. So at first I thought it was what I wanted—'

'But it isn't?'

'It was just that sense of wanting to get straight back on the horse, you know? Prove I was still up to it. Now I've had time to reflect, I'm not sure it would be healthy to go back there. Given what I went through.'

'I can see that,' Murrain agreed. 'Not sure it's the healthiest of lifestyles at the best of times. You think you'd prefer a move back into investigatory work?'

'If I were talking to HR about this,' she said, 'I'd be saying things like: I think it's time for me to broaden my experience, increase my skill-set.'

Murrain shrugged. 'There's no need to talk bollocks with me. What is it you really want?'

'I'm a police officer not a bureaucrat. I want to do things I find satisfying. That make me feel I'm doing something worthwhile. I've worked in CID before. I enjoyed it and I think I was good at it. So, yes, I'd like to come back to it.'

'I suspect you won't escape the bureaucracy,' Murrain said. 'That's the future of policing. But you come well recommended. We're short of experienced officers. I'd be very happy to take you.' He paused. 'Not being a bureaucrat, I don't know about the ins and outs of this. Are you technically still a police officer?'

'I don't think so. But I still have my warrant card. Triple-warranted, in fact.'

'If you want to come, I'll get Joe to check it out. Might have to be a secondment to a police staff role, at least to start with. But I'm sure we can make it work.'

'I want to come,' she said, surprised at her own certainty. 'I'd like to join you.'

'Sure you don't want time to think?' He laughed. 'People usually want time to think before they come to work for me.'

'No,' she said. 'It feels like the right thing.'

'I'll set the wheels in motion.' It felt like the right thing to him as well, Murrain thought. He'd known from the moment Milton's car had turned into the car park. He couldn't have said how or why but he had no doubts. 'Now you've passed the rigorous selection process, I ought to give you a sense of what you're letting yourself in for. This isn't typical but it's quite a case.' He climbed to his feet and led her over to where Milton was concluding what had appeared to be an endless series of calls.

'Nearly there,' Milton said, cheerily. 'The Incident Room's being set up. I've gone for one of the meeting rooms in Fred Perry House. Not quite on the doorstep, but nice and sizeable and it won't tread on anyone's toes. Got us a good Office Manager, two of the best analysts, good forensics guy—'

'The thing I didn't mention is that our Joe is never one to hide his light under the proverbial bushel,' Murrain said.

'If I don't sing my own praises, no-one else round here's going to bother.' Milton smiled at Donovan. 'Are you coming on board, then?'

'Assuming we can sort out the paperwork.'

'Another job for Joe, then,' Murrain said. 'Never happier than when he's sorting out paperwork. Speaking of which, we should see how the interviews are going.'

Donovan and Milton followed him out into the hotel reception. Ferbrache and the team of SOCOs were standing outside the entrance having a final chat while one of them smoked a cigarette. He probably needed the fresh scent of nicotine after the time he'd spent in that hotel room, Murrain reflected. 'You done, Neil?'

'All yours,' Ferbrache called back. 'Leave it tidy, won't you? I'll get the salient points to you as quickly as I can.'

Murrain waved his thanks to Ferbrache, then turned back to Milton. 'OK, Joe. You reckon we've got ourselves properly organised?'

'Pretty much,' Milton said. 'I've got a few loose ends to tie up, but I'll do that in a bit. Then it should all run like clockwork.'

'And he's not even joking,' Murrain said. 'OK, shall we go and take a proper look at the crime scene? See if it gives us any inspiration.' He began to make his way up the stairs.

Milton watched him for a moment, and then turned back to Donovan. 'The thing you need to understand,' he said, in what might have been a stage whisper, 'is that, when he talks about inspiration, he's not entirely joking.'

CHAPTER FIVE

Murrain felt the sensation again as soon as he entered the room, stronger this time. He hesitated in the doorway, almost as if there were a physical barrier to his entry. It was Marie Donovan, he thought, somehow she was a part of this. But there was no point in forcing it. All he could do was ride with it, keep his attention focused, hope that some sense would emerge.

He continued into the room and stood for a moment. There was a stiff chill breeze blowing in through the open window but still no disguising the rich mix of blood and putrefaction. The body had been removed and the wide brown bloodstain on the carpet was fully exposed. There were further splashes of blood all around it—on the bed, on the dressing table and stool, on the walls behind. No doubt Ferbrache and his team had gleaned some information from the patterning. For Murrain, all it did was confirm the ferocity of the attack.

'Jesus,' Milton said, from behind him. 'And you say the guy sat and ate his breakfast in here?'

'Apparently,' Murrain said. 'Don't know whether he managed the black pudding.' As he spoke, he wandered around the room, apparently aimlessly, peering behind the television, out of the open window. He crouched and peered under the bed, keeping himself carefully away from the bloodstains. He pulled open the doors of the fitted wardrobe and stared inside. The wardrobe was empty except for some unused hangers and a spare blanket, which had been examined by Ferbrache's team and then left on the ground. Murrain continued gazing into the space for a few moments as if about to identify some overlooked clue. Then he slammed the doors shut and turned back to Milton and Donovan.

'Everything cleared out,' he said. 'Ferbrache reckoned it was a very thorough job. Fingerprints wiped. Everything rigorously cleaned down.'

Donovan was standing in the middle of the room, looking round her, as still as Murrain had been restless. 'It has a familiar feel,' she said, finally.

'Go on.'

'I don't know. I'm probably talking rubbish.'

'I'm big on feelings. Instinct. Joe will tell you that.'

'He's very big on feelings and instinct,' Milton agreed. 'Much bigger on that than on filling in forms. Or remembering appointments.'

Murrain ignored him. 'So go on.'

'I've had contact with professional killers. I mean, the real pros. The contract merchants. One time, I got much too close to one.'

'You're not saying that this is the work of a pro?' Milton said.

'The killing doesn't seem that way, no. But—well, my experience is that the people who do that kind of work are highly functioning psychopaths. They don't think like the rest of us. They don't have the same kind of empathies, the same connection with their fellow human beings. There's no emotional connection. But they know how to hide it. They know how others expect them to behave and they play the game.'

'I don't see—' Milton began, and then stopped at a glance from Murrain.

'The pros don't normally kill like this because—well, why would they? They get no personal satisfaction from the killing, any more than they feel any moral disgust or revulsion. It's just a job. Their only real question is whether the price is right. So they just want to make it as simple and risk-free as possible.' She paused and looked around the room. 'So the killing itself doesn't feel like a pro job. It feels more personal. But we're dealing with the same kind of individual. The sort of person who can sit and finish breakfast while there's a mutilated corpse lying feet away. The sort of person who can calmly make sure everything's thoroughly cleaned before leaving.'

Milton gave Donovan a wry smile. 'Your specialist subject, is it? Psychos and professional killers?'

'Like I say, I got much too close to one once. Worked alongside him without realising it. It's a long story. But it made me want to find out what sort of person could do that. I had a—well, I took a career break after my last major field assignment and used it as an opportunity to kick off an MSc in Criminal Psychology. I've been researching a dissertation. So, yes, I suppose it is my specialist subject.'

'You'll be a whizz on Mastermind,' Milton said. 'But I still don't understand the breakfast thing? Isn't that just taking an unnecessary risk?'

'It's about control. If most of us had committed that sort of act, we'd be in an almighty panic and just want to be out of the place. This sort of person often reacts differently. They calm themselves down, force themselves to think logically. Once they've done the deed, they want to act as normally as they possibly can. The breakfast might have been a conscious way of creating a pause between the act and the clear-up. Like stepping back into real life.'

Milton was looking sceptical. 'Sounds a scarily cool customer.'

'I can tell you,' she said. 'The real ones are exactly that.'

Murrain was still wandering, apparently aimlessly, around the room, as if he were absorbing everything he was seeing and hearing. 'So if this is one of your highly functioning psychopaths, the question remains—why kill like this? You reckon it could be because they'd lost it and weren't functioning quite so highly after all? Or because they wanted it to look amateur?'

'Or because they wanted it to be high profile?' Milton added. 'I mean, if they'd just quietly pushed this woman under a bus, we might not even have recognised it as murder. If it had been a discreet professional killing we'd have probably assumed it was an underworld thing and treated it accordingly. Might not even really have made the media. But this—' He gestured around the blood-drenched room. 'Until we prove otherwise, we have to treat this as a real threat to public safety. We can't keep it quiet.'

Milton gestured towards the bed which Ferbrache's team had now stripped off its covers. 'Small point, and I'm sure Ferbrache will provide us with the details, savoury or otherwise, but do we know if the bed was slept in?'

Murrain thought back to when he'd first entered the room. 'It was disarrayed, as if someone had slept in there. I suppose at the moment we've no reason to assume the victim and the killer didn't spend the night in here together. Seems the most likely scenario. Why?'

'I was just thinking about Marie's theory. A crime of passion is one thing. But it's another to spend the night with someone knowing you're going to top them in the morning.'

'As you said, a scarily cool customer.'

Murrain had moved to stand by the window, as if seeking inspiration from the view of the now emptying car-park or the rows of grey Victorian houses beyond. 'It raises another question, though,' he said, slowly. For a moment, he felt as if some image was appearing before his eyes, something he could half-glimpse behind the mundane landscape below. But as he blinked it was gone, its significance still unknown. He turned back into the room. 'If he was going to kill her anyway, why wait till morning?'

Oh, for Christ's sake.

Beth threw down her pen and stomped back from the tiny studio into the main part of the house. It was the fourth time the phone had rung in the last hour. The first one had just been a click and then silence, the familiar sound of some marketing company's autodial failing to connect. The second had been a distant voice enquiring if she'd recently had an accident that wasn't her fault. She'd assumed the caller had been selling legal services rather than enquiring out of curiosity, but she hadn't stayed on the line to find out. The third had been an automated caller with an incongruous American accent requesting that someone she'd never heard of should call the number of what Beth imagined was a debt collecting agency. No-one of the given name had lived in this house for the last ten years at least, so Beth assumed they'd just conjured up a wrong number from somewhere. Whatever, she had no intention of calling back and engaging with them.

She hardly even knew why she bothered with a landline number. The only real, non-junk calls she received on it were from her parents.

They were old enough still to assume that mobile phones were ruinously expensive and to be used only in emergencies. Twice a week, she'd receive that dutiful call from the depths of the West Midlands. 'Just checking that everything's OK, dear.'

Yes, of course. Why wouldn't it be? Just because she hadn't been in a serious relationship for the last three years, her business was slowly going down the pan, and she wasn't sure where her next mortgage payment was coming from. But, of course, she shared none of that with her parents. 'Everything's great. You don't need to worry.' As she well knew, however disastrous her own life might currently be, in the next few years it would be her turn to start worrying about them.

Now, she snatched up the phone fully prepared to bark some obscenity at the time-wasting caller.

'Beth Monk?' A male voice, she thought, though slightly high-pitched. Odd-sounding, slightly distorted. A mobile and not the best of lines, she thought. An accent she couldn't quite place. Perhaps slightly camp.

She bit back her intended response and took a breath. 'I'm sorry. Who's this?'

A pause. 'You don't know me. I'm a friend of Mac's.'

Mac. Hearing the name was like receiving a sharp blow in the solar plexus. She found that for a moment she could hardly speak. 'Mac?' She realised that, simply by repeating the name, she'd answered the caller's opening question.

'Yes, I understand you know him?'

The present tense was anything but appropriate. Three years. Three years in which she'd been alone, apart from a handful of calamitous dates and a couple of even worse one-night-stands. 'I've no idea where he is, if that's what you're asking.' She could feel the coldness in her voice. Unfair to direct it at this caller, who might have his own reasons for wanting to track down John McKendrick. But she couldn't bring herself to care.

'No, no that's not it. Like I say, I'm a friend. I'm in contact with him.'

She could feel her hand tighten on the cordless phone. In contact. After three years of nothing. 'Look, I'm sorry. I don't know why you're calling, but I'm really not interested—' She was lying, of course. But she knew that, for the sake of her sanity, she couldn't allow this to go any further.

'Can you at least give me a minute to explain? I know you must be busy, and I really don't want to waste your time.'

'You already are doing,' she pointed out. 'Look, it's not your fault, I'm sure. But I really don't want to hear anything from John fucking McKendrick.'

She was on the point of ending the call, but the voice said: 'He said you'd say that. It's just that he wanted the chance—'

Her finger hesitated, momentarily but fatally, over the cut-off button. 'He deserves no fucking chance. You tell him that. You make sure he fucking understands that.'

'He's dying.'

There was a long moment's silence while Beth absorbed what the caller had said. 'Is this some sort of game?'

'No. Mac's dying. That's what I called to tell you. Bowel cancer. They reckon three, four months, max.'

Still clutching the phone, she slumped down on her worn sitting-room sofa, feeling as if all the breath had been knocked from her. Moments before, her hatred for McKendrick had been pure and straightforward. Now it felt clouded and confused. She hated him no less, of course. Nothing the bastard had done was changed by what he might now be facing. But she'd loved him once, and now he was dying. 'Christ, I'm sorry,' she said. 'That's an awful thing to happen to anyone.' Even John fucking McKendrick, she added silently to herself.

'Yeah. Poor bugger.' There was perhaps a touch of Australian in the accent, she thought now. The voice of an ex-pat Brit who'd spent a few years living in the lucky country. That would make sense.

She took another breath and readied herself to end the call. It was dreadful news, but news about someone who no longer concerned her. That had always been Mac's way. He sucked you into things, into his life, his circle. He got you to do things you'd never intended. He got

46

you tangled in the mess of his existence. He'd landed her in the mess she was in now, she reminded herself. She'd probably made it worse, but Mac had set the downward wheels in motion.

'Look, I'm really sorry to hear that. But, with respect, I'm really busy and—'

'He wanted me to meet up with you. So I could explain—'

'What?' She could feel her temper fraying. 'I don't need any explanations. We're way, way past that.'

'No, that's not what I meant. He doesn't expect anything from you—'

'He's already taken fucking plenty.'

'That's partly what this is about.'

'So what is it about? I'll give you two minutes.' She knew, now, she should have ended the call long before.

'I met Mac in New Zealand. Dunedin. I've been out there doing some consultancy work—'

'I don't need your life story. One minute.'

'He's living out there now.'

'I could have guessed. As far as possible from his responsibilities here.'

'Mac and I met in a bar. Got talking. We got on OK. He was living out there on his own. I'm travelling out on business regularly, stuck in hotels by myself. So we meet up whenever I'm visiting. I was out there last week.'

Jesus, she thought. He really is going to give me the whole shebang. She was tempted just to leave him rabbiting on, but she knew she was past that point now. 'And?'

'That's when he broke the news. It was a real shock. I mean, he looks fine. You wouldn't know—'

'Yeah. I get it.'

'I hadn't seen him for a couple of months. He'd only had the diagnosis confirmed a few weeks before. It had hit him hard. Made him reflect on his life.'

'That's a first, anyway. He's got a hell of a lot to reflect on.'

'He knows he's treated people badly—'

47

'He's always known that. It's never stopped him doing it again.' It was only after he'd gone that she'd realised what an unmitigated, wide-ranging shit Mac had really been. For months, one revelation after another had popped out of the woodwork, each exposing some new and deeper level of duplicity and selfishness. 'Look, I don't know who the hell you are. But you know nothing about what McKendrick did to me. Whatever he's told you, the reality was ten times worse.'

'However much you despise him, he despises himself more.'

'I sincerely doubt that.'

'He just wants to make some peace with himself. With the world.'

She had a sudden inkling of where this was going. 'Christ, he's found God, hasn't he?'

She knew from the pause she'd hit the bullseye. 'It's given him some comfort in the face of this awful news.'

'Jesus, a bloody deathbed conversion. I should have guessed it. That's just bloody typical. He's probably setting himself up to do some deal with God or St fucking Peter.'

'That's not—' The voice sounded genuinely pained.

'What are you then? Some sort of vicar?'

'Since you ask, I'm a Christian. I introduced Mac to this.'

She almost found herself laughing at the pompous piety of his tone. 'OK,' she said. 'You've had well over your two minutes now, and you still haven't told me why you're calling.'

'Mac's stuck out there,' the caller said. 'A long-haul flight's beyond him. He knew I was coming home this week, so he asked me to contact some people on his behalf.'

Some people. She wondered quite how many people Mac had screwed over and whether he was directing this crap at all of them. 'There's nothing I want to hear from him.'

'He's written a letter. I mean, hand-written. He wanted me to deliver it personally.'

'He might as well have just stuck it in the post. I'd still have thrown it straight in the bin.'

'And I've some items. Things he said belonged to you.'

Beth couldn't bring herself to speak for a moment. 'What sort of things?'

'Various things. Some envelopes which look like they're full of photos. He didn't say exactly what was in there, but said you'd want them. And some personal items. Some jewellery.'

She was tempted for a moment to tell him just to dump the whole lot. But she knew, or she thought she knew, what would be in there. The photographs would be a whole load of personal pictures, some of them intimate, that McKendrick had taken during their time together. Photography has been one of his enthusiasms and he'd used a professional non-digital camera he'd bought years before, carrying out his own developing. He was good at it, and she'd been flattered by the quality of the pictures he'd taken. He was a sweet-talker and the poses had become increasingly daring. She knew there'd be some in those envelopes she wouldn't want anyone else to see. She wondered whether Mr Born-Again Christian had been tempted to have a peek.

She hadn't been surprised when the boxes of photographs had disappeared along with McKendrick. It was his collection, after all, and at the time his disappearance had had far more immediate consequences for her. It was only a few days later that she'd realised McKendrick had also walked away with those potentially embarrassing images. She consoled herself that they weren't digital and were unlikely to end up spread across the internet. Even so, knowing what she knew now about McKendrick, it had felt like another form of violation.

The jewellery was something else again. That, almost as much as the emptying of their joint account, was what had been most devastating. Most of it wasn't hugely valuable—although, for someone in her financial position, the value wasn't negligible—but it had included items that meant a lot to her. There was a bracelet she'd inherited from her late grandmother, presents her parents had bought for her on significant birthdays. She'd assumed McKendrick had just taken the lot and flogged it. She couldn't imagine why he wouldn't have done. But there was a lot about McKendrick she'd never understood.

49

'And I have a cheque for you?'

'A cheque?'

'Mac says that you loaned him some money. I don't know whether this covers the whole amount. But it's a sizeable sum.'

Jesus. It sounded as if McKendrick really was trying to make his peace with God. Loaned. Well, that was one word for it. Waltzing off into the unknown with the entire contents of their joint accounts. She'd even contacted the police at the time but they'd shown only token interest. He'd done nothing strictly illegal as far as the money was concerned, and the taking of the jewellery sounded more like a domestic dispute between an estranged couple. In the end, she'd let it drop, too exhausted to pursue whatever avenues might be open to her.

The truth was, whatever she thought of McKendrick, she couldn't afford to ignore this. She was as good as broke. The design work wasn't coming in, and she'd more or less exhausted her limited savings. The money that McKendrick had taken wasn't a fortune by some people's standards but it was money she'd saved up over several years before she'd met him. It would be enough to tide her over for a good few months. Maybe enough time to get the business back on its feet.

'You can't just send me this stuff?' She was conscious she'd been silent for too long.

'I promised Mac I'd deliver it personally. That seemed important to him.'

'Where are you based?'

'I live in London. But I'm staying up in your neck of the woods for work this week, if you're around. I'm fairly tied up with business meetings but we could meet Tuesday or Wednesday lunchtime, if either of those is good for you. We could meet at my hotel or I can come to you if that's easier?'

She had no intention of inviting this stranger to her house. 'No point in dragging you out here,' she said. 'Why don't we meet at your hotel? Where are you staying?'

He gave her the name of an upmarket chain hotel out on the edge of the Peak District. 'Why don't we meet in the hotel bar? We can go through the stuff and grab a bite to eat.'

'That's fine,' she said. It seemed churlish to refuse. Whatever she might think of McKendrick, at least this guy seemed to be trying to do a good deed. 'I'm sorry,' she added. 'I didn't catch your name.'

'My fault,' the voice said. 'I don't think I gave it. Jack Brennan.'

'Look forward to meeting you, Mr Brennan. I'm sorry if I was a bit abrupt.'

'I understand entirely. Mac seems to have been—well, whatever he was, he's a changed man now.'

She made no response to that. 'Shall we say Tuesday, then? About twelve-thirty?'

'I look forward to it.'

She ended the call. It was only then, as she was standing with the phone in her hand, that it occurred to Beth to wonder how Jack Brennan might have got hold of her ex-directory landline number in the first place.

CHAPTER SIX

'How the other half live, eh?'

'I've seen worse,' Murrain said. 'Much worse.' He glanced across at Will Sparrow with mild amusement. Back at the ranch, they referred to him as 'posh boy'. He wasn't really posh, and he was hardly a boy any more. But he was from relatively upmarket Bramhall and he was still, if only by a few months, the youngest member of the team. He seemed to enjoy living up to the nickname. He'd put on a few pounds since he'd joined them, and it wasn't difficult to imagine him, in twenty or so years time, as a potential Chief Constable.

It was actually a moderately respectable terraced row, tucked into the network of side-streets just off the main A6 on the south side of Stockport. Some of the houses looked more neglected that others, and Murrain guessed there was a divide here between renters and owner-occupiers. The houses were small, opening directly on to the street with maybe a small garden or yard at the rear. Nothing fancy, but nothing too shabby either.

Their destination was one of the better maintained properties, though Murrain imagined that Ivana Berenek might well fall on the rental half of the divide. The house was brightly and recently painted. The sparkling clean windows suggested a house-proud occupant. The road was quiet, and Sparrow was able to park the pool car immediately outside the front door.

The door opened before Murrain could press the bell. Inside, there was a smartly dressed young man, perhaps twenty years of age. He was wearing a dark grey business suit that, to Murrain's inexpert eye, looked bespoke and possibly expensive. His open-necked white shirt gleamed as brightly as the windows. 'Yes?'

'We're looking for Mrs Berenek. We understand she lives at this address.'

The young man leaned forward and glared at them suspiciously. 'Who's asking?' He had neatly trimmed dark hair combed back from a slightly sallow forehead.

Murrain held his warrant card out an inch or so from the young man's nose. 'We'd like to talk to Mrs Berenek, if she's in.'

The young man stared at them for a moment and then looked past them, with the air of someone expecting other visitors. Finally he turned and bellowed: 'Mum! Someone to see you.' He looked back at Murrain. 'She'll be down in a minute. I was just off out.' He pushed his way brusquely past, and Murrain watched with mild curiosity as the young man climbed into an aged but high accessorised BMW and pulled out into the road, slightly too quickly for the conditions. 'Good to meet you, too,' Murrain murmured to himself. He wasn't sure why, but he'd made a point of memorising the car's registration number before it sped away.

'Can I help you?'

Murrain turned back to the doorway. 'Mrs Berenek?'

'Yes?'

He held out his warrant card again, less aggressively this time. Ivana Berenek looked anxious and the sight of the warrant did nothing to change her expression. It occurred to Murrain that a mature Eastern European woman might find nothing reassuring in a visit from the police. 'You're aware of the incident at the hotel?'

She nodded, and now there was some relief in her face. 'Yes, of course. Mr Callaghan was good enough to call me. This is my day off from the hotel, you understand.'

'Of course. May we come in? We just need to ask a few questions. I hope it won't take long.'

She stepped back to usher them into the narrow hallway. 'I'm afraid it's a little untidy,' she added, apologetically. 'My son—'

The small sitting room looked far tidier than Murrain's own house ever managed. The only visible signs of recent human occupation were a folded copy of The Sun on a formica coffee table and a pair of new-looking trainers left incongruously in the middle of the carpet. Mrs Berenek picked them up disdainfully and tucked them behind the sofa. 'Can I get you some tea?'

'No, thanks. We won't keep you any longer than we need to.' Murrain lowered himself on to one end of the sofa, and watched as

Sparrow, having considered the available seating options, chose a high-backed wooden chair by the window. He had the air of someone who'd been thrown unexpectedly into a totally alien environment.

Mrs Berenek perched on the front edge of an armchair facing Murrain. 'How can I help you?'

'We understand you were on duty over the weekend?'

She nodded. 'I do the day shift at the weekend. Eight till five, usually. Mr Callaghan likes to have someone experienced there for the weddings and other events. It's usually our busiest time.' She spoke good English, with only the faintest trace of a foreign accent. Murrain wondered how long she'd been living in the UK.

He'd normally have delegated this kind of interview to more junior members of the team. Sparrow and his colleagues had spent most of the afternoon systematically interviewing the hotel staff and remaining guests, and were now making telephone contact with the guests who'd checked out that morning before the body was discovered. In principle, the interview with Ivana Berenek was simply another in that sequence.

But Murrain, being Murrain, was keen to meet face to face with the one witness who had, as far as they knew, actually met the killer. He wanted to look her directly in the eye, hear what she had to say, listen to the sound of her voice. So he'd left Milton busy overseeing the establishment of the Incident Room and the collation of the information they'd gathered to date, and headed down here with Will Sparrow for company.

'So you were working on Saturday afternoon?'

'Yes, it was busy. We had a big wedding. A big buffet, you know, and then the disco in the evening. People coming and going. The wedding guests who were staying wanted to get checked into their rooms. And then we had another party arrive. A hen party. They'd already been drinking, I think. It was chaos.' She looked momentarily exhausted even from describing it.

The killer had picked his moment, Murrain thought. 'Do you remember checking other people in on the Saturday afternoon? I mean, apart from the wedding and the hen party.'

She nodded and tapped the side of her forehead. 'I have a good memory. There were four other couples checked in, I think. I know that because all the wedding guests had a discounted rate, so I remember the ones who were not part of that.'

'Do you remember checking in a Mr James?'

She frowned. 'I don't remember names so well.'

'We think he paid in cash upfront, rather than using a credit card. Does that ring any bells?'

Her face brightened. 'Oh, yes. I remember that. He kept trying to use his card, but it was refused by the system. He said that he'd been having problems with it for a few days so he'd taken out some cash just in case.'

'That must be unusual?'

'We get older customers who want to pay cash, but it's not common. People sometimes have problems with their cards but we usually sort it out. They use an alternative card or they contact the bank, or whatever.'

'So Mr James will have stuck in your mind?' Murrain was watching her carefully. He'd half-expected a recurrence of the sensation he'd experienced in the hotel but so far there was nothing. No connection.

'He'd have stuck in my head anyway,' she said. 'I mean, not his name. But the way he looked.'

'Go on.'

She closed her eyes, as if trying to summon back the memory. By the window, Sparrow was frantically scribbling notes though Murrain had no idea what he might be writing. 'There was something odd about him. Something not quite right.'

Finally, as she said that, Murrain sensed something. Some image that refused to come into focus. Some sound he couldn't quite recognise. He could almost taste the incongruity she was describing. 'Tell me what he looked like. As best you can.'

She closed her eyes again. 'He was—medium height. Not as tall as you. Maybe as tall as your colleague.' She gestured towards Sparrow. 'His hair was dark. Black or very dark brown. Quite long.'

She paused. 'That was one of the things that seemed not right. The hair. I wondered if it was perhaps a wig. Or perhaps just dyed. But, you know, not quite natural.'

Murrain nodded, encouraging her to go on. If it had been a wig, then her description, however good it might be, wouldn't get them very far.

'He had glasses. The kind that turn into sunglasses, you know.'

'Photochromic,' Sparrow offered from across the room. 'I used to wear them. Before I got contacts.'

'He'd come in from the sunshine,' she said. 'So they were still quite dark. I couldn't see his eyes properly.'

'Was he clean-shaven?' By now, Murrain was half-expecting that 'Mr James' might also have been wearing a false beard.

'Yes. He looked—quite young. Not much more than a boy.'

Murrain judged that Mrs Berenek was in her early sixties. Her definition of youth was probably even more elastic than his own. 'How old would you say?'

'I don't know. Mid-twenties, maybe.' She stopped again, and Murrain could see she was thinking. 'That was another odd thing,' she said. 'He dressed older than he looked, if you see what I mean. His clothes looked middle-aged.'

'Young people can still dress smartly,' Murrain said. 'Like your son for example.' He'd intended it as a mildly ingratiating compliment, but Mrs Berenek's reaction was almost one of disgust. 'Hah. That one. Takes after his father.'

Murrain thought it wiser not to enquire more deeply. 'But when you say his clothes looked middle-aged—?' he prompted.

'I'm not sure how to describe it. He had a big raincoat, and a suit with, you know, stripes.' She waved a hand in the air to illustrate a vertical stripe. 'He was wearing a tie—blue and white stripes, I think. It looked like it might be something official, like a club or a college or something. I don't know. The whole effect just seemed old. Not the clothes you'd expect a young man to be wearing.'

Murrain nodded. 'You've a very good memory, Mrs Berenek. I wish all our witnesses provided this level of detail. If you don't mind,

I'd like to sit you down with one of our experts to put together a detailed description and perhaps a photofit picture.'

The anxiety had returned to her expression. 'I would have to come to the police station?'

'That would be best,' Murrain said. 'But we can drive you in and bring you home, or take you there from work tomorrow. I'm sure Mr Callaghan won't mind.'

She was still looking worried. 'OK. I am keen to help you. You believe this Mr James is your murderer?'

'He checked into the room where the killing occurred,' Murrain said, carefully. 'That's all we know at the moment.' He stopped to allow her a moment to recover herself. 'Do you remember anything about the person who was with this Mr James?'

For a second, she looked puzzled. 'There was no one with him,' she said.

Murrain glanced across at Sparrow who was still engrossed in his note-taking. 'You mean he checked in as a single guest?' The check-in card, he recalled, had referred to 'Mr and Mrs James'.

'No, sorry. I am not being clear. He checked in with his wife. But she was not there. Not when he checked in.'

'Did he say where she was?' The sensation he'd felt was still there, no stronger or weaker than before. He felt, as he did so often, as if there were some understanding or knowledge that was tantalisingly out of reach.

'He said he'd left her in the town centre, shopping. He said she loved it and he hated it so he'd left her to get on with it while he checked in for a rest. He was supposed to be picking her back up at around five. I didn't think much of it at the time. I was more intrigued to see what sort of woman would have married such an odd man.'

'You didn't see them come back later?'

'I went off at five—well, probably half-past before I got away. There was a lot to hand over, you know? I didn't even see him go out again, if it was before I went off. But it was very busy. I was probably in the middle of dealing with someone else when he went past. It was young Michelle on the desk after me. She might have seen something.'

'We'll check,' Murrain said. The Michelle in question would no doubt be on their list of interviewees, and might already have been seen. He'd have to make sure that this was checked out with her. But it seemed more likely the whole story was a fiction. That there had been no wife, shopping or otherwise. Which took them back to the question of who the victim was and how she'd ended up in the killer's room.

They'd taken nothing for granted, of course, but until now their working assumption had been that the killer and the victim had arrived together. That they'd been, in whatever strange sense, a couple. But if that wasn't the case, it opened up new possibilities, some of them far from comfortable.

'Thank you, Mrs Berenek. That's been most helpful.' He made a move to rise. 'We'll be in touch about getting a more formal statement and description from you.' He registered the way her hands tightened on the arms of the sofa. 'It really is just a formality. But an observant witness like yourself could make all the difference in catching whoever did this.'

'Yes, of course. I will do my best to help.'

'We're very grateful.' Murrain stood in silence for a moment while Sparrow packed his notebook and pen into his briefcase. 'Your son seemed in a hurry. Was he off out?'

Mrs Berenek shook her head. Her expression had hardened and it was impossible to decipher it. 'He tells me nothing. Work, I think.'

'Ah. What line of work is he in?'

She was already at the front door. 'Like I say, he tells me nothing.'

Murrain followed her into the hallway. 'Children,' he said, aiming for a light-hearted tone. 'It's always the way, isn't it? Only come running when they want something.'

She opened the door in what was unmistakably a gesture of dismissal. 'He will get nothing from me.'

Murrain was on the point of offering some rejoinder, but then he caught her expression. 'Well, thank for your time, Mrs Berenek. We'll be in touch.'

As they walked back to the car, Murrain risked a glance over his shoulder. Mrs Berenek was still standing at her front door, as if to ensure that they really had departed. 'What was that all about?'

Sparrow shrugged. 'Other families are always a mystery.'

Murrain watched while Sparrow fumbled for the car keys. 'Do me a favour, though, Will. When we get back, run Berenek and his car reg through the PNC. See if we've anything on him.'

'You think he might have something to do with this?'

'I can't see it, can you? But there might be something there that's of interest to us. Worth a look, anyway.'

Murrain paused for a moment and looked back to where Mrs Berenek was still standing. The sensation was stronger now. Something in the air, taking shape.

Definitely worth a look.

CHAPTER SEVEN

'Think we're just about there.'

'That's good, Paul. Then all we have left to do is catch the killer.'

It took DS Wanstead a moment to realise that, as so often, Milton was joking. 'Bugger off, Joe. I've been working my socks off this afternoon.'

'No, I can see that. Seriously, you've done a bloody good job.' He waved Marie Donovan forward to meet the florid-faced DS. 'Come and meet DS Paul Wanstead. Kenny thinks I'm the bureaucrat, but Paul's the only truly organised person we have round here. Paul, this is Marie Donovan, who we hope is coming to work with us.'

Wanstead was probably only a little older than Donovan herself but had the air of an old-school copper. He was overweight and dressed in clothes that, in varying degrees, seemed either too large or too small for his bulky frame. He managed somehow to look both physically uncomfortable and yet entirely at ease. 'Please to meet you,' he said. His gaze moved up and down her body with an expression that stayed marginally on the right side of salacious. 'Hope you don't regret the decision. Where are you coming from?'

'The NCA,' she said. 'On secondment. That's if everyone can swing it.'

Wanstead raised an eyebrow. 'Thought the traffic was all the other way,' he said. 'You're supposed to be the elite.'

'Not sure it works that way,' she said. 'Depends what sort of policing you want to do. Anyway, it's a long story.'

'Well, look forward to working with you, if you haven't changed your mind now you've met Joe.'

'We'll see.' She smiled. 'I've been impressed so far.'

'Paul's going to be the Office Manager for the case,' Milton said. 'He's done all the real work in getting the MIR set up today.' He gestured towards the array of desks and equipment that filled the Incident Room. 'Like I say, a bloody good job.'

The place certainly looked well-organised. There were rows of workstations and computer terminals, a line of filing cabinets, two electronic whiteboards and a couple of traditional notice-boards. Everything the modern murder enquiry could want. 'You got the staffing sorted, Paul?'

'Still waiting to hear back on who Admin are going to provide, but other than that I think it's all in place.'

'That's good.' He turned to Donovan. 'You wouldn't believe how difficult it is even getting the basics in place sometimes. Everybody says it's a priority, but in this place everything's a priority. Mind you, it's easier now we're here. We'd never had got a room like this in the old station.' The force had moved a couple of years earlier to share accommodation with the local authority. Everyone had complained about the move and many continued to complain about the proximity to non-police staff, but most acknowledged that the new building provided a substantially better working environment. Even if, as Donovan had discovered, its meeting rooms did not always offer easy access to the casual visitor.

She'd come back up here with Milton because she was still keen to find out more about how this team worked. In particular, she wanted to find out more about Murrain. She'd asked a few questions on the journey back but Milton had deftly batted them away with non-committal responses. In any case, he'd been on the hands-free for much of the drive, getting an update from Murrain on the visit to Mrs Berenek and from Paul Wanstead about the general progress of the investigation.

'Anything new, then, Paul?' he asked, now, though it was only fifteen minutes or so since they'd spoken over the phone.

'What do you think? Same old same old. Nothing significant coming out of the interviews so far. Still waiting on the reports from the SOCOs and the doc.'

'Still no clues to the victim's identity?' Donovan asked Wanstead.

'Nothing. We've been checking back through all the Manchester mispers for the last year or so. There are one or two possible matches that we're following up, but nothing that leaps out at you. There've been no relevant reported missing persons in the last few days as far as we can see, not even nationally, though obviously we're still getting up to date info from other forces on that.'

'What about the hotel guests? Or even the staff?' Milton asked. 'Any chance that anyone's gone missing there? Given what this Berenek woman told Kenny.'

'Yeah, that's a scary thought, right enough. If the killer and the victim weren't an unhappy couple and the killer checked in by himself, it does raise the question of how he got her into the room, doesn't it? Difficult to see how he could have dragged her through the whole hotel against her will.'

'Which suggests,' Milton said, 'that either she went there willingly, or he didn't have to drag her very far.'

'We're going through the hotel guests and the staff to double-check that. But it's hard to see how someone could have disappeared without being missed.'

'I don't know. I mean, weddings are always a mix and match of groups that don't really know each other. The bride's relatives. The groom's relatives. Bride and groom's own friends who don't know any of the relatives. People from their workplaces who don't really know anyone. You know what I mean. If someone was on their own, they might vanish and people would just think they'd slipped off or crashed out early. It's possible.'

Wanstead gave a visible shudder. 'I've never liked hotels. Something unnatural about all those strangers sleeping so close together.'

Milton regarded him curiously. 'You know, Paul, I get new insights into your character every day. We'll need to think about the CCTV footage as well. See if there's any footage of our Mr James checking in or sign of the two of them coming into the hotel or in reception. We've assumed they spent the night in that room together, but I suppose it's conceivable she might have come early Sunday morning.'

'Much less likely,' Wanstead said. 'Hotel normally locks up overnight. Midnight in the week but not till one am at the weekend. Wedding festivities officially finished at midnight and there was some to-ing and fro-ing after that, but apparently the doors were locked at one as usual. Then reopened at six. We've interviewed the night porter. He's sure no-one came into the hotel between one and six. He was on the desk then till he went off duty at eight. Says it was even quieter than most Sunday mornings. He saw no-one at all apart from staff coming on duty, until the first guests started drifting down to breakfast around seven-thirty.'

'Makes sense,' Milton said. 'Still, we should check the CCTV for the whole period.'

'Already got someone working on that. It's not great quality. Cheap digital cameras. But they've got several, covering the main doors, rear fire exits, car parks, as well as reception. Usual stuff. But they're fairly visible. If someone wanted to avoid them, it wouldn't be difficult.'

'That was my impression, too. And given how thorough this guy was at clearing up after himself, I'm not investing too much hope in his carelessness.' He shook his head. 'Still, it's the only way to go. Hope for a chink of light somewhere.'

'Yup,' Wanstead said. 'Either that, or wait till Kenny goes off with the fairies.'

Donovan had been watching the exchange with interest and she was tempted to follow up Wanstead's remark, but she guessed from Milton's expression that it was a joke not to be shared with someone who, for the moment, was still an outsider. It reminded her that she was still only a visitor here. 'I'll get out your hair,' she said to Milton. 'I imagine you're going to be around here for a while yet.'

Milton surveyed the room. 'Looks like it. Kenny's on his way back in, so we'll have a confab and see where we go next.'

'Wish I could join you,' she said. 'Sounds like there's a lot to do.'

'Me too. But Kenny will pull the requisite strings, I'm sure. He's good at that. Understands the politics.'

She wondered about that. Murrain had struck her as a rather unworldly figure, certainly by the standards of senior police officers. But perhaps that quality stood him in good stead. Maybe people had a tendency to underestimate him. Donovan, at least, was already beginning to recognise that there was more to him than met the eye.

'You sure you'll be OK, sir?'

Murrain turned his gaze slowly back towards the young man. 'Contrary to many people's assumptions, Will, I'm not entirely incapable. I think I'll manage.'

'No, I didn't mean—' Sparrow's face had already turned a deep beetroot.

Murrain laughed. 'No, I know you didn't. I also know what a lot of people think about me.'

'I'm sure nobody—'

'Best not to dig yourself in any deeper, son. Shall we go in and see how things are going?'

On their return from the interview with Mrs Berenek, Murrain had received a call asking if he could spare Sparrow to assist with the final interviews at the hotel. The evening shift had now turned up for duty and the team of interviewers were busy collecting statements from all those who'd been on duty the previous weekend. Murrain had diverted back to the hotel and—uniquely, in Sparrow's experience of working with more senior officers—had suggested that Sparrow hang on to the pool car to get himself back to the office later. 'There might be others who need a lift,' he said. 'Better than having to bring someone else out later. I can always just hop on a bus. There're plenty going up the A6.'

Sparrow's response had been intended as no more than a discreet prompt about whether this was really in keeping with Murrain's status, but as soon as he'd spoken he realised the question could be misinterpreted. There were those who thought that, when his mind was elsewhere, Murrain wasn't safe to be allowed out.

Murrain certainly seemed distracted today, though that was unsurprising given his leadership of the case. His other, more extended telephone conversation in the car had been with the Assistant Chief overseeing the media liaison on the case in conjunction with the force's Head of Communications. Their inclination for the moment was to release only the bare minimum of information. That was fine by Murrain who just wanted to get on with the investigation, but he had no illusions that this line would hold for very long. In any case, if they failed to make progress in identifying the victim—much less the killer—they might soon be actively seeking the media's co-operation. None of that was likely to be comfortable.

In part, he wanted some time alone because he needed time to think. Or, more accurately, time to stop thinking. Time to switch off his conscious mind, however briefly, and get in touch with whatever lay beneath. He couldn't do that while he was driving—to that extent, his detractors were right about his being a potential danger to others. He couldn't do it while he was having to interact with his colleagues. He needed just a few minutes by himself. Maybe something might emerge.

The hotel seemed much calmer than earlier. The main function room had been cordoned off as the venue for the continuing interviews, but otherwise the place had returned to business as usual. There was a guest checking in at the desk, an older couple sitting chatting over tea in a corner of the lounge. It was likely that the murder had not yet reached the local TV news or the front page of the local paper. When that happened, later this evening or in the morning, the atmosphere here would no doubt change again. For the moment, even if they'd spotted the couple of marked cars parked discreetly behind the building, most of these newly-arrived guests were still unaware of what had happened in a room above their heads.

Members of Murrain's team were arrayed in the four corners of the large function room, each interviewing a member of the hotel staff. When in use, the place would no doubt be rendered intimate and atmospheric by the skilful use of room dividers and atmospheric lighting. In the chilly light of an autumn afternoon, it was a bleak space with down-at-heel decor and a random assemblage of utilitarian conference furniture. Immediately inside the door, DC Roberta Wallace, one of the newest and most enthusiastic recruits to the team, was collating the notes from the interviews to date.

'How's it going, Bert?' Sparrow asked. Murrain winced inwardly. He was never sure whether DC Wallace was happy with this inevitable nickname. He couldn't bring himself to use it but found equally that 'Roberta' congealed in his mouth. So he ended up calling her nothing and she probably assumed he simply couldn't recall her name.

'As well as can be expected,' she said. 'By which I mean we're getting through them, but almost nothing of interest has come out so far. Most of them had no contact with the victim or the killer, saw and heard nothing, and basically have three-fifths of bugger all to tell us. If you'll excuse the language, sir,' she added, for Murrain's benefit.

'Mild by my standards,' Murrain said. 'Bound to be the way. For the moment, all we can do is keep plugging onward in the hope that something will turn up. All we need is one lead from somewhere.'

His mind was still wrestling with Mrs Berenek's revelation that the killer had checked in alone. That might mean nothing at all, but his instincts, elusive as they always were, were suggesting otherwise. 'Have you interviewed someone called Michelle? One of the receptionists.'

Wallace consulted her list. It was neatly hand-written on one page of her notebook, each name appended with a series of codes which presumably carried significance for Wallace herself. 'That's her over there,' she said. 'She'd just come on duty. Does evenings.' She pointed towards a young-looking blonde woman sitting alone at one of the round conference tables. 'She's next up to be interviewed.'

Murrain glanced at Sparrow. 'There you go then, Will. Your first one. See whether she's any memory of seeing our Mr James leave the hotel that evening.'

'Not much chance, is there?' Sparrow said, glumly. 'Given all the comings and goings for the wedding.'

'You never know. Sounds like our Mr James was the memorable type.'

He watched as Sparrow made his way unenthusiastically across the room then turned back to Wallace. 'Have you got a list of the weekend guests there?'

She nodded and slid a stapled sheaf of papers across to him. 'Callaghan pulled them off the system for us. We asked for anyone who was here over Saturday or Sunday night, and they're sorted by check-in date.'

Murrain scanned down the printed list. 'You've presumably not been able to interview most of these face-to-face?'

'No, but we've sent the list back to DS Wanstead. We saw the handful who hadn't checked out when the body was found this morning. Most of them were wedding guests who'd made a weekend of it. They're the ones I've checked on the list.'

'Get anything from them?'

'No. You know what weddings are like. Meal, speeches, disco. Everyone ratted. No-one saw anything unusual.'

'Imagine not.' Murrain was checking through the list. Largely couples. Mr and Mrs This and That. The odd unmarried pair. A few with children in the family rooms. One solo female. A Ms Kathy Granger.

For the briefest of seconds as he read the name, Murrain felt the familiar pulse through his body. Perhaps his fears had been justified— that the killer had simply snatched a random lone female from among the wedding guests. But then he registered the other information on the list he was holding. Kathy Granger had checked out, safe enough, at 10.53 on the Sunday morning. That made sense. It would have been an extraordinary coincidence if the killer had managed to select the one individual who wouldn't have been immediately missed.

But, as ever, Murrain was reluctant to dismiss his own instincts. Kathy Granger's room was on the same floor as the room in which the killing had occurred, although at the opposite end of the hotel. Maybe she'd witnessed something, perhaps when she'd been returning to her room on the Saturday night or when checking out on the Sunday morning. He made a mental note to check with Wanstead whether they'd managed to contact her.

He pushed the list back across the table to Wallace. 'Thanks. How many more have you got to get through?'

'Not many. Maybe another hour.'

'OK. Don't work later than you need to. You'll all need a break.'

She looked at him curiously. 'You'll be going off yourself soon, will you, sir?'

He smiled. 'Do as I say, not as I do, Bert. A good lesson to learn.' It was the first time he'd used her nickname. It sounded false in his mouth, but she looked gratified, as if he'd finally noticed her existence.

'Thanks, sir.' She was smiling back. 'I'll bear that in mind.'

As he left, Murrain paused for a moment in the hotel lobby, taking a last opportunity to soak in the atmosphere of the place. The elderly couple were still sitting in the corner of the lounge finishing their pot of tea but otherwise the place was now deserted. There was nothing remarkable about the hotel. Just a typical mid-range place to stay. A superannuated Victorian or Edwardian villa that had been expanded over the years, with an ugly 1970s extension at the rear. Whatever resonance Murrain had felt earlier had disappeared. There was nothing to see. Nothing to feel.

As he stepped out into the car-park, he felt his mobile phone vibrate in his pocket. As he took the call, he glanced at the number on the screen. 'Hi, El. You home now?'

'Cheeky bugger,' she said. 'It's only half-five, you know.' A characteristic pause. 'But I'm just about to leave. I'm guessing you're pulling a late one tonight?'

'Looks like it.' There were some men—many of Murrain's colleagues, in fact—who might have resented being married to a substantially more senior officer. Murrain had never been one of them. He'd watched Eloise's relentless rise up the greasy pole with a mix of wonder and pride. When they'd married, fifteen years before, they'd both been Sergeants, Murrain in CID and his wife in uniform. They were seen as something of a golden couple—both able, well-regarded, apparent high-flyers. In the intervening years, Murrain had made DCI while his wife had reached the dizzying heights of Chief Super. That was fine by Murrain. He was happy doing what he did, and had no illusions that he was cut out for senior management. Eloise was an organiser, a trouble-shooter. She went in and sorted things out. Improved performance, hit targets, got herself noticed. Some resented her success, but she was generally respected for her abilities. For his own part, if he hadn't been married to her, Murrain might have found himself hating her. As it was, he loved her almost unconditionally. Even so, he could occasionally bring himself to resent the fact that, the more senior her role, the earlier she seemed to leave the office.

'This the Stockport thing?' she asked, though he knew she'd know exactly what it was. 'How's it going?'

She wouldn't expect him to give her any details over the phone. 'About as you'd expect,' he said. 'You know the circumstances.'

'Yeah. I heard. I'll cook something that won't spoil, then. Assume you're not planning to stay up all night?'

'Don't think there'd be much point,' he said. 'Not that sort of case.'

'Your sort of case, though.' It wasn't a question.

'I suppose. That's what scares me.'

'Me, too,' she said. 'You knew, didn't you? Yesterday, I mean.'

'I guess. But I didn't know what I knew. That's always the problem.'

'I know the problem. I've lived with you long enough.'

'You have,' he said. 'Some would say too long.'

She laughed. 'I'll give you a while yet. Text me when you're on your way.'

'I will. Love you.' He spoke the last words like an incantation, and waited until she repeated them back.

As it turned out, his expectations of the bus service had been more than optimistic. The next bus, as promised on the electronic signage in the shelter, seemed to have gone AWOL, and there was a twenty-five minute wait for the one after that. Sighing, he resigned himself for a wait at the bus-stop, thankful that at least it wasn't raining. After all, he'd told himself that solitude was what he needed.

He knew the way this worked. He couldn't force it. Maybe something would come of it, maybe it wouldn't. Even if it did, the 'something' might well turn out to be worthless, or, worse still, misleading. That had happened once or twice. He'd misread the signs and ended up chasing some untamed goose. But that was rare. Mostly, it helped.

All he could do was relax and go with the flow, hope it would lead him in the right direction. At least the bleak environs of the A6 at this end of Stockport offered little in the way of distraction. In one direction there was a row of Edwardian housing, most now converted to offices or subdivided into flats, in the other a stretch of apartment blocks that could have been built any time in the last thirty years, flanked by a petrol station and a row of shops and takeaways. Why here? Why that hotel? Did the location have any significance, or was it simply an anonymous backdrop to a random act?

He couldn't tell, except that it didn't feel random. His instinct told him there was some pattern here, some sequence that needed decoding, that might give them the lead they needed.

He closed his eyes for a moment and tried to allow the thought to develop. But nothing came. And then, momentarily, there was that same familiar crackle through his body.

He opened his eyes. A car had pulled up at the kerb opposite, the driver's window sliding down.

'I thought it was you. Can I give you a lift anywhere?'

Murrain blinked. Marie Donovan. He knew she'd headed back to the office with Milton. She was presumably now on her way home. 'I think I'm going the other way,' he called. 'Back into the office.'

'I can still give you a lift if you like. It's only five minutes back up the road. Better than waiting for a bus.'

He hesitated for a moment. He'd wanted the time to himself, to see what emerged, to see if he could find some sign, some indication of where to go next.

And perhaps he'd found one.

CHAPTER EIGHT

She executed a perfect U-turn—no mean feat, considering the volume of traffic on the A6—and came to a halt beside the bus-stop, leaning over to open the passenger door.

'Police driver training?' Murrain asked as he climbed cautiously into the car.

'I've done all that stuff in my time,' she said, her eyes fixed on the rear view mirror as she waited for an opportunity to pull out. 'High speed pursuit. Surveillance. You name it.'

'Very good. We're a bit short on those skills in the team, apart from Joe.' The tightening of Murrain's fingers on the edges of his seat suggested he might be happier to keep this unchanged.

She smiled across at him. 'Don't worry. I'm actually a very cautious driver. How come you'd been left at the bus-stop?'

'My idea,' Murrain said. 'I hadn't realised the bus timetable was a work of fiction. Thought I'd be back at the office by now.'

'Least it's not raining.' She signalled and pulled out neatly into the traffic. There was a steady stream of cars heading out of town, but the road was relatively quiet heading north.

'I wouldn't have tried if it had been,' Murrain said. 'I'm optimistic, but not stupid.' He eased back in his chair, feeling slightly more comfortable now he realised that Donovan wasn't a speed-demon. She was a more sedate driver than Sparrow, certainly.

'By the way,' he said, after a pause, 'I wanted to ask you about your knowledge of professional killers.' He was conscious that, however he might phrase this, there was no way to make it sound a casual question. 'The stuff you were talking about back at the hotel?'

'Yes?'

He sensed a tightening in her voice. 'Tell me to shut up if I'm out of order.'

'I will,' she said, shortly. Then she added: 'I'm sorry. This is a sensitive area for me.'

'I appreciate that. I'm not being gratuitously nosey.'

She didn't respond for a second, her gazed fixed on the road. 'OK. Go on.'

'I've been thinking about what you—and, for that matter, Neil Ferbrache—said about this looking like a pro job—'

'The clearing up, anyway.'

'Yes, exactly. It's not a world I know much about. Even in Serious Crimes, we only tend to come across the amateur stuff. Very amateur, generally.' He hesitated, wondering how to phrase what he wanted to say. There were times when he just wanted to tell the truth—that he was only following his gut. It was just that, figuratively speaking, his gut was noisier than most. 'You worked undercover, I understand?'

'I'm not really supposed to discuss the detail of that,' she said. 'Even with other officers. You understand?'

'Yes, of course.' In his experience, most undercover officers weren't shy about shooting their mouths off. 'I'm not interested in the detail. It was just what you said about coming into contact with a professional killer.'

'More than once,' she said. Her grip had tightened on the steering wheel. Perhaps this wasn't a good subject to raise with someone driving through rush-hour traffic.

'Right.' He was tempted to change the subject. But his instinct—that same bloody instinct that had got him into this conversation in the first place—was telling him that, really, she wanted to talk.

'I worked closely with someone who—well, he wasn't what I thought he was. I thought he was someone I could trust. One of the few people I could trust, in fact. And then he tried to kill me. Cold-bloodedly. On a contract, just to shut me up. Someone I'd worked with, just the two of us, for months on end. I'd never guessed. And it meant nothing to him when he was about to pull the trigger.'

'Christ,' Murrain said. 'I'm sorry. I shouldn't have—'

He could see that there were tears in her eyes. 'No, don't worry. It's helpful to talk about it. They gave me counselling after everything that happened. And that's been helpful. But, you know, it's the nature of the job. You have to bottle it up.'

'Who was this guy? I mean, not his name. But what sort of person? What sort of people was he working for?'

'It's organised crime, isn't it? Big business, but on the wrong side of the law. I was getting too close to the wrong people, so they brought in a contractor. And it wasn't just me.' She stopped, but Murrain said nothing. 'I escaped. But they got someone I was close to. It was the same guy behind it. I can't prove it. I can't even prove it was murder. But I know it happened, and I know it was him.'

'Look, I'm sorry,' Murrain said. 'I shouldn't have raised this. I just wanted to understand—'

'The mindset? The mentality? Yes, so did I. That's what set me off doing the research. I wanted to understand how someone could do that to another human being.'

'And did you? Understand, I mean.'

'Not really. The psychologists talk in jargon. They pretend they're explaining but all they're doing is labelling. And the labels don't tell you much. High functioning psychopath. What does that mean? It doesn't explain why someone ends up like that, or how they can do what they do. It doesn't tell you *anything*.'

They were approaching the office now. At the next set of lights, she indicated and pulled over into the right-hand lane. 'Is it OK if I drop you at the back? Then I can go round the block and head back south.'

'That's fine. Sorry to have dragged you out of your way. And sorry if I've been insensitive.'

Don't worry,' she said. 'On either count.' For the first time, as they waited for the lights to change, she looked at him and smiled. 'It's just hard to talk about it dispassionately, you know?'

'It must be.' He knew he'd already pushed things too far. 'Thanks again for the lift. I'll be in touch on the job front but take it as read that you're part of the team.' He paused. 'Assuming you still want to be.'

'You haven't put me off.'

She pulled into the small drop-off bay by the rear entrance to the office block and Murrain murmured his thanks again as he climbed out. He stood by the roadside as she drove away, watching until she'd turned the corner that led back on to the main road.

He'd felt it, definitely, as she'd been talking. Especially as she talked about the killing of someone close to her. That sense of a link, a connection. He'd been right to ask the questions.

Murrain looked around him as if, until that moment, he'd forgotten where he was. The setting sun, crimson between the buildings, was catching the windows of the office block behind him, deepening the shadows along the street. The road was, in that second, empty of cars and people, and Murrain caught himself feeling an unaccustomed unease.

A killer who could dispatch life savagely but without emotion. A vicious but dispassionate slaughterer. And some link, that he couldn't yet fathom, to the arrival of Marie Donovan.

He remained motionless for a moment. And then he turned and pushed through the double doors into the brightly-lit building.

CHAPTER NINE

'Holly?'

Donovan closed the front door gently and stood in the hallway listening. After all these years, she'd developed a sixth-sense for the presence of another human being. She couldn't have explained how she knew the house wasn't empty. Maybe she'd subconsciously heard something. Maybe she'd registered some unfamiliar scent. She had no idea. She just knew she wasn't alone.

It was barely six. It would be unusual for Holly to be back this early and her car wasn't on the road outside. But no-one else could be in here.

She realised she was holding her breath even though she'd already revealed her presence by calling Holly's name. For a moment, after her conversation with Murrain, this felt almost like a flashback.

She pushed open the first door on the left.

'Jack?'

He was sitting on the sofa in the living room, flicking through some woman's magazine Holly had left on the coffee table. He looked up, smiling. 'Oh, hi. You're earlier than I thought you would be.'

She bit back the angry response that was halfway out of her mouth. There was no point, not with Jack. It washed over him. She just had to be clear and assertive. 'How did you get in?'

He burrowed in his pocket. 'You gave me a key, remember?'

She did remember, and she also remembered asking him to return the key the last time they'd met. He'd claimed not to have it with him and had promised to stick it in the post. Needless to say, he'd never done so. 'I don't want you just letting yourself in here, Jack. In fact, I don't want you here at all.'

He put on his little-boy-lost face. Not so long ago, she'd have been taken in by it. 'I thought we were still friends.'

'I never said that, Jack. Not the way you mean. I just wanted us to be civilised.' She was pretty sure she'd never used the word 'friends', but Jack's memory was always selective.

'Look, Marie. I'm not trying to take us back to where we were—'

'That's good, Jack. Because it's over.' As far as she was concerned it had been over almost before it had begun, but that was something else Jack had never been prepared to acknowledge. 'What are you doing up here, anyway?'

'Just paying a visit,' he said. 'Got a big job on. London outfit, but seems to have links up here, so likely to be up here a lot.' He smiled. 'Was looking out for you today. They reckoned you'd be in later but you didn't come back.'

She wondered how much her colleagues had told Jack about where she was. Probably everything. Everyone in the office loved Jack, except for those few who detested him. Ironically, she seemed to be the only one who, by now, was genuinely indifferent to his presence. 'Something came up,' she said.

'That's why I came over,' he said. 'Didn't want to go away without seeing you.'

'No, well, now you've seen me.'

'Don't be like that, Marie. OK, so it's over. We don't have to hate each other.'

'I don't hate you, Jack. But there's nothing between us. There never was. It was just a fling.' She'd tried to be this blunt before, but he never quite seemed to take it in.

'It was more than that, Marie. You know that. Whatever you might feel now.'

They'd been round this loop countless times and sometimes she'd found herself almost believing him. But she knew he was wrong. There'd never been anything between them. They'd just briefly fallen in with each other. She'd been an emotional wreck, traumatised, alone. He'd been on his own in London and had turned on the charm. It had taken her just a few weeks to realise it was a mistake. She was in no state to embark on a relationship, and, for all his charm, Jack Brennan was the last man she needed. Brennan cared about little but himself. Even in those few weeks, she'd begun to feel she was being used—sexually, socially, professionally. She was providing him with company in a strange town and with the insights and contacts he

76

needed to establish himself in the Agency. But she knew he'd discard her as soon as he'd taken what he needed.

Even so, she couldn't quite bring herself simply to dump him. She had the impression that that would be a first in Brennan's life and she had no idea how he'd take it. For a while she allowed things to drift on, hoping that the relationship, such as it was, would fizzle out or—more likely—that Brennan would turn his attentions elsewhere.

Fortunately, she'd already made the decision to sell up and move. After everything that had happened, she wanted a new start. She'd originally thought this might just involve a change of role and a move across London, maybe even into the unchartered territories north of the river.

But there'd been the offer of a job in the regional office up here and she'd decided it would be prudent to put some distance between herself and Brennan. For a while, that had worked. Brennan hadn't exactly taken the hint—there'd still been more than a few phone calls and a couple of visits which was how he'd ended up with a key to this place. But from what she'd heard, it hadn't taken him long to find a replacement among the females in the London office. She was happy for him to give others the impression that it was he, rather than she, who'd done the dumping.

Even so, Brennan had never quite seemed to acknowledge that they were finished, assuming they'd ever really started. Maybe he liked the idea of stringing along a relationship up here while playing the field down south. Maybe he just wanted to demonstrate he was the one in control. Either way, there'd been previous occasions when he'd left voicemails or sent texts that had implied that their relationship was in some way ongoing. He'd made a couple of visits to the office and behaved towards her in a way she'd found uncomfortable—a little bit too intimate in the presence of others, a little bit too tactile. Others might easily have assumed that there was still something between them.

'Jack,' she said now, 'whatever relationship we might or might not have had, it's long gone. We're done. I don't want you here. I'd like you to leave.' She could feel her stomach churning as she spoke but she tried hard to keep her voice steady.

He pushed himself up from the sofa and took a step towards her. Involuntarily, she found herself moving away from him. She'd never felt physically threatened by him. Not exactly. But she'd seen glimpses of his temper when something hadn't fallen his way. 'It doesn't have to be this way, Marie. We can still—'

'This is exactly how it has to be, Jack. Don't you get it? I want you to leave. Now.' She felt her body tense as she made an effort not to retreat from his looming presence.

'Not until we've talked about this properly,' he said. 'Not until you've *listened* to me.' He took another step forward and she could sense the restrained anger in his voice. She'd seen him in this kind of mood, usually after a few drinks, but the anger had always been directed at someone or something other than her. Now, she felt caught in its full glare.

'Look, Jack, if you just—'

She had no idea what she'd been about to say, what kind of proposal she might have been about to make. They'd both heard the sound. The front door opening.

'Marie?'

'In here.' It took her a moment to articulate the words, as if she'd forgotten how to speak.

'Oh, right. I was just wondering if—' The woman stopped as she entered the room. 'Jack Brennan. Bloody hell.'

Donovan had taken the opportunity to take a step away. It hadn't occurred to her that Holly would know Brennan but she supposed it wasn't so surprising. Brennan's reputation, like her own, tended to go before him. 'You've met, then?'

Holly smiled at Brennan and there was something in her expression that Donovan couldn't read. 'We go back a way, me and Jack. Or, more accurately, Jack and Ben went back a long way. A very long way.'

That explained it, and it perhaps also explained the ambivalence in Holly's expression. Ben had been Holly's partner, yet another copper, in the days when both had worked for GMP. Holly had always seemed reluctant to discuss that part of her past, and Donovan had never really wanted to enquire. All she really knew was that Ben had been working as an undercover officer and had left Holly, done a bunk one day. She'd heard various versions of the story—that there'd been another woman, that Ben had been facing some disciplinary enquiry, that he'd gone over to the other side, even that he'd been topped. Whatever, no-one really seemed to know what had happened and Holly never discussed it.

It had all been before Donovan's time up here, and she'd really only got to know Holly a few months before. Holly had been a Crime Scene officer up in Lancashire, but had made the decision a year or two before to transfer into the more sedate lifestyle of an analyst role in the NCA. She'd subsequently got together with an agency investigator, an ex-Immigration Officer called Garry Meadows. Donovan had known of Meadows a little from her London days because they'd had some joint involvement in an undercover investigation into people-trafficking rings. She hadn't liked him much and had been surprised to discover that he and Holly Finch, the smart intelligence analyst in the north-west office, were an item. She'd been less surprised when, just a few weeks later, she'd learned that the two had had an acrimonious break-up.

That was how Holly came to be living here. After Ben's death, she'd sold up the house she and Ben had bought together out in Altrincham and had been renting a flat in Salford Quays, relatively convenient for the Agency offices. Then, just a few months before, she'd made the mistake of ending her tenancy there to move in with Meadows. It was only after she'd moved in, she'd told Donovan, that she realised it was the last place she wanted to be. When the break-up had left her temporarily homeless, Marie Donovan, who'd begun to recognise that Holly's rather intense demeanour concealed an appealingly dry sense of humour, had offered her a spare bedroom and a shoulder to cry on. It had been intended as a short-term solution but a few months on neither had shown any great inclination to end it.

It was clear to Donovan that Brennan hadn't been expecting to meet Holly here—he'd presumably failed to pick up on that bit of gossip while he'd been in the office, even if he'd run into Holly herself—and didn't look entirely comfortable. Donovan didn't want to think too hard about the possible causes of his discomfort. There were more than enough skeletons in Brennan's cupboard. 'I didn't realise,' he said, finally.

Holly shrugged. 'Marie's been good to me. I can't say that about many people.'

To Donovan's ears, that sounded pointed enough. 'Jack's just leaving,' she said. 'Aren't you, Jack?'

Brennan's gaze flicked between the two women. If there had been any fight in him—figurative or literal—it had been extinguished by Holly's arrival. 'Just off,' he agreed. 'Heading back south tonight for a day or two.' He looked theatrically at his watch. 'Suppose I'll have missed the worst of the traffic by now. Good to see you again, Holly. Been a long time. We should catch up.'

'Yeah,' she agreed. 'Sometime.' It didn't sound as if she felt the need to be very urgent.

'And you, Marie. I'll be in touch. *Au revoir,* then.'

'Goodbye, Jack.' If she had any say in the matter, there wouldn't be a next time. If nothing else, she'd be changing the locks. 'Don't let us keep you.'

As the front door closed behind him, Holly began to laugh, unexpectedly and uncontrollably. It sounded like the sound of relief bordering on hysteria, but after a moment Donovan found herself joining in.

'Jesus,' Holly gasped after a few seconds, 'what the hell was that all about?'

Donovan shook her head, momentarily unable to respond.

'I'd heard that you and Jack had—well, been a thing. But I'd assumed it was all over.'

'We were never really a thing,' Donovan said, finally. 'And we're certainly not now. Jack just doesn't like to take no for an answer.'

Holly's laughter had faded as quickly as it had begun. 'You can say that again,' she said. 'You can bloody well say that again.' She took a breath and shook her head, as if surprised by her own vehemence.

There was some history there, Donovan thought, and she was tempted to probe further. But it wasn't her business and she knew there was no point in pressing Holly to reveal more than she wanted. If she felt like talking, she would, probably some late evening after a few glasses of wine. If she didn't, well, who the hell cared about Jack Brennan anyway?

'Anyway, he's gone,' Holly continued, almost as if speaking to herself.

'I'm sorry,' Donovan said. 'I didn't expect him to be here. He won't be back.'

Holly nodded, though her expression suggested she hadn't really heard. After a moment, she walked over to the window and stared out, as if to reassure herself that Brennan really had left. Then she turned back. 'I'll tell you what, though,' she said. 'He was really shocked to see us together, wasn't he? He didn't know what to make of *that*.'

Murrain was constantly impressed by the speed with which an investigation team could transform a pristine meeting room into something resembling a semi-organised rubbish tip. In this case, he'd missed the interim stage in which the meeting room had been designated the MIR but the human impact was already in evidence.

There were workstations piled high with files and paperwork. There were scatterings of discarded, unwashed mugs, a few cardboard cups from the local coffee shop, the odd soft-drink can and plastic water bottle, and—presumably for the benefit of those expecting to work late—a couple of takeaway pizza boxes crammed into the nearest rubbish bin.

Murrain knew that, for the most part, the chaos was only apparent, just as it had been at the crime scene earlier in the day. It wasn't his way of doing things. He preferred everything neat and in its place. But he knew that was really only because, left to itself, his head was much more scrambled than those of his colleagues, as today's missed appointment demonstrated. The members of his team knew full well what they were about.

By now, the room was relatively quiet. CID officers didn't work shifts and everyone knew that the overtime budget was almost non-existent these days. Even so, they'd willingly work whatever hours were needed on a case like this. But this didn't yet have the feel of an all-nighter. Once they'd finished conducting and writing up today's interviews, there wouldn't be much else they could sensibly do before the morning. By then, he hoped, they'd have at least the bare bones of the SOCO report from Ferbrache, and Warwick would be fast-tracking the post-mortem. On the basis of the telephone discussions he'd had with the two experts earlier in the afternoon, Murrain wasn't optimistic that either would provide much more in the way of substantive leads but for the moment it was all they had.

Milton and Wanstead were sitting at the far end of the room, apparently cross-checking a sheaf of spreadsheets. It wasn't policing as Murrain had once known it but it was the way things worked nowadays.

'Any progress?'

'Not so's you'd notice,' Milton said. 'We're checking what interviews have been completed and what's still outstanding. You wouldn't believe how little information you can get from that many people. Dozens of hotel guests and staff and no-one saw or heard anything.'

'I'd believe it,' Wanstead offered. 'Hotel staff are trained not to notice anything, and most of the guests will have been pissed on Saturday night and hungover Sunday morning.'

Murrain pulled up a chair and slumped down opposite them. 'Nothing from the CCTV, either?'

'Not yet. Lots of coming and going in the car-park as you'd expect, but nothing we can tie in to anything. Maybe a shot of our Mr James checking in but only from the rear. Tells us nothing we don't already know.' Milton's puppyish demeanour seemed to have temporarily deserted him. 'We're getting some of the footage enhanced but I'm not holding my breath.'

'No other sightings of our mysterious Mr James, I take it?'

'Nothing. Sparrow just sent over his notes of the interview with the receptionist.' He scrutinised the print out for the details. 'Michelle Fenton, apparently. She'd no recollection of seeing him leave or return to the hotel later that evening. She was on Sunday morning too, apparently, and didn't see him leave then, either. But Saturday night the place was heaving. Sunday morning was quiet but she wasn't always on the desk.'

Murrain nodded. 'Jesus, this is a strange one, isn't it? How's it possible to commit that kind of murder in a building full of people without anyone having an inkling?'

'Hotels, isn't it?' Wanstead said, morosely. 'No-one wants to know what's happening in the next room.'

'And we've literally nothing else?' Murrain flicked aimlessly at the pile of papers on Wanstead's desk, as if hoping the answer might fall into his hand.

Milton exchanged a glance with Wanstead. 'There is one thing, boss.'

'Go on. Make my day.'

'Well, it's probably something and nothing. But it's an odd coincidence.' He burrowed among print-outs for a sheet of paper. 'This wedding. I mean, the reception in the hotel function room. They were police.'

Murrain looked up and blinked. He'd felt something, then, as Milton had uttered that last word. 'Police?'

'We didn't spot it at first. Obviously, a lot of the guests were just relatives and random friends, the same mix that you get at any wedding. But when we started to track down contact numbers, we spotted—well, to be honest, Bert Wallace pointed it out—that there were quite a few police types among them.' He held out a printed list for Murrain. 'Some officers. One or two had even put their rank on the check-in form.'

'Probably hoping to get the bar kept open late,' Wanstead added.

'And one or two others mentioned it when we called to talk to them. We eventually got hold of the groom's father. Turns out the groom's a DI in the Lancashire force. Bride also works for the force in some kind of IT role. So a fair number of the guests were past and current colleagues. Bride's family comes from Stockport which is why the wedding was down here.'

Murrain said nothing for a moment. 'Have you managed to speak to the happy couple?'

'Not yet. They've flown out to the Maldives. I wasn't keen to interrupt their honeymoon unless I had to.' Milton peered at Murrain. 'You think this might be important?'

'Christ knows. Like you say, it's an odd coincidence, but it could just be that. There's nothing to suggest the killing's connected to the wedding at all.'

'Papers'll have a field day, though,' Wanstead said. 'Murder committed in a hotel full of coppers and nobody notices a bloody thing.'

Murrain was scanning the list of interviewees. 'I think we should bear it in mind, anyway. Maybe it's not time to disturb the honeymoon just yet, but worth thinking about in terms of possible motives, if nothing else.' His finger traced down the list and stopped. 'Anyone managed to get hold of this Kathy Granger yet?'

Wanstead leaned over and squinted at the name. 'Not sure,' he said. 'Hang on.' He tapped at his keyboard and waited for the details to appear. 'Who is she, anyway?'

'The one solo female staying over Saturday night. Not our victim, though.' Murrain had to stop himself adding the word 'unfortunately'. 'She checked out safely on Sunday morning. She has an address in Bury so assume she was heading back home.'

Wanstead was scrolling through the records on the screen. 'Looks like we've not managed to get hold of her yet. Called the number she'd given at check-in, but no answer.'

Milton was gazing at Murrain with interest. 'You think she's worth following up, boss? One of your tingles?'

Murrain laughed. He usually felt uncomfortable with others making light of his idiosyncrasies, but he'd learned to make an exception with Milton. When it came to it, Milton had always been prepared to take seriously whatever Murrain had to say. 'Something like that,' he said, after a pause. 'May be nothing. Probably is nothing. But keep trying her.'

'Only too happy to, boss. Frankly, we could do with all the tingles you can offer.'

CHAPTER TEN

'I did a *boeuf bourguignon*,' Eloise said, as he stomped up the stairs to get changed. 'If you're still hungry.'

'I'm starving,' he called down. 'I could eat anything. Even your beef stew.'

It was a familiar joke. In addition to her many other talents, Eloise was a highly skilled cook. Murrain could hold his own in the kitchen, particularly by comparison with his male contemporaries, but she was something else. It had started as a vague interest but Eloise's interests rarely remained vague. Either she dropped them quickly or, more commonly, she began to take them very seriously indeed. In this case, as with so many of her accomplishments, she'd begun by reading, progressed to practising, and then, when she felt confident enough, had embarked on a series of high-powered training courses. Some men might have found the process intimidating but Murrain was content to enjoy the fruits of her labours. In fairness, he probably cooked at least half the time and she always accepted his lesser offerings with good grace.

'How's it going?' she asked, when he reappeared in the kitchen dressed in his usual worn sweatshirt and jeans.

'It isn't. Not at all.' While she brought the food out of the oven, he poured them both a glass of red wine. 'We've nothing. No leads. No clue as to who the victim is, let alone the perpetrator. Nothing.'

He'd said as much to the ACC and the Head of Communications in an impromptu telephone conference during his drive home. He hated telephone conferences at the best of times—you couldn't see who you were talking to, you couldn't read the expression on their face, you didn't have a clue what anyone was really thinking. This one, conducted on a hands-free in busy traffic while trying to justify his work to his boss's boss, was close to Murrain's idea of hell.

'No, nothing,' he'd said. 'Not a single lead worth speaking of. Or even not worth speaking of, to be honest.' He'd wondered whether to mention the wedding's police connection but even to Murrain that sounded like clutching at straws unless something more substantive emerged from it.

'So what next?' the ACC had asked. He was an operations man who'd spent the shortest possible part of his career in CID.

'We hope for the best,' Murrain had said.

Even listening to the resulting silence on his hands-free device, he hadn't had too much difficulty gauging what the ACC thought of that response. 'That's all we have?' the ACC had said, finally. He'd sounded genuinely pained.

'We have to hope either the SOCO report or the post-mortem gives us something to work with,' Murrain had explained. 'Either that or we get something from one of the interviews. All we can do is take it step-by-step and make sure we don't miss anything.'

'In the meantime,' the Head of Communications had asked, 'what do you suggest we tell the media?'

Murrain had—just—resisted the temptation to say that he'd assumed that was her job. 'What have we said so far?'

'Nothing much. We've just said that a body's been found in a Stockport hotel. And that it's being investigated as a potential unlawful killing. Nothing about the manner or circumstances of the death.'

'Can't we keep it like that?' he'd asked, already knowing the answer.

'For tonight, probably,' she said. 'But too many people already know about the killing—the cleaner who found the body, the hotel manager, by now probably the whole bloody staff there. And their families. And their friends. And anyone they've met in the pub. It won't be long before it all leaks out. Somebody might even get the bright idea of trying to sell it to one of the tabloids. Then we're stuffed. We'll be left trying to explain why we kept quiet about a potential threat to the public.'

'We don't *know* there's a threat to the public,' the ACC intervened.

'But we don't know there *isn't,*' Murrain said. 'I get that. And if it gets out the wrong way, the media will have a field day. So, yes, you're right. We need to announce something in the morning.'

87

'And just hope that the tabloids aren't already working on it overnight,' the Head of Communications had said. 'I've put out one or two discreet calls to sound out if it's leaked, but if I do too much of that it'll just pique their interest.'

'Let me sleep on it,' Murrain had said, realising as he spoke that sleeping was likely to be the last thing he'd manage that night. 'We might want to make some sort of appeal for information anyway by then. If we do nothing else, we at least need to identify the victim.'

There had been another silence after that and then the ACC had added, with a cold finality: 'I think, Kenny, that we're expecting a little more from you than *that.*'

Now, though, sitting here with his glass of merlot and his plate of casserole even that felt beyond his powers. Eloise was watching him with apparent concern. 'I've never seen you quite so dispirited by a case,' she said. 'This is usually when you come to life.'

'I must be a bundle of fun to live with the rest of the time, then.'

'Don't get me started on that one. You'll only regret it. But, seriously, I've not seen you like this before.'

'I've never had a case like this before,' he said. 'Usually there's something to go on. Some dangling thread you can begin to tug. This time, there's nothing. Nothing we've found so far, anyway.'

'There's you,' she said. 'And your—sensitivities. Are you telling me the spider-sense isn't tingling?'

He usually had no difficulty with Eloise, like Milton, joking about these things. She'd had to live with the consequences long enough. Tonight he found himself feeling irritated. 'It's not like that. You know that, El,' he said. 'Well, it is, sort of. But it's not something I *want.*'

'I know that,' she said, more gently. It was at times like this that he seemed most child-like, when he allowed her at least to glimpse what he had to live with. Once, when they were first getting to know each other properly, he'd called it a curse. She hadn't understood that at the time. She'd thought he was exaggerating what she'd seen then as little more than the usual copper's instinct. Now, years later, she understood much more about what he had to endure. 'But you can't ignore it.'

'It's like static. It tunes in and out. Mostly it means nothing.'

'You don't know that's true,' she said, thinking of all the times when he'd argued the opposite. 'You just don't know what it means, most of the time. What have you felt this time? When have you felt it?'

He took a breath, as if about to disagree with her, but then he said: 'You mean, after Sunday morning?'

'Yes. After that.'

'I felt it at the hotel, definitely. It was strongest there. I don't know whether it was just a confirmation of what I—experienced on Sunday, or whether there was some other significance. It was the whole place—not just the crime scene, though it was strongest there. I could almost *see* something. It was unnerving.'

'Go on.'

'There was something when we went to see the receptionist. The woman who'd checked in our Mr James.' He paused, and frowned. 'Not so much her, though. Her son. That was the odd thing. I hadn't really registered that till now.'

'You think he—'

Murrain shook his head. 'I mean, anything's possible, obviously. But that's not how this works. If it did, I'd be the perfect detective, wouldn't I?' The peevish tone had crept back into his voice. 'Just made me think he was worth having a closer look at.' He stopped again, trying to force himself to think. 'Then I felt it about this woman—the one solo female staying in the hotel. I don't know what that means. Maybe she's our breakthrough witness. Perhaps she's one person who saw or heard something significant. We've no other material witnesses. Even the couple in the next room didn't hear anything odd. When we questioned them, at first they said they'd heard nothing.' He paused and allowed himself a thin smile. 'Then the wife said she thought she might have heard a baby crying on the Sunday morning.'

Eloise stared at him. 'Jesus. That's a chilling thought, isn't it?'

89

He didn't ask her exactly what she'd found chilling. He still wasn't sure if she'd really heard that sound, whatever it was, or if she'd just been humouring him. 'Then there's Marie Donovan,' he said.

She raised an eyebrow. 'Marie Donovan? Who's she?'

'Potential secondee to the team from the NCA. Saw her this morning.'

'Why would she want to join your lot from the NCA? With respect,' Eloise added. Then she nodded. 'Oh. Right. Donovan. Thought the name sounded familiar.'

'The whistleblower. Famous, or notorious, wherever two or three coppers are gathered together.'

'Jesus. She's been hounded out? That's scandalous. From what I read, she did everything by the book. Went through Professional Standards, formalised everything. And the bent cop she exposed was sent down. What the hell more do they want?'

'You know how it is. I'm sure *they've* done everything by the book, too. Even gave her a commendation. But people like that always end up as an embarrassment. I don't think she's been hounded out. It's more that no-one quite knows what to do with her.'

'The effect's the same,' Eloise said, bluntly. 'So she's going to become another of your wounded animals, is she?'

'I don't know what you mean.' He avoided her eyes by concentrating on the last few mouthfuls of the casserole. 'Great stew, by the way.'

'Of course you don't. But she's another one. Like me. Like Joe Milton. You take us in, sort us out, mentor us until we go on to bigger and better things. It's what you do, Kenny, though I'm not sure you even realise it.'

'If you say so. Anyway, the point about Marie Donovan is that I felt it when she was around. Stronger than ever.'

'I'll bet you did,' she said. 'But, you mean, the same thing? Connected with this case? The old spider-sense?'

'I think so. Not just randomly. I mean, as far as I can judge. But it definitely felt as if she was part of it, somehow.'

'But how can she be?'

'I've no idea. She has a pretty colourful background. I suppose it's possible. Neil Ferbrache has this theory that it was a professional job.'

'I didn't think Neil dealt in theories.'

'He doesn't. That's why I'm taking it seriously. And maybe that's where the link with Donovan comes in. She was an undercover officer. She reckons she had some dealings with a contract killer. So who knows?'

If anyone else had been talking like this, Murrain thought, Eloise would have dismissed it as bollocks. She might still think that in his case but at least she had the grace not to show it. He rose and gathered the plates and cutlery to load the dishwasher. 'I think I'll stay up to watch Newsnight.'

She swallowed the last of her wine. 'I know you. You're going to sit up and fret. If you do go to bed tonight, you'll be up at the crack to get back into work. Which is fine, as long as you don't disturb me if and when you do come to bed and as long as you don't wake me before seven. More than your life's worth.'

'I'll do my best.' He was burrowing in the cupboard under the sink to find the dishwasher tablets.

'You'll do better than that,' she said. 'Unless we want to have another murder on our hands—' She stopped, watching him. 'You OK, Ken?'

It took him a moment to reply. Then he turned to her, still crouched awkwardly on the floor. 'I felt it, then. Again. Just when you were speaking.'

'What? When?'

'Just then. When you spoke.' He climbed wearily to his feet and stood looming over her, his ungainly body looking too large for the compact kitchen. 'When you said we'd have another murder on our hands.'

She looked back up at him. He had the same lost expression he'd had on the Sunday morning in the hotel. 'Oh, sweet Jesus,' she said.

Milton sat gazing tiredly around the deserted MIR. He felt an urge to tidy the place up, to throw away the discarded drink cans and fast-food containers, straighten up the tottering piles of paperwork, hang up the jacket that someone had abandoned on the back of a chair. But no-one would thank him for it. At best, they'd feel intimidated. At worst, they'd blame him for losing some key document or piece of information.

Murrain had ordered the team home an hour or so before. Many of them hadn't really wanted to go. They preferred to stay and beaver away at something—paperwork, checking data, anything—to give themselves the illusion of progress. Going home was like an admission of defeat. These were the supposed golden hours, and yet it seemed that there was really nothing more they could do.

But Murrain had been right. He'd told them they'd gone as far as they realistically could for the moment. They'd all be more effective for a decent night's sleep. Some had looked relieved at the absolution, one or two had made a token protest, but no-one ever challenged Murrain on matters like that. Or much else, come to think of it. Murrain was a quiet gentle figure, these days at least, but he never had any difficult in asserting his authority. Ten minutes later, the room had been empty.

Milton had drifted out along with the rest but made it only as far as his own shared office. He suspected that Murrain knew full well that his deputy had had no intention of heading home yet. Sometime soon, Murrain would no doubt be wanting to have a conversation about Milton's circumstances. That tended to be Murrain's management style. He was smart enough to notice when something was wrong and sensitive enough to pick the right moment to address it. For the moment—and particularly in the face of this latest case—he'd be content to let it ride. But not for long.

The truth was that Milton had no desire to head home, tonight or any other night. There was nothing much for him to head home to. A couple of weeks ago, there'd have been Gill, waiting to welcome him with her liveliness, her humour, her unabashed sexiness. Not to mention a takeaway and a bottle of wine.

But Gill was in Paris, beginning what she insisted was only an intermission in their relationship. Milton knew she meant it sincerely but he still didn't really believe it. It was too big a step, and she was too good at what she did. The six-month temporary contract would be extended, and then become permanent. She'd talk to him about his moving out there but they'd both know it would never happen. And slowly, step by step, they'd drift apart and it would all be over.

When she'd asked him if she should apply for the job in the OECD, of course he'd said she should. Her career was taking off. It wouldn't be right to get in her way. Privately, he'd hoped she wouldn't be offered the job but he'd always known that they'd select her. Why wouldn't they? She was, after all, wonderful. And so they had. But even then he'd managed to fool himself it wouldn't happen. That she'd turn down the job or that it would somehow fall through. That her current employers would make her a better offer. That she'd realise how he really felt and change her mind.

But of course he hadn't said any of that to her. Everything had trundled on until, just over two weeks ago, he'd waved goodbye to her at Manchester Airport and the whole thing had finally become real. He'd driven back from the airport to a new-build townhouse in Sale that suddenly felt much too big for his solitary presence. He'd lived on his own before but he'd been with Gill for five years or more. She'd moved in with him when he'd finally come through his troubles and it had felt like a symbolic moment. Now, he wondered about the implications of her departure, temporary or not.

Since then, he'd been drifting through his days as if semi-conscious. He'd lived on takeaways and supermarket meals-for-one, drunk too many bottles of wine and cans of beer in the evenings, and thrown himself back into his work. He and Gill spoke on the phone most days but even that felt hard work. Her life was full of new beginnings—a new flat in a supposedly up-and-coming *arrondissement*, new colleagues, new work challenges, a whole new lifestyle. His was more of the same. Even when something dramatic happened, like this new case, there was little he could tell her. The calls had already become a sequence of awkward silences, embarrassed bursts of conversation, uneasy and unshared laughter. He suspected that soon even the calls would become less frequent, and the ending would have begun.

He found the last dregs of a carton of milk in the office fridge and made himself a strong coffee. Then he made his way back into the now-empty MIR and slumped at his workstation, wondering what to do. There was no point in going home. He wouldn't sleep. Even on the best of nights now he found himself lying wide awake, staring at the ceiling in the semi-dark, listening to the burr of traffic on the main road. He was up half the night, watching mindless TV, playing computer games, listening to music through earphones so as not to disturb the neighbours beyond the thin walls. Tonight, there'd be no point in even pretending he might sleep. Murrain would be in the same position, he knew, but at least he had Eloise to take care of him.

There were still things he could do, if only just more re-reading and double-checking. He spent a few minutes working aimlessly through the interview reports, hoping to spot something, however trivial, they might have missed the first time through. According to the clock over the meeting room door it was 9.30pm. Maybe time for one more shot at getting hold of the elusive Kathy Granger. If she'd been out straight from work, maybe she'd be home by now. He found the number in the records and dialled. There was still no response. He allowed it to ring for several minutes in case she might be in the bathroom or even already asleep, but there was no answer, no voicemail.

Frustrated, he ended the call and sat back. After a moment, he pulled out his mobile and flicked through his address book. He found the number he was looking for and pressed Call.

This time, the phone was answered almost immediately. 'Hello? Joe?' Then, before Joe could answer: 'Blimey, mate, long time no hear. How you doing?'

'Not so bad,' Joe said, deciding that his wasn't the moment to start discussing his relationship issues. 'All good with you?'

'You know. Same old same old. But, yeah, OK.'

Milton had met Rob Fletcher when they were both on a High Potential Development scheme course at Bramshill. Both had apparently been marked out as future leaders, whatever that might mean, and had undertaken the required mix of academic and hands-on training. That had been two years before, and both of them had now reached the dizzy heights of Detective Inspector. Fletcher was based up in Lancaster and, after the training course, they'd occasionally met up for a drink if either had reason to be in the other's patch.

'Given the time of night, I'm assuming this isn't a social call, Joe.'

'Yeah, sorry to disturb you—'

'No problem. You've just dragged me away from the most mawkish bit of a chick-lit DVD so frankly I'm going to be eternally grateful, whatever you're about to ask of me.'

'Just after a bit of information, really.' Milton briefly outlined the background to the case. 'Can't say a lot more because it's not really hit the media yet, but you get the drift.'

Fletcher whistled gently. 'Christ, yes. Nasty one. And you've got nothing at all?'

'Except what I've told you, no. We're pretty much clutching at any straw we can find. Hence the interest in the wedding.'

'I can see that. Though I can't really see how it's likely to be relevant. Who were the bride and groom?'

'Groom's a guy called Andy Barton.' He paused, peering at the screen. 'Ha. Only name we have for the bride so far is Julie Barton. She must have proudly signed into the hotel that way. So don't know the maiden name.'

'Julie Welling,' Fletcher said instantly. Then there was a pause. 'And that'd be DI Andy Barton.'

'You know him, then?'

'Everybody up here knows good old Andy. He's a piece of work.'

'You're not making that sound like a good thing.'

'No, well, we've had one or two run-ins, me and Andy. But then a lot of people have had run-ins with Andy.' There was another silence, as Fletcher was clearly contemplating what to say. 'You know the type.

Arrogant little prick. Not prepared to listen to anyone else. Makes himself look big by making others look small. Full-time tosser.'

'You're not a fan, then?'

'Not a huge one, since you ask. My impression, for what it's worth, is that he was probably an effective copper but he's out of his depth as a manager. He talks a good game and he gets his way by bullying. That's how he's got as far as he has, despite a few blots on his copybook.'

'What sort of blots?'

'Kind of stuff that gets hushed up. Suggestions that he's been on the take. One or two complaints against him. Inappropriate behaviour. By which I mean borderline sexual harassment. Another officer. A witness in a burglary. Never proven. You know the drill.'

'I can imagine it.'

'Didn't seem to stop him progressing, though. Moved into CID with you lot. Then took a side-step into an undercover role.'

Milton felt his hand tighten on the phone. He couldn't imagine how this might be significant, but he felt somehow as if he'd just had a glimpse of light. Not a lead exactly, but something that might take them in a new direction. Jesus, he thought, I'm turning into Kenny Murrain.

'Since then he seems to have gone from strength to strength,' Fletcher went on. 'Made DI a couple of years ago. I think he's more than reached his level of incompetence, but he has his champions on high.'

'Right,' Milton said, trying to absorb this. 'And what about his new wife?'

'Julie Welling, as was,' Fletcher said. 'I can't claim to know her except as someone to nod to in the corridor. Works in intelligence. Bit of a looker, and knows it. Maybe ten years younger than Andy Barton. Not difficult to see what he sees in her. Not so clear what she sees in him. Father figure, maybe, or sugar daddy. Or am I being too cynical?'

'I've never known you be cynical, Rob,' Milton said, drily.

'She's wife number two,' Fletcher added. 'First one divorced him on the grounds of multiple infidelities, I hear. So I wouldn't give the marriage much chance if Julie's expecting him not to play away.'

'It's never easy to fathom other people's relationships,' Milton said. Or even, he added silently to himself, your own. 'That's really interesting.'

'Maybe. Can't see that it's likely to shed much light on your murder, though. Unless you're suggesting that Barton got up to some really serious no good on his wedding night. Even for Barton, that doesn't seem likely. In any case, if I know Andy Barton, he'd have been too pissed to raise a knife.' He paused and laughed. 'Or much else for that matter.'

'I'm happy to take your word for it. But, no, I can't see he's a serious suspect. But there might be a connection with someone who was there. It just feels like an odd coincidence. You know how it is. You pursue any avenue.'

'Yeah, I can see that. Anything else I can do for you?'

'Does the name Kathy Granger mean anything to you?'

'Don't think so. Should it?'

'Probably not. She was another guest at the hotel. The only solo female staying in the hotel that night, which is why we first noticed her.'

'She's not your victim, presumably?'

'No, she checked out safely on the Sunday. We assume she headed back home. She gave a Bury address. We've been trying to make contact but there's been no response on the number we have.'

'Why the interest?'

Good question, Milton thought. Because Kenny Murrain's instincts have pin-pointed her? Not the kind of thing you can say to a hard-headed Lancastrian DI. 'Nothing really. She's just another witness we want to speak to. Was staying on the same floor as the crime scene. But we've no reason to think she'll be able to tell us any more than the others have. Just occurred to me that she might be another Police colleague. She's not one of ours, so I wondered if she was with you.'

97

'She could well be,' Fletcher said. 'There are a lot of us. Do you want me to find out?'

'It's not urgent but, yeah, if you could, that would be helpful. We'll keep trying the number she gave with her booking, but if she's one of yours it might save us time.'

'Shouldn't be a problem,' Fletcher said. 'If she does work for us, she'll be in the internal phonebook. I'll have a look in the morning.'

'Cheers, mate,' Milton said. He wasn't sure he had a lot in common with Fletcher, but they got on well enough after a pint or two. Always paid to keep on the right side of people. 'I'll do the same for you sometime.'

'Can't imagine we'll ever have the need to call for help from you spoiled city types,' Fletcher said. 'No, seriously—it's no problem. We going to grab a pint sometime?'

'That would be good. I'll let you know when I'm next up your way.'

'You do that, old son.'

Milton ended the call and sat silently in the empty MIR, his mind still running over what he'd heard. Andy Barton sounded a real charmer but it was difficult to see how he might be linked to this killing. Even so, Milton felt a growing unease. This case had felt wrong from the start. This was a unique killer committing a unique murder. In a building filled with serving police officers. That felt like a strangeness too far.

The clock said ten-thirty. Suddenly, the building felt cold and empty and Milton felt, for the first time in years, a clutch of those old familiar anxieties.

Time to go home, he thought. Definitely time to go home.

Even if it wasn't really home any more.

TUESDAY

CHAPTER ELEVEN

'You're sure?'

Pete Warwick gazed at him without speaking. It was Murrain who, literally, blinked first. 'Yes, of course you're sure,' Murrain said. 'Dumb question. But it does change our thinking.'

'I spotted them yesterday, but I didn't want to say till I'd had a closer look,' Warwick acknowledged. 'It was quite subtle.'

'Subtle,' Murrain repeated. It wasn't the word he'd have used, but he and Warwick had different perspectives on the world.

'It looks to me,' Warwick went on, 'as if he put something round her ankles and wrists to protect them. A padded bandage, that sort of thing. There weren't the lesions that you might normally find in that kind of situation. But there was some surface bruising. On all four limbs. So I don't think it's a coincidence.'

'She was tied up,' Murrain said, as if to convince himself of the fact. 'Does that square with what you found, Neil?'

They were in a small meeting room along the corridor from the MIR. It was what Joe Milton insisted on calling a case conference, but which Murrain just saw as an opportunity to share the few ideas they had. It also put pressure on Pete Warwick and Neil Ferbrache to share what they had even if they hadn't yet had time to finalise their formal reports.

'Difficult to say,' Ferbrache said, pushing his glasses back up his nose as he peered at his notes. 'There's nothing inconsistent with that. She wasn't tied to the bed because the headboard was a solid unit and there was no footboard, so nothing to tie her to.'

'I'd say her wrists and ankles were tied together, maybe with her wrists behind her legs to incapacitate her. Probably with those self-sealing plastic tie things,' Warwick said. 'But that's just a guess. There's no strong medical evidence.' He spoke as if this was a quite unacceptable state of affairs. 'And I think she was gagged. Not tightly. Again, there's just slight evidence of bruising. But I found some traces of cotton in her mouth.'

'Enough to muffle any screams, though,' Milton offered.

'I'd imagine so.'

'It all indicates premeditation,' Murrain said, voicing the obvious point that they'd all been contemplating. 'Not a crime of passion.'

'Very much so,' Warwick agreed. 'And the plastic ties suggest someone who had some idea what they were doing.'

Murrain glanced at Ferbrache, who nodded. 'Links in with what we were saying yesterday.'

Milton was frowning, working through the implications in his head. 'So she wasn't taken by surprise. When he stabbed her, I mean.'

'Well, if she'd been tied up, I'm imagine she'd have had an idea his motives weren't wholly honourable, if that's what you mean,' Warwick said drily.

Milton had had sufficient dealings with Warwick's brand of superciliousness not to be intimidated. 'Well, not exactly. I meant that yesterday we'd all drawn the conclusion that she'd been taken by surprise while sitting at the dressing-table, or some similar scenario. But that can't have been the case.'

'It would seem not,' Warwick agreed. 'The angle of the knife wounds indicates she was stabbed from behind and slightly above. I think we'd assumed—we'd *all* assumed—that she'd been sitting at the dressing table with the killer standing behind her. Maybe she wasn't. Maybe she was kneeling and he was crouching behind.' He looked across to Ferbrache for support.

'I think,' Ferbrache said cautiously, 'that's consistent with the blood patterns. Probably more consistent than if she was sitting at the dressing-table. When I came to map out the patterns, that didn't look quite right.'

'So what are we saying?' Murrain asked. 'That he made her kneel down before he stabbed her. Was she still tied up at this point?'

'My guess would be yes,' Warwick said. 'Though I should stress that there's—'

'No strong medical evidence, no,' Murrain finished, wearily. It was one of Warwick's catch-phrases. He was a skilled pathologist, but he was even more expert at ensuring his own backside was well-covered. 'Why do you think he protected her wrists and ankles? Seems odd to be concerned about that if he was going to kill her anyway.'

'That's more your territory than mine,' Warwick said.

'Maybe he didn't know he was going to kill her,' Milton said. 'Maybe initially he had some other agenda.'

'There's no evidence of any sexual assault, if that's what you mean,' Warwick said.

'I don't know what I mean,' Milton went on, patiently. 'I just mean that perhaps he didn't start with the idea of killing her. Or that he didn't see that as the inevitable outcome. So he wanted to look after her at first.'

'Or maybe he wanted to confuse us,' Murrain said. 'Make us think it was unpremeditated. That it was a crime committed in the heat of the moment.' He shook his head. 'None of it really hangs together, does it? Premeditated, carefully planned, by someone who apparently knew what they were doing, and knew how to clean up the scene afterwards. But he commits a murder like that.'

It was the same incongruity Milton had been wrestling with the night before, that had driven him from the deserted building with a taste of the panic attacks that had plagued him years before. He'd made it home OK but sleep had eluded him and he'd been back in the office at first light, feeling washed-out but wanting to press on. Murrain had turned up half an hour later, looking less tired but similarly driven.

'Anything else, Neil?' Murrain said.

Ferbrache shuffled through his papers. 'Nothing of significance. More of the same, really. But, if you want my opinion, the room was too clean. Forensically speaking, I mean. The bed was like it hadn't been touched, let alone slept in or on. If the victim was tied up all night—and especially if she was terrified—there was no new contamination of the carpets, if you get my drift.'

'I get your drift,' Murrain said. 'So what's that telling us? And don't just say that's our territory.'

'It suggests to me first that the killer took some care of the victim overnight, maybe. But it suggests more that the killer was going to some length to minimise any risk of being identified. I suspect some protection was placed on the bed and maybe on the carpet too. Some sheeting the killer took with them. And, as before, that they cleaned up very thoroughly.'

'The victim's bowels and bladder were relatively empty,' Warwick said, 'however that might have been achieved. I'd estimate she ate early the previous evening.'

Murrain looked up. It was a question that, stupidly, he hadn't thought to ask yet. No doubt Warwick had been waiting smugly to point out his omission. 'Do we know what she ate?'

Warwick smiled benignly. 'I was wondering when we'd come to that. It looks like her last meal was a nice poached salmon with some new potatoes and a salad. Most nutritious. There were some traces of alcohol in her bloodstream. I'd say she'd had a couple of glasses of wine.'

Murrain gazed back at him for a moment with a faint smile. 'Any views on the grape variety or vintage as well, Pete?' Then he turned to Milton. 'First sighting of a lead, I suppose.'

'I'll be on to it, boss. Though if she ate in town, it'll be a long-shot.'

'Better than a no-shot, anyway. Seems to make even less sense. The victim enjoyed a pleasant meal before being very gently tied up and then killed.' He shook his head as if trying to clear it.

There was a sudden, unexpectedly loud buzzing from Milton's mobile phone on the table. He shrugged apologetically. 'Excuse me if I take this. Might be relevant.'

Murrain nodded. 'Think we've gone about as far as we can, anyway.'

Milton left the room, already beginning to talk into his phone as he exited. Murrain turned back to the others. 'Thanks for your efforts, people. Just wish we were making a bit more progress.'

'I'll get the full report to you later today,' Warwick said. 'We all understand the sensitivities here. But I can't pretend it's going to tell you anything more.'

'Same here,' Ferbrache said. 'On both counts.'

'Neither of you fancies working any kind of a miracle, then,' Murrain said. 'Bloody typical.'

Beth climbed out of the car and stood for a moment, drinking in the fresh air and the view. She'd been here before, a couple of years previously, for a Christmas do with the marketing department of a company where she'd been freelancing. As a freelancer, it was unusual to get invited to any kind of office Christmas party, and this had been a pretty upmarket affair, more of a dinner-dance than the usual drunken disco. She'd almost declined the invitation as she really knew only a handful of the attendees. In the end, though, she'd had a good time. She'd drunk enough to be relaxed but not so much that she'd found herself doing or saying anything embarrassing. The food had been good and the company, on the whole, even better. She'd got on particularly well with one bloke there—Gid something, she recalled—and she'd harboured vague hopes he might contact her afterwards. But he never had, and she'd concluded he was probably married though he hadn't given that impression on the night. Even so, her memories of this place were positive.

The hotel's setting had been impressive enough even on a cold December night. She remembered how, after the taxi had dropped her off, she'd stood, just as she was now, gazing into the vast openness of the Cheshire plain. That night, the landscape had been little more than a black space filled with constellations of lights, the orange glow of Manchester rising in the distance. Now, on a clear autumn day, she could see the full panorama from the hazy city towers in the north to the Cheshire pasturelands in the south. In the far distance, north of Manchester, she could make out the curve of Winter Hill. Much closer, there was the brick-built railway viaduct cutting through the heart of Stockport. It was a glorious day, but the chill wind already tasted of winter.

She turned and looked around her. On this Tuesday lunchtime, the car-park was almost deserted, with only a couple of brightly polished executive vehicles to accompany her own battered Ford Fiesta and a Renault Clio of a similar vintage. She wondered whether the mysterious Jack Brennan was the owner of the Audi or the BMW. It seemed likely. Whatever business had brought him to stay in a hotel like this would be more lucrative than her own brand of freelancing. Still, maybe she'd get a free lunch from him, alongside the return of at least some of what Mac had taken from her.

The interior of the hotel felt cosily warm after the open moorland. She walked past the reception desk, feeling, as she always did in places like this, as if she were about to be exposed as a charlatan, unfit to be allowed in somewhere so luxurious. It was ridiculous, she knew. In reality this was little more than an upmarket chain hotel—the sort of place that fleeces bored business travellers in the week and offers bargain breaks to young couples and families at the weekend. Even so, it was more upscale than anywhere she normally frequented.

The hotel bar was situated beyond the reception, forming an anteroom to the restaurant beyond. She'd half-expected that Brennan would be sitting waiting for her, even though she was a few minutes early. But the only other occupant of the room was an earnest-looking business-woman, a year or two younger than Beth herself but looking utterly at home in this context. She was tapping at a laptop, pausing for an occasional sip of coffee, and had glanced up only briefly as Beth had entered the room. Her expression confirmed that she too was waiting to meet someone, but that Beth had definitely not fitted the bill.

Beth sighed to herself and took a seat as far as possible from the other woman. Beforehand, she'd felt intrigued about this meeting. About who Brennan might be, and what more he might know of Mac and his current circumstances. She'd even been looking forward to the prospect of a lunch with someone who, whoever and whatever he might turn out to be, was at least another human being. It seemed quite a while since she'd had much social interaction with one of those.

Now she was here, in this alien-feeling environment, she felt much less comfortable. The prospect of a leisurely lunch seemed unenticing. All she wanted was get back what McKendrick owed her, if that were possible, and then put him, and any of his friends, firmly out of her life forever. She just wanted this over with.

105

'Joe?'

'Yes?' He was standing in the corridor outside the meeting room. Through the glass Murrain was finishing off with Warwick and Ferbrache.

'It's Rob. Rob Fletcher.'

'Oh, Christ, sorry, Rob. It said: 'number withheld'. I thought you were selling double-glazing or payday loans.'

'Not till after retirement. I'm on the office landline. I was following up your call last night.'

'That's good of you.' He meant it sincerely. He hadn't really expected Fletcher to get back to him and certainly not so quickly. In the light of day, he was feeling almost embarrassed he'd interrupted Fletcher's evening in the first place.

'Never like to let down you city types when you come crawling to the real workers for help.'

'Thanks. Imagine it makes a change from dealing with sheep-rustling, anyway. Or whatever it is you woolly-backs do with sheep.'

'You asked me about Kathy Granger?'

'Right. Does she work for you lot, then?'

'Looks like it. Found her in the internal phone book. Assume it's the one you're looking for. Seems she's an administrator in HR.'

'Oh. Right.' Milton jotted down the phone number, slightly taken aback. 'Hadn't expected that, somehow.' He remembered just in time that Fletcher's partner worked in HR for some Preston law-firm. 'Not that I've anything against HR.'

Fletcher laughed. 'You're the only one, then. No, I was a bit surprised. I mean, there's no reason why not, but I'd have expected that most of the guests would be colleagues of dear old Andy Barton or his new bride.'

'Must have known one of them from somewhere, anyway. Suppose we'll find out when we talk to her.'

'No doubt. Well, hope she helps cast some light on your mystery.'

'Can't really see it, but you never know. Thanks for tracking her down, anyway.'

'No problem, mate. Just don't forget you owe me a favour.'

'I won't.'

Milton ended the call and stood for a moment, watching Murrain still chatting with the others in the meeting room. No time like the present, he thought. He couldn't imagine that Kathy Granger was going to add anything significant to the sum of their knowledge. But he knew better than to ignore Murrain's instincts. He thumbed in the number Fletcher had given him.

The phone rang just once, then a voice said: 'HR. How can I help?'

They'd obviously been taught to answer the phone like that. Milton thought. Wasn't it one of the great lies? 'I'm from HR and I'm here to help.' 'Hi,' he said out loud, 'I'm trying to get in touch with Kathy Granger.'

There was a pause. 'Who's calling, please?'

Milton hesitated, wondering how much to say. 'My name's Joe Milton,' he said. 'Is she available, please?'

Another pause, longer this time. 'She's not available at the moment. Can I ask what it's in connection with?'

There was no point in beating about the bush, Milton thought. 'Actually, it's DI Milton from Greater Manchester Police. I need to speak to Ms Granger about an ongoing investigation. It's quite urgent. Can you tell me how I can contact her?' Not that invoking the name of GMP was likely to cut much ice up there.

'Well—' The speaker stopped again. 'I'm afraid I can't, exactly. She's not in work today.'

There was something odd in his tone, Milton thought. 'Are you expecting her in tomorrow?'

'This investigation,' the speaker said cautiously. 'Kathy's not in some kind of trouble, is she?'

'Is there any reason you think she might be?'

'Well, no, not Kathy. But this isn't like her.'

'What isn't?'

'It's just that she hasn't turned into work today. Or yesterday. And she's not called in either. She never usually takes a day's sick.'

Through the glass partition, Milton saw Murrain turn towards him, almost as if he'd been listening in to the conversation. 'Have you tried calling her?'

'Well, yes. We were all a bit anxious. But it just rings out. And then when you called—'

'Yes, I understand, Mr—?'

'Cartwright. Keith Cartwright. I'm the payroll manager. Kathy's boss.'

'Thanks, Mr Cartwright. We just want to speak to Kathy as a potential witness in a case we're investigating. Not even a material witness, most likely. She was just one of a number of people who were in the locality at the time the crime was committed.'

'I see. Well, I can pass on a message when she does come in.' Cartwright sounded disappointed that the story wasn't more exciting. 'Funny, this is about as close as we've ever got to real policing.'

'Funny,' Milton agreed. 'And you reckon it's unusual for Kathy to behave like this?'

'Not like her at all. She's never sick. And if she's ever delayed or anything, she's always scrupulous about letting us know where she is.'

'She didn't give any indication she wouldn't be in this week?'

'Not at all. We knew she was going away for the weekend. Some old friend's wedding or something.'

Milton made a mental note that Granger hadn't told her colleagues that the old friend in question was either DI Andy Barton or his new bride. That might or might not be significant. He had no idea whether Barton's name carried any cachet in the rarefied realms of Human Resources.

'Is anyone planning to check she's OK?' he asked. 'Pay a home visit, I mean.'

'We don't normally do home visits till someone's been off sick for a couple of weeks. That's the procedure.' Cartwright sounded like someone who would be a stickler for procedure. 'So I don't really know—'

'From what you've said, these don't sound like ordinary circumstances. Is there any family you can contact? Neighbours?'

'Not that I know of. Kathy lived alone. I think both her parents are dead. Not sure there's anyone else. I can check the file.'

'If I were you, I'd get someone to visit her. It's almost certainly nothing. But if it's out of character—well, you can't be too careful, can you?'

'No, I suppose not,' Cartwright said, doubtfully. 'But I don't want her to think we're snooping.'

'She'll be pleased you're concerned about her, I should think.'

'You're probably right. And I'll tell her you want to talk to her.'

Milton gave his number and ended the call. He looked up to see Murrain still sitting in the meeting room, alone now. He was still gazing at Milton through the glass, and Milton could tell from the older man's expression that he already *knew*. Not the detail, not what Milton had just been hearing, not about Granger's absence from work.

But Murrain knew something had happened, and he knew it mattered.

CHAPTER TWELVE

Donovan had worried that Jack Brennan might be waiting when she walked into the Agency office the next morning. But there was no sign of him and, when she checked his on-line office diary, his meeting schedule confirmed he'd been telling the truth about heading back to London the previous night. That was some small relief. She and Holly had spent the evening knocking back too much red wine, watching some crappy old film on TV, and studiously avoiding making any reference to the man who'd unexpectedly invaded their home.

Now, Donovan was feeling mildly hungover and dreading the thought of another day pretending to carry out a non-job in this place. As it turned out, though, the fates—which had already done a decent job of ensuring that Brennan was at the other end of the country—were on her side for once. She hadn't even finished booting up her computer terminal when Murray Graham poked his head round the office door. 'Must have gone well yesterday, then?'

Graham was the poor bugger who'd been left managing her when the last burst of organisational music had stopped. He was a decent enough man but out of his depth in a political organisation like the Agency, which was no doubt why he'd ended up with Donovan. His background was as a financial investigator with Her Majesty's Revenue and Customs, and the ways of policing seemed a perennial mystery to him.

'The interview?' she said. 'Well, I liked what I saw.'

'They must have felt the same,' Graham said, 'given how quickly they've responded.' He held up a sheet of paper. She had a suspicion he printed off every e-mail he received. 'They seem keen on you.'

It sounded as if Murrain had been as good as his word. 'What did they say?'

'If we can release you, they want to offer you a twelve-month secondment. Same pay and conditions but them picking up the tab. This chap Murrain reckons he can sort the paperwork. Rather him than me.'

'What sort of start-date are they talking about?' She knew that nothing in this environment ever moved quickly.

'As far as he's concerned you can start immediately. Reckons they've some big investigation on and he needs all the bodies he can get. He's putting pressure on to release you as quickly as we can.'

She nodded. This was usually the point at which, having stuck you in a non-existent role for weeks on end, they suddenly decided you were indispensable. 'And how do you see that?'

He looked momentarily embarrassed and she waited for the inevitable refusal. 'Look, Marie, you know I rate you really highly. But, frankly, we both know you're wasted here. I wish I could offer you something better, but—well, I think it's better if you go as soon as possible.'

'And as soon as possible means what?'

'Up to you, really. Do you have anything you need to finish off?'

'Not really.' He knew as well as she did that there was nothing she couldn't hand over immediately. None of it was important, and much of it hardly constituted serious work.

'My sense was that Murrain would take you straightaway if he could.' He shrugged, the embarrassment still evident. 'I can call him. Say we can release you immediately in the circumstances. If that's OK by you.'

'Fine by me,' she said. It would be good to be out of here, good to be doing a real job again. Good, she thought, to be working alongside Murrain and Milton.

'Just hope he's right about the paperwork,' Graham said, as he turned to leave. 'Need to get the funding sorted ASAP. It's hitting my budget.'

Thanks, she thought. Nice to be just an unwanted financial overhead. Whatever the future might hold for her, it had to be better than this.

'Sir?'

Murrain had seen Sparrow hovering by his desk, ostentatiously standing out of earshot but close enough to be noticed. Murrain had been on the phone for a long time—half an hour or so—trying to sort the administration for Marie Donovan's transfer, but Sparrow had shown no sign of departing. Something important, obviously, if only to Sparrow.

Sure enough, as soon as Murrain replaced the receiver, Sparrow appeared in front of him. 'Sir?'

Murrain looked up wearily. He'd persuaded HR to agree to the transfer, despite it being 'highly irregular' and 'outside normal procedures'. Murrain hadn't really seen the problem. He was carrying enough unfilled vacancies to ensure there was plenty of budget to pay for her. He'd managed, without too much difficulty, to get sign off from his Chief Superintendent. The only thing preventing the move was bureaucracy, but that of course was the biggest hurdle of all.

'We can't afford to be setting a precedent?' the HR Business Partner had intoned.

'What sort of precedent?'

'Well, encouraging managers to act outside normal procedures.'

'Why not?'

'There'd be chaos.'

'There's already chaos. Because we don't have enough staff.'

It had taken another thirty minutes to persuade the HRBP that it really was possible to step outside procedure. It was a victory and a significant one, in that Murrain needed all the experienced hands he could get, but it had felt like an unnecessary diversion of his time and energy from the task at hand. Around him, officers were collating information from the interviews and other sources, but still nothing of substance was emerging.

'Sir? Sparrow said again.

'Sorry, Will. Miles away. What can I do for you?'

'You asked me to check that car numberplate, sir?'

Please just call me Kenny, Murrain wanted to say. The old hierarchical certainties were gradually being eroded and most officers were happy to be called simply by their forenames these days, whatever their rank. But that tended to leave some of the younger ones, like Will Sparrow, unsure where they stood. 'Car numberplate?' For a moment, he had no idea what Sparrow was talking about.

'When we made the visit to Mrs Berenek,' Sparrow explained. 'The son's car. As we were leaving.'

'Right.' He remembered now. There'd been something about the son. It had been he, rather than the mother, who'd triggered the response. 'Find anything?'

'Maybe. I'm not sure. I only just got around to looking because— well—' He gestured apologetically at the activity around them.

'It's probably not a priority, given everything else we're dealing with. Just curiosity, really. But you found something?'

'Well, the car's not his for a start. Looks like it's a company car.'

'Unusual vehicle for a company car.'

'That's what I thought. Owned by an outfit called Paradise Holdings. Registered office in Alderley Edge.'

'Ah,' Murrain said. 'That makes more sense.'

'You know them, sir?'

'Only too well. One of the trading names of one Patrick Henessey. Name mean anything to you?'

'Rings a bell,' Sparrow said, though his face suggested the opposite.

'Long been of interest to us, Henessey, and of even more interest to the NCA, I'd guess. Local businessman. Import-export stuff. Some of it legit—he supplies stuff to half the restaurants in Chinatown. But there's a disparity between Henessey's published accounts and the lifestyle he leads.'

Sparrow nodded. 'I remember him now. Wasn't there an attempt to prosecute him?'

'A couple, at least. One fell at the first hurdle because the CPS thought the case wasn't strong enough. Another got to Court but the case was thrown out on the grounds that there'd supposedly been some collusion on the evidence. He had the best lawyers. You can imagine.' Murrain sighed.

113

'Yes, I can imagine.' That was so often the problem. They all knew who the villains were. The problem was building a case that would satisfy the CPS and then stand up in Court. Officers could be tempted to cut corners to get a result. Sometimes it worked, whatever you might think of the morality. More often, it left everyone with egg on their collective faces. 'What's Henessey's line of business? The illegit side, I mean.'

'Anything he can make money from. Drugs, money laundering, VAT fraud. I've heard rumours of people-trafficking. Last I heard, he was getting himself alongside the Eastern European gangs in the city. Risky territory, but Henessey reckons he can look after himself.'

'So Karl Berenek's on his payroll?'

'Sounds like it. Maybe Henessey finds Berenek's connections useful. Would explain why he was prepared to give him a car.'

'Pity he allowed Berenek to choose the model,' Sparrow said. 'Though I can't envisage Berenek driving a Mondeo.'

'What about Berenek himself? Anything on him?'

'He has a record,' Sparrow said. 'Nothing big. Petty theft, early on. Then drug dealing, but only softer stuff, supposedly. And he was once arrested for GBH, but the case was dropped.'

'Recent? That last one?'

'About a year ago.'

'Wonder why it was dropped. Maybe Henessey intervened. Smart lawyers, a bit of pressure on the witnesses. Who knows?'

'Do you want me to try to find out more, sir?'

'Don't think it's a priority at the moment,' Murrain said, though his instincts were still suggesting differently. 'Keep him on the back burner, though. I reckon there's something there.' He paused. 'Thanks, Will. Good work.'

He watched as the young man made his way back to his desk, looking pleased with himself. They were a good team, he thought, a good mix of talents and personalities. Eloise reckoned that was down to his own management abilities but he'd never quite been able to see that. He didn't think of himself as a manager. He was just a copper who'd been promoted to the point where he couldn't avoid being responsible for a team. He wasn't aware he'd done anything with this group of individuals except treat them as mature human beings. But maybe that was rare enough in this environment to make a difference.

'Boss?'

Joe Milton was standing in front of the desk, a folder of papers in his hand. 'How's it going, Joe?'

'Nothing much new, sadly. We've got the reports through from Ferbrache and Warwick. Nothing significant they haven't already told us.' He flicked through the papers. 'Ferbrache managed to get a fair few decent prints in the room, but they've been able to match most of those either to the usual room cleaners or the victim herself. The others don't match anyone on file.'

'Oh, well. Can't say my hopes were high.'

Milton gestured towards the phone. 'Any luck with Donovan?'

'She'll be joining us from tomorrow, despite HR's best efforts.'

'Tomorrow? She must be keen.'

'You know how it is. She wants out. They want her out. If we pay for her, everyone's happy.'

'And you reckons she's what we need, despite all that?'

'Don't you think so?' Murrain sounded genuinely interested.

Milton laughed. 'I'm more than happy to trust your instincts, boss. But, yes, since you ask, I think she knows what she's about.'

'I'll blame you, then, if it all goes pear-shaped. Speaking of instincts, what are you going to do about Kathy Granger?'

'Granger?' Milton had filled Murrain in about his conversation with Granger's boss. Murrain had nodded, taking in the information but initially offering no response. It was only now, out of the blue, that he'd returned to the topic. 'You think I should do something?'

'What do *you* think?'

Milton lowered himself into the seat opposite Murrain's desk. He had the sense that this was going to be a serious conversation. 'If we're talking about instincts, mine are that we should follow it up, to be honest. Whether we can persuade our colleagues up north of that is another question.'

'I'd always recommend following your instincts,' Murrain said, all flippancy gone. 'Test them out. Find out what's driving them. When you can trust them and when you can't.' This was typical of Murrain, Milton thought. Some people thought he was a bit of an old hippy, with his visions and his feelings. But at heart he was a pragmatist. He knew that what detectives refer to as instinct is usually the accumulation of all their years of experience, the stuff they don't even know they know. But instinct can be a euphemism for other, less positive influences—prejudice, untested assumptions, personal bias. The trick, he said, was to follow where your instincts led but always to be questioning them, asking yourself what it was, really, that had brought you down this particular road.

'Is that how it works with you?'

Murrain hesitated. There were few people with whom he'd ever felt comfortable discussing these issues. His late mother, a couple of the siblings he hardly ever saw these days. Eloise, of course. And, increasingly, Joe Milton. He wasn't sure why he was prepared to invest so much trust in Milton. Perhaps, he thought, simply because his Christian name was Joe. Joseph. 'Not really, no,' he said, finally. 'Not with the real stuff. I mean, I get a gut feel about some things, just like anybody else, whether it's right or wrong. But the real stuff, the real *feelings*, those are different. I don't have any doubt. I know they're there and I know they mean something. The question, usually, is working out what.' Another pause. 'Often, it's not what you expect at all.'

'And you have this—feeling about Kathy Granger?'

'I had it from the moment I saw her name on the list of guests that Bert Wallace was using. It was there, no doubt. But it might mean anything.'

'But it's worth following up?'

'I'd say so. But, like you say, it might take more than that to persuade Lancs Police to take it seriously.'

'They don't need to take it very seriously,' Milton pointed out. 'Just get the local PCSO to check it out. She's one of their own, after all.'

'That argument might carry more weight than the fact that we want to talk to her,' Murrain agreed. 'Can you get that mate of yours to pull some strings?'

Milton sighed. 'I suppose. I hope there's something in this, though. He's already got us marked down as big-city numpties.'

'Probably better not to mention that this is all down to your boss's instincts, then. That might confirm his view that we're operating in a Mancunian lala-land.'

'I'll just tell him that she might be a more material witness than we originally thought. I'll steer clear of any reference to séances or psychic insights.'

'Good move.' Murrain smiled. They'd shifted the gears of the conversation back into their more usual banter. But neither had any doubt that the discussion had been deadly serious. As Milton rose, Murrain leaned forward and added: 'As soon as you can, I think, don't you?'

'With respect,' Kev Anderson said, 'isn't this a matter for HR?'

'With *respect*,' his Sergeant responded, 'it's a matter for you. I just allocated it to you, or did you miss that?' Irony was largely wasted on Anderson, he knew, but he kept trying to find some way of penetrating that thick skull.

'Yeah, but—well, if she's absent, it's a home visit, isn't it? That's HR's business.'

Anderson would know all about the absence procedure, given his own frequent non-attendance. 'I don't think they're concerned she's had a couple of days off, Kev. I think they're concerned about her welfare.'

'She's HR herself, isn't she? Typical. One law for them—'

'They're concerned because she's not called in.'

'That's a disciplinary matter, then—'

'It's also out of character. That's why they're worried. Just bugger off and do it, Kev. It's on your beat, anyway.'

'So what am I supposed to do, exactly?'

'Just ring the doorbell and see if there's any sign of life.'

'And if there isn't?'

'Then report back and they can decide what to do next,' the Sergeant said, wearily. He'd no more desire to get landed with this one that Anderson did, but he knew that when the order came from on high you had to show willing.

'If you say so, boss.'

'I say so.' The Sergeant sighed. There were people out there, he knew, who still thought this was a command-and-control structure. Not with some PCSOs, it wasn't.

In truth, Anderson wasn't too reluctant to take on the task. It was, as the Sergeant had said, on his beat anyway. It would make a break from the usual routine. It would give him the chance to skive off for a smoke. It would remove him, at least temporarily, from having to interact with that most troublesome of groups, the general public.

The place wasn't difficult to find. A new block of flats in a moderately upmarket Bury suburb. A decent enough place, he thought, wondering vaguely how she could afford it on the salary of an HR Officer. You could never fathom others' finances. Maybe she'd inherited something. Maybe she was divorced and had managed to take this place from her husband.

He was thinking these random thoughts as he approached the front door of the block. It was one of those places with security locks on the doors, a row of doorbells, and a speakerphone to announce your presence. He scanned down the bells until he found the name he was looking for: Granger.

Even before he'd pressed the bell, a voice from behind him said: 'She's not there.'

He turned, surprised by the interruption. The man behind him was elderly, probably in his seventies if not older. He was a cheerful looking figure, clad in a long old-fashioned raincoat, slightly rotund, with a crown of unruly white hair. He was clutching two bulging Tesco bags.

'I'm sorry?'

'She's not there,' the man repeated. 'That's Kathy's bell.'

'How do you know she's not there?'

118

'I'm her next door neighbour. George Canning.' He made as if to shake hands then realised he was carrying the shopping bags. He looked up and down Anderson's uniform. Anderson was substantially overweight, and his protective vest and equipment made him look even more stocky and ungainly. 'Is she all right?'

'That's what I'm here to find out,' Anderson said, solemnly.

'I know she was away for the weekend,' Canning added. 'But she doesn't seem to have come back yet. She usually lets me know her plans.' He sounded aggrieved that he'd not been kept informed.

'How do you know she's still away?'

In response, Canning placed one of the carrier bags by his feet and pressed a code number into the key-pad by the front door. The door buzzed open and he pushed his way inside. Taking his cue, Anderson picked up the bag and followed Canning.

'There.' Canning pointed to a row of wooden pigeon holes. 'She's not collected her post.' The boxes were lockable, but it was possible to see the small stack of what looked like junk mail inside. 'She always collects her post straightaway. And I can hear when she's moving about in the flat. She's not been there since Friday morning.'

'Right,' Anderson said. It sounded as if his duty here was almost done. He turned to hand the bag back to Canning, who made no effort to take it.

'Why are you here, then?' Canning asked. 'Is it because she works for you lot?'

'I suppose so,' Anderson agreed. 'I was just asked to check she was all right.'

'You'd better do that, then, hadn't you? I'll take you up there.' It was clear that Canning's real agenda was to obtain some help carrying up his shopping, but Anderson could see no escape other than the sort of outright rudeness that might prompt a complaint. Canning struck him as the sort who might take action at the merest hint of a slight.

'OK. Lead the way.' He followed Canning into the lift and up to the third floor. Canning's flat was, inevitably, at the end of the corridor, furthest from the lift. Anderson followed him in, noting the mild chaos of what he imagined was a widower's residence.

'There you go, then, Mr Canning. I'll leave you to it.' The idea of a crafty cigarette was becoming more attractive by the second.

'Don't you want to check inside?' Canning fumbled in his pockets. 'She leaves me a spare key. In case there are any problems. We had a burst pipe once—'

'I don't think that would be right,' Anderson said. 'I don't have a search warrant or anything.' He had no real idea of the legal niceties, but the lure of the nicotine was growing stronger.

'To be honest,' Canning said, 'I'm a bit concerned myself. It's not like her. I hope nothing's happened to her in there.'

For the first time, it occurred to Anderson that this might be a possibility. That perhaps Kathy Granger had returned on Sunday after all, and had suffered some accident or illness. Perhaps he ought to check. If she was in some kind of difficulty, that was the kind of thing that might get you a commendation. Anderson had long harboured ambitions to become a fully-fledged Constable but so far, for some unknown reason, he'd been unsuccessful at the selection events. This might make the difference.

'She doesn't mind you going in there?'

'I go in there all the time when she's away,' Canning said.

This wasn't exactly an answer to Anderson's question, but he didn't much care what Canning might get up to. 'I suppose we should just go in and check there's nothing wrong.'

Canning led Anderson back along the corridor to Granger's flat. Before Canning could stick his spare key in the lock, Anderson made a point of hammering loudly on the door. 'Anyone there? Police!' No-one could accuse him of not doing this by the book.

'Told you,' Canning said. He twisted the key in the lock and pushed open the door.

By this point, Anderson had almost persuaded himself that they would indeed find Kathy Granger sprawled out on the floor or languishing on the bed with some serious illness. Or, even worse, perhaps she'd been the victim of some violent crime, a burglary that had gone horribly wrong.

But the flat was deserted. It was neat and tidy, with a minimalist modern decor a world away from Canning's clutter. The double-bed in the solitary bedroom had been left made up. The kitchen was clean, although the dish-washer was turned on, at the end of its cycle, as if Granger had left it running when she departed. The sitting-room looked pristine. Everything seemed in order, other than the absence of an occupant.

'Well, that's it then,' Anderson said to Canning. 'Wild goose chase.' He was already heading for the door, fumbling for his cigarette-packet. 'Don't worry, I'll let myself out downstairs.'

CHAPTER THIRTEEN

Later, when the police and the manager were asking those endless questions, she thought she might get into trouble. She was used to that from her younger days, when she'd been a teenage girl in what she still thought of as home. It was the default position when the authorities didn't know what to do. Muddy the waters, harass and intimidate anyone on the scene, demonstrating their ineptitude while supposedly asserting their authority. Making sure that, whoever was blamed, it would never be them.

It was different here. She knew that well enough. The police had their faults, and she still did her best to steer clear of them. But most of those she'd dealt with over the years had been well-intentioned enough, just trying to do their job. Some had been helpful to her, others less so. The kindly policewoman who'd helped keep her sane after Ronnie had been attacked, in those bleak few days when she'd been sure he was going to die. That policewoman had probably just been doing her job too, taking care of their only witness. But she'd felt like a genuine friend, the only one, except for Ronnie himself, that Marika had.

That was a few years ago now, and things had moved on. Ronnie had survived, but he'd never worked again and, she thought, had never been quite the same man she'd first loved. But they got on well enough and managed to scrape by, pooling her small salary and the benefits he was entitled to. She still hoped that one day he would ask her to marry him, but it hadn't happened yet and the prospect seemed more distant with every year that passed.

That was why she'd made a mistake that afternoon. Her mind had been elsewhere. She'd been thinking about Ronnie, about their lives together, about what might have been and what still might be. She was carrying out her work, as she so often did, largely without thinking. It wasn't, after all, work that required much thought. There was a set routine for cleaning each room, which she'd learnt in her first days here and which she always followed to the letter. There were times when she felt that the prescribed routine was insufficient, when the room really needed a more thorough clean. But she knew that the supervisors didn't want her to exercise that kind of initiative. If she took longer than specified to clean a room, she fell behind schedule and no-one would thank her, much less pay her, if she had to work late to get it done.

So she did what she was asked to do. A quick run over with the vacuum cleaner, the surfaces wiped down, bathroom cleaned, crockery and glasses washed, the sachets of tea and coffee replaced. Tick it off, and get on to the next one. You could do it with your eyes closed, and most days she did it with her brain switched off.

They were running late that day, anyway. A couple of the other women were off sick, and more than usual of the guests had left it to the last minute before checking out. Usually, they got most of the rooms done in the morning, and finished off the remainder in the brief window before new guests started checking in. Today, it was already past two and there were still rooms that needed to be prepared. The supervisor had been hassling all morning, and there was no point in complaining that they were short-handed.

That was why she missed the sign, she told herself. Thinking back, she'd already been down this corridor once and had noted the 'Do Not Disturb' notice on the door. She'd returned in the afternoon to deal with a couple of neighbouring rooms that had now been vacated, and this time, her brain still not engaged, she'd moved automatically on and had the door half-open before she registered that the sign was still in place.

It wasn't a mistake she'd ever made before. She was on the point of calling out an apology and retreating when something made her pause. She didn't know what it was at first. Afterwards, she thought she'd picked up the scent without realising. Whatever it was, it was enough to make her hesitate, her trolley still half in the room, listening.

There was no sound she could detect. From the doorway, she could see the television was off. Beyond that, she could make out only the foot of the bed and the single armchair by the window. The bed appeared undisturbed.

It was only then that she registered the smell. It puzzled her at first. It was nothing she immediately recognised, but it seemed oddly familiar. Rich, pungent, on the edge of unpleasant. And, for some reason, it made her afraid.

It took her another moment to realise the truth. She knew that scent only too well. It was the scent that had soaked into the air in that grim alleyway the night Ronnie was mugged. The scent that had lingered in her nostrils for days so that she could taste in it in every mouthful that she forced herself to eat or drink. The scent she'd thought she would never forget.

The scent of spilled blood.

Murrain could, just about, recall a time when policing involved something other than meetings and paperwork. These days, they seemed to dominate everything. He understood why the bureaucracy was needed. It was just he wished that he didn't need to be involved. Even though he tried to delegate all those activities to Milton, he still found himself wasting most of his time on work that seemed peripheral to actual policing.

Today, he'd spent much of the morning in yet another session with the ACC and the Head of Communications. Neither was impressed with progress on the case to date, though he'd resisted the temptation to point out that it wouldn't be improved if he had to spend every working hour discussing how to handle the media.

'We need to make an announcement,' the Head of Comms had said, bluntly. 'We've held them off as long as we reasonably can.'

'Be my guest,' Murrain said. 'What do they want to know?'

'They want to know the nature of the killing, who the victim is, what the circumstances are, what progress we've made—'

'Everything, then,' Murrain said.

'They're journalists, Kenny,' she explained patiently. 'Of course they want to know everything. So far, most of them have assumed that this was some gangland thing, but that's only because we've said so little. Once we give them the full story, we'll have the nationals on the doorstep.'

'Wanting to know,' the ACC added, 'why we haven't yet identified even the victim, let alone the killer.' He leaned forwards across the desk. When he wanted, the ACC was adept at combining his usual urbanity with a distinct sense of threat. It had probably been a very effective style in the days when he'd been involved in actual police-work. 'Making any progress there, Kenny?'

You know exactly how much progress we're making, Murrain responded in his head, because you've been demanding and receiving hourly updates. Out loud, he said, 'Nothing new yet.'

'Jesus.' The ACC banged his fist on the desk, surprising all three of them. 'How is it possible we can't identify someone in this day and age? I thought we were all on a million databases.'

'Once we get a name, we'll no doubt be able to discover everything we need to. But we've nothing to go on yet. No obvious mispers, no local reports of anyone missing. No matches we've found to fingerprints or DNA—' He knew that the ACC knew all this, but saw no harm in reminding him.

'So—' the Head of Communications interrupted. 'An announcement. What are we going to say?'

'What do you think we should say?' Murrain asked, pointedly. It was supposed to be her job, after all.

She looked only momentarily flummoxed. 'I think it's up to you to tell us what it's appropriate to release operationally, Chief Inspector.'

He noted the use of the rank, presumably to remind him in his turn what his job was supposed to be. 'To be honest, I think we can release pretty much anything we've got, given it's almost nothing. The nature of the killing. A female victim. There's not much more.'

'That'll be plenty to get the tabloids frothing,' she said. 'If we don't give them a context, they'll assume the worst. Or, rather, they'll encourage their readers to assume the worst. Crazed killer on the loose.'

'But we can't give them a context,' Murrain said. 'We can't pretend we know it's a domestic or gang-on-gang stuff. We don't know that.'

'And we can't tell them we've not yet identified the victim,' the ACC added, gloomily. 'They'll think we're idiots.' His expression suggested he wouldn't necessarily defend Murrain against this accusation.

The Head of Communications shuffled her papers in a professional-looking manner. 'I don't think we've much choice, then. We'll go for the enigmatic, nose-tapping, we know more than we're letting on approach. Report the nature of the killing and say that we're pursuing a number of lines of enquiry which, for operational reasons, we're currently keeping under wraps. That'll buy us time at least for a day or two.'

Murrain nodded. 'But in the longer term it puts even more pressure on us to come up with a quick result, because they'll want to know what these 'lines of enquiry' actually were.'

'Something like that,' she responded with an icy smile. 'But I'm assuming that won't be a major problem for you, Chief Inspector. Once you've a name, you'll no doubt be able to discover everything you need.'

Bluff well and truly called, he thought. But she was right of course. They had to tell the media something and he couldn't come up with anything much better. It was just that, as always, it would end up with his neck on the block. There were times when he almost envied Eloise her promotions.

By the time he arrived back at the MIR, the room was almost deserted. Some of the team would still be at lunch, but the majority would be out carrying out the duties assigned to them from that morning's planning team. There was a full-scale search of the hotel and its grounds taking place, in the hope of finding either the murder weapon or other relevant material. More extensive statements were being taken from the most material witnesses. Local business owners in the area were being approached to obtain access to their CCTV recordings. The intelligence team was poring over the records of telephone calls made from or in the hotel during the relevant period. Data from the Automatic Numberplate Recognition cameras in the regional road network was being reviewed. In short, they were going through all the prescribed routines, and Murrain had no confidence that any of it would result in a shred of relevant information.

Milton called across: 'Boss. Something you need to know.'

'Anything you've got. No matter how trivial.' He slumped down into the chair opposite Milton's desk.

'Just had a call from Robbie Fletcher.'

'Your mate up in Lancs? Go on.'

'They sent a PCSO out to check on Kathy Granger's flat. She's not there. There's no sign of her. Not been there since before the weekend, apparently.'

'They're sure of that?' Murrain could feel it already, that pulse, that indescribable surge through his body. Stronger than ever. And the image behind his eyes, not quite discernible.

'Looks like it. Some bloke next door had been left a key. Sounds like he was the nosy neighbour type and insisted on letting the PCSO into the flat to check.'

For the first time, Murrain could almost see the image. Like pixels slowly aggregating into recognisable shapes. The woman kneeling. The raised knife. 'It's her,' he said, quietly. 'She's the one.'

'She's our victim?'

'She's our victim.' It was a statement of fact, as if Murrain had received documentary evidence. But then he paused, the picture in his mind shifting slightly. 'Unless we have two killings.' He could still feel it, like an extra beating heart pounding through his blood. Growing stronger.

'But we know Granger checked out—'

'Someone checked out. Maybe someone checked out on her behalf.' Murrain's eyes suggested that his head was still elsewhere. 'We need to speak to whoever was on reception Sunday morning. If they were busy, I guess they might not have registered who actually checked out. If this is Granger, I'm assuming whoever it was checked out using her card.' He paused. 'And her PIN.'

Milton nodded, following the train of thought. 'If the killer had her tied up all night, I imagine it wouldn't have been difficult to get the PIN out of her.' He shook his head. 'She might have thought that was all the killer wanted. That if she handed over all her financial stuff, money and cards, he might let her go. Jesus.'

Murrain shook his head hard, as if to clear the vision that had coalesced behind his eyes. 'OK. We need to get back to Lancs, see if there's anyone who can identify the body as Granger's. They must have her ID photo on file—they could maybe e-mail that up so we can get an initial confirmation. And we need to talk to that receptionist.'

'I'll get on to it,' Milton said. 'But what did you mean about two killings? You can't think—'

'I don't know what I think. I don't *think*, that's the trouble. I'm just feeling. And my feeling is there's something else. More to come.' He shook his head again, with the air of a dog shaking off rainwater. 'Christ, I can almost *see* it.'

'Kenny?' DS Wanstead was standing behind Murrain, shifting his substantial weight from foot to foot.

Murrain twisted on his seat, glad of the interruption. 'You OK, Paul?'

'Just had a call from the Control Room.' He took a breath, as if struggling to find oxygen. 'Looks like we might have another one.'

'Oh, Jesus.' Murrain barely whispered the words. The worst thing was that this wasn't any surprise to him. 'Where?'

'You know the hotel-spa place in the hills above Macc?'

Murrain recognised the name. He'd been up there, years before, for some training seminar. He remembered nothing of the seminar itself, not even the title or subject-matter. But he remembered the views from the hotel itself, the aura of the setting sun across the Cheshire plain on a winter's afternoon. 'Something similar?'

'Not much doubt,' Wanstead said. 'Stabbing. Nasty piece of work, according to the uniforms on site.' He paused. 'Thing is, it sounds like this time we might have a name for the victim. She'd booked the hotel room herself, and the killer doesn't seem to have made the same effort to hide her identity.'

Murrain glanced across at Milton, who shrugged. 'Maybe got interrupted?'

'Maybe,' Murrain said. 'What's the name?'

'That's the point,' Wanstead said. 'The clincher. The victim was on our list.' He paused, in the manner of a magician building up to his climactic reveal, but Murrain was already ahead of him.

'Kathy Granger,' he said.

CHAPTER FOURTEEN

Bloody typical, she thought.

They expected her to be meticulous in everything she did— follow all the protocols, carry out the risk and security assessments, make sure she could account for every second of every day, and maintain all the bloody paperwork no-one would ever refer to again. Even her bloody expenses had to be justified line by line, every sodding penny recorded.

Then, when it suited them, they pulled a stroke like this.

She was almost tempted to ignore the summons. Stay in her tiny flat in Levenshulme with her phones turned off, the TV turned up to maximum, and a bottle of Pinot Grigio next to her. That would bloody teach them. She could imagine them sitting there, smug smiles on their faces, glancing at their watches and then glancing at each other, until it dawned on them that she'd actually had the bottle to stand them up.

Except, of course, that she didn't. Well, it wasn't a lack of bottle exactly. She'd never lacked that. It was more that she knew it wasn't worth the hassle. The one thing she'd learnt was that the ability to screw others around was one of the perks of seniority. Even the good guys behaved like that once they got promoted, no doubt because that was what their bosses were doing to them. And so on, up the line.

So you learned just to grin and bear it. It was easy enough in her job, after all. She didn't have much to do with them, other than make sure she complied with the bureaucracy when necessary. If they said jump, you jumped, but you expended as little energy as possible.

So when the summons had come, she wasn't surprised. Irritated, but not surprised. She'd had other things planned for that evening, obviously. And, for once, it wasn't even just a personal inconvenience. She'd arranged to meet some lowlife she'd identified as a potential informant. He was only a foot-soldier but he had contacts in the right places. Better still, he'd got himself into trouble, owing sizeable gambling debts to the wrong people so he was running shit-scared. With a few nudges in the right direction, she could get him on board.

But you had to be subtle. He was long enough in the tooth not to put his trust in just anyone, however desperate he was. She'd met him a few weeks earlier in the shabby city centre pub he frequented, making sure he saw her in the right company. Inevitably, he'd tried to chat her up. In any other circumstances, the idea would have been laughable, but she feigned interest and eventually, on the fourth or fifth time of pestering, had given him her mobile number. They'd met once more since then, for a couple of drinks in the slightly more upmarket pub she'd insisted on. She'd spent most of that evening fending off his advances, as she'd known she would, but had left him with the impression that it would be only a matter of time before she succumbed to his dubious charms. She'd strung him along just long enough, and tonight she'd planned the big reveal. He'd be disappointed that his amorous ambitions would remain unfulfilled, but she'd hoped the promise of a substantial financial retainer would prove ample compensation. She knew these people. He'd snap at the bait.

But then she'd received the summons from on high and had had to postpone the meeting. It wasn't ideal. He'd think she'd dumped him, and then he might get jittery, and she'd have to start building his trust all over again, if it wasn't already too late. Still, there was nothing she could do about it. They'd said jump, so she jumped, and they could deal with the consequences.

The summons had come in the usual way. A brief text on the secure mobile line. Time, place. Nothing more. No explanation. No enquiry as to whether she was available or whether the time was convenient. No opportunity to say no.

She didn't even know who'd be there. The meeting had been called by her handler, her sole official point of contact back to the ranch. If it had been just him, that would have been fine. More than fine, in fact, depending on what sort of meeting he had in mind. But Jack, risk-taker as he was, wouldn't have used the official channels for anything other than an official meeting. These short-notice meetings were generally more that the usual catch-up sessions. If they called a meeting outside the usual routine, it was because some big-wig had got involved. Maybe they wanted to change her current assignment. Maybe they wanted to curtail it for some reason best known to themselves. Maybe they'd got something new for her, or they wanted her to get hold of some specific intelligence. Even more than when fending off the lowlife's wandering hands, she'd probably have to spend the evening finding polite ways to say no.

So that, pretty much, was what she was expecting when she pulled up outside the hotel that evening. It was a pity they couldn't have found somewhere more salubrious for the meeting. That was par for the course, too, though, and confirmed her suspicion that there'd be someone more senior there. Jack rotated their meetings round the business hotels that fringed the city centre, ensuring that their recurrent meetings were unlikely to pique anyone's interest. But he chose the best places he could find within his limited budget, so they could get a half-decent meal and glass of wine.

When some senior manager tagged along, Jack made a point of meeting in the cheapest, nastiest budget hotel he could find. She wasn't sure why. Maybe to demonstrate he was being parsimonious with the Agency's budget. Maybe to help keep the meeting short. Most likely— and she could entirely sympathise with this—it was just another small way of kicking back at the people in charge. She didn't imagine that Jack enjoyed having to drive all the way up here for this, any more than she did.

If that was his intention, he'd more than succeeded on this occasion. Even by the standards of budget hotels, this was at the lower end of the scale. It looked to be a privately-owned place, rather than one of the big chains, tucked away at the arse-end of a would-be business park that itself looked barely half-occupied. The hotel building was purpose-built, maybe twenty years old. She suspected it had originally been built by one of the chains but been sold off when the expected market had failed to materialise in the surrounding neighbourhood. She wondered how profitable the place could be now. From what she knew of this location, it might well double as a knocking-shop.

Brilliant choice, Jack, she thought, raising a mental glass to him. If he was accompanied by some top brass tonight, it should be a gloriously uncomfortable meeting. She'd initially been surprised that he'd asked her to meet in one of the hotel rooms, rather than in the bar or restaurant as they usually did. But any bar or restaurant in this place would be worth avoiding.

The fine autumn weather they'd been enjoying had finally broken. By the time she pulled into the hotel it was raining heavily, a strong wind whipping the last leaves from the trees along the main road. The uneven surface of the car park was dotted with murky-looking puddles, and a steady stream of water poured from a broken gutter over the hotel entrance. Perfect, she thought. So she'd turn up at the meeting looking and feeling like a drowned rat.

There were more cars outside the hotel than she had expected, most of them the kinds of vehicles that might be driven by an unsuccessful sales representative, though one of them was presumably Jack's pool car.

God, this was a depressing place. She assumed that Jack would have booked the room just for the meeting, and that neither he nor his supposed colleague was planning to stay the night here. It did look like the kind of place that would be accustomed to letting rooms by the hour. The staff would draw their own conclusions about her presence. Maybe that was another of Jack's little jokes. Well, as long as he never brought her back to this place outside work.

Her impression of the place wasn't improved by its interior. She imagined that its original designers had aimed for cheap and cheerful. Well, one out of two wasn't bad. The reception was shabby, the carpet worn and stained. The receptionist, a young Asian man, glanced up without interest as she pushed through the creaking double-doors. For whatever reasons, he didn't seem remotely surprised to see a solitary woman walk straight past him towards the lifts.

Room 316, the text had said. She hesitated momentarily before entering the battered-looking lift, wondering whether it was capable of reaching the third floor under its own steam. But she couldn't bring herself to return to the reception to find the stairwell.

The lift worked well enough, although the mirrors lining its interior reflected back a depressing image of her rain-soaked head and shoulders. Whatever the reasons for calling tonight's meeting, she wasn't sure she was entirely going to forgive Jack for dragging her out to this dump.

The corridor on the third floor was as bleak as the reception. Fading wallpaper, peeling at the corners. A row of blank doors. A fire escape at the far end that looked as if it had been chained shut. And, inevitably, Room 316 was at the end, the last room on the left.

As she walked towards it, a sudden unease struck her. She glanced back over her shoulder, as if someone might have emerged, unseen, from the lift. But the corridor was empty and silent.

In any other circumstances, this would be the dumbest of moves. Allowing herself to be invited to a hotel room in a run-down dump like this, not even knowing for sure who was waiting behind that door.

But there was no risk, of course. The summons from Jack had come on the secure line. No-one else could have invited her here. And, whatever she might think of Jack, he was professional enough.

She reached the end of the corridor, noting that her suspicions about the fire-escape had been correct. Let's hope there's no fire this evening, then, she thought.

Then she turned and knocked firmly on the bedroom door.

CHAPTER FIFTEEN

'I assume you've not joined us expecting a quiet life?'

'I don't remember that line in the job description. Mind you, two murder scenes in two days is an impressive strike rate by any standards.'

'You can say that again,' Milton said. They were in the entrance to the Wentworth Moor Hotel and Spa, looking out at the haze of lights scattered across the Cheshire plain. The rain was pounding down and a fine mist was settling across the moorland. Lost in a cloud, Milton's mother used to say, and that was how it felt.

Murrain was inside, negotiating access to the crime scene with Ferbrache, whose team were finishing up. After catching a glimpse of the room and its contents, Milton had needed a blast of clean damp air and had retreated out to the entrance, where a couple of his colleagues were taking the opportunity for a quick cigarette before things got properly started. He'd met Marie Donovan in the lobby, coming in the other direction.

'Didn't expect to see you here tonight,' he said. 'Thought you weren't joining us till tomorrow.'

'I got the summons from DCI Murrain, didn't I? He thought I might want to be in on it. That I might be interested to see what was going on.'

'Interested, eh?' Milton nodded. He knew the way Murrain's mind worked. Though 'mind' probably wasn't the right word. He'd have wanted Donovan here to see what response that provoked in him. The same as at the Stockport hotel, or different? Some connection here, or none? Something he should follow up, or not?

'He was lucky I was available,' she said, half-serious. 'I'd almost embarked on a serious date with Mr Merlot.'

'Good job we caught you, then.'

'Probably. My housemate was out tonight, though, so it was always going to be an abstemious evening.'

'If you say so.' He was on the verge of asking her about the housemate and her domestic circumstances but couldn't think of a discreet way of probing further. A moment too late, it occurred to him to wonder why he was interested.

'Anyway, I'm here now, sober and alert. Well, sober, anyway.' She had wandered away from the main doors, still sheltered by the glass awning that dominated the front of the hotel. The rain was teeming down, sweeping across the car-park in waves as the wind buffeted over the moors. The entrance was surrounded by an untidy cluster of crime-scene vehicles, pulsing blue lights smeared by the rainstorm. 'What is it about Murrain, anyway?'

'How'd you mean?' As if he didn't know.

'This 'intuition' stuff. Feelings.'

'All cops work on intuition. We all work from the gut.'

She stepped back into the light. 'Not like Murrain.'

'You've spoken to people about him.' It wasn't a question, and it sounded almost accusatory.

'Not really,' she said. 'I asked around a bit when the possibility of this job came up. You'd expect me to do that.'

'And what did people say?'

'Positive stuff, mostly. Well-regarded. Good track record. A lot of integrity. Decent guy. Hands-on copper rather than a pen-pusher.'

'But?'

'But?'

'You sound as if you're leading up to a but.'

'Not really. That was what people said. A good manager, too. Everyone said that. Good to work for. A great mentor.'

'I can't argue with that,' Milton said, 'but I can still sense that 'but' hanging in the air.' He'd followed her out into the semi-darkness, gazing past her at the downpour, the thickening darkness.

'People reckoned he was a character. I wasn't sure what they meant by that. It felt like a euphemism for something, but I could never get anyone to say what.' She paused, as if choosing her words. 'Unorthodox, that was another word. And I was told he picked up the cases that others had given up on. When everyone else had reached a dead end.' She stopped and smiled. 'Someone reckoned he was called 'Terminal' Murrain.'

Milton was smiling now too, as if he'd decided to trust her. 'That might be because it's where he leaves your career. I'd go with unorthodox.'

'So what is this stuff?'

'I should tell you to ask him yourself, but he'd never tell you. He doesn't talk about it.'

'So you don't want to either? That would be disloyal.'

He shrugged. 'Not really. It was Eloise, his wife, who told me, and there's no-one more loyal to Kenny than she is.'

'That would be Chief Superintendent Eloise Carter? She told you?'

'That would be the one. She thought I ought to know, if I was going to work with Kenny on a long-term basis. She'd do the same for you. If you stay with us, she will, eventually. But I'll give you the heads-up for the moment.'

'Go on.'

'The way I understand it,' Milton said, 'it's what some people call 'second-sight'.'

'Seriously?'

'Seriously. It's genetic, apparently. Kenny's family is Scottish. An old Highland family, from up in the Black Isle, north of Inverness. Remote bloody place, by all accounts. Fisherfolk, craftsmen. And some of them, so Eloise told me, had the gift. Kenny's grandmother. Great grandfather. Somesuch. There's some family legend about an ancestor who was a seer. You know, fortune-teller.'

'You're taking the piss, aren't you?'

The clouds had descended and the moorland had vanished into the mist. It was as if nothing else existed. 'It's not for me to say,' Milton said, finally. 'I mean, I'm the ultimate sceptic about this stuff. But then I'd have said the same about Kenny and Eloise. And they seem serious enough about it.'

'Useful quality for a detective,' she said, still not quite sure if he was making fun of her.

'You'd think so, wouldn't you?' Milton said, but the smile had vanished. 'But I don't think it's that simple. The way I understand it,

Kenny gets these—I don't know—feelings, sensations, sometimes even visions. He takes them seriously. He reckons that every one means something. It's just that mostly he doesn't know what they mean, what their significance is. Sometimes they go nowhere, sometimes they lead to something useful.'

'It sounds like it could just be coincidence,' she said. 'With respect.'

'Like I say, I'm as sceptical as you. If you disregard all the false positives, the occasional success seems remarkable. Who knows? But Kenny thinks there's something there and he's no fool. And it has worked.' He jerked a thumb back towards the hotel. 'I saw him when he first read Granger's name in that list of hotel guests in Stockport. He felt something then.'

'She was the only solo female on the guest list,' Donovan pointed out. 'Maybe it was nothing more than that.'

'Maybe. I'm not trying to prove anything. Just telling you what Kenny thinks. What he believes. How he works. It's not magic, it may be entirely explicable, and it's mostly not what he's about. Ninety-five percent of what he does is standard, rock-steady detective work. But it's the five percent that makes him special.' He hesitated. 'There's one other thing you ought to know about this.'

She was stuck by the sudden change in his tone of voice. 'Go on.'

'Don't know whether you've picked up on this from anyone else, but Kenny and Eloise had a son.'

She registered the past tense. 'What happened?'

'Bright kid, apparently. Studious type. Did fine till he got to secondary school, then got badly bullied. In part, maybe, because of who his parents were. Or what they were. He kept it to himself so his mum and dad didn't realise what was happening till too late. I don't know the full story, but he was attacked one night after he'd stayed back at school. Beaten up in an alleyway, apparently. Probably not intended as anything serious, but he hit his head somehow. Unconscious when they found him, and was in a coma for weeks. Didn't pull through.' He stopped, as if he'd run out of words.

'Jesus. Did they get the bastards?'

'Kenny had had one of his—you know, feelings that day. Had almost been persuaded to go and pick the boy up from school instead of letting him walk home. But something had come up, the way it does in this job. So he blamed himself. Probably wasn't thinking straight at all. He wasn't involved in the investigation, obviously, and he was getting frustrated because they weren't making progress.'

'They must have known who did it, surely?'

'They had a good idea. They pieced together the background, found out about the bullying. It was a sizeable group involved, though everyone knew who the ringleaders were. The real question was who was involved in the attack. The front-runners all managed to concoct solid alibis, maybe genuine, maybe not. Parents had their own reasons for disliking the police. Should have been open-and-shut, but we couldn't get anything to stick. Nothing the CPS was prepared to run with, anyway. Kenny got more and more frustrated. His kid was still lying in a coma, he's blaming himself, the perpetrators looking like they're going to get away scot-free. And he reckoned he knew—not just suspected, but *knew* —who was responsible.'

'I can see how he might persuade himself of that,' she said, immediately aware that her words sounded too cold, too sceptical. 'I mean, in the circumstances.'

'Maybe. Or maybe he was right. Either way, he tried to do something about it. Went round to one of the houses. Started throwing about accusations. Got into some sort of altercation. Ended up assaulting one of the kids' parents.'

'Not smart.'

'No. I understand Kenny had a bit of a reputation in his younger days. Headstrong. Bit reckless. Also a bit of a drinker. Managed to curb all that after he met Eloise. But this was enough to make him lose it. He got off lightly in the end. He was suspended but managed to avoid prosecution. Fortunately he'd been stopped before too much damage was done, and a few strings were pulled. IPCC did their thing, but everybody recognised the extenuating circumstances, especially since by that point Joe had died.'

'Joe,' she said.

He allowed himself a faint smile. 'It has occurred to me. Anyway, Kenny just got a relatively mild ticking-off in the end. But it put an end to any prospect of a prosecution for Joe's killing. In fact, I've a suspicion that was how they persuaded the father not to press charges.' He looked past her to the hotel entrance, from which a couple of Ferbrache's team had emerged carrying their boxes of equipment. 'I don't know if I should have told you all that. But it helps to have an idea what makes Kenny tick.'

'It's an awful story.'

'It's one reason why I don't take his—whatever it is, his supposed *gift* too lightly. I get the impression that for him it's as much a curse as it is a benefit. He seems tortured by what he doesn't know. What he can't do.' He looked momentarily embarrassed. 'We should get back inside,' he said, finally. 'Looks like Ferbrache's lot have just about finished.'

She followed him back into the hotel reception, equally glad of the chance to change the subject. 'So what's the story here, then? When the DCI called me, he didn't say much. He just said they reckoned the body here was Kathy Granger. How does that work?'

'Christ knows. Story is that she checked in here last night. Booked on-line yesterday afternoon. Same credit card she used to check out of the hotel in Stockport. Don't seem to be any further signs of her last night or this morning, though obviously we've not talked in detail to any of the hotel staff. Body was found by a cleaner this afternoon. We're waiting for Pete Warwick to give us a time of death, but Kenny reckoned it looked relatively recent. Maybe only an hour or two before the body was found.'

'So different from the first killing?'

'Yeah, though the killer might have expected it to remain undiscovered until tomorrow. The room was booked till then, and there was a Do Not Disturb sign on the door that the cleaner missed. But this time the killer seems to have made no effort to conceal the victim's identity. Everything still there. Clothing. ID.' He gestured across the rain-soaked car-park to a vehicle ringed with police tape. 'Even her car parked over there.'

'Maybe got interrupted somehow?'

'It's possible. But Neil Ferbrache reckons there's been a similar clean-up operation here. Killer has fairly successfully removed all traces of himself. Subject to whatever Neil might find on the forensic front, of course, but he didn't sound optimistic.'

After the cold and gloom of the night, the hotel seemed dazzling and welcoming, a haven of polished surfaces, plush upholstery and endless mirrors. The hotel guests had been corralled into the restaurant and the lounges, plied with complimentary food and drinks by the hotel management while the police took control. Murrain was sitting in the lobby with Ferbrache and Warwick, obtaining a debrief before the two experts departed.

Milton had already kicked off the process of systematic evidence gathering, allocating members of the team to conducting interviews and taking statements from potential witnesses. Murrain had fended off three calls from the Head of Communications who was revising and amending her press release almost by the minute.

Murrain gestured for Milton and Donovan to join them in the corner of the lobby. Ferbrache took the opportunity to excuse himself, wanting to help his team finish packing up. Warwick remained where he was, watching the three police officers with mild interest.

'Pretty much what we thought,' Murrain said. 'Stabbing carried out with the same sort of ferocity as in Stockport. Approach looks the same. The victim was kneeling by the bed, stabbed from behind and above. Similar sort of clear-up afterwards, though not where the victim's concerned. All surfaces carefully wiped down. Some sort of protective sheeting apparently used. The same care we saw in the first killing.'

'So the failure to conceal the victim's identity—' Milton said.

'Looks deliberate. There's no sign that the killer was interrupted or was rushed.' He paused. 'So, from the killer's perspective, Granger's identity must be important. This isn't random. She's the only clear link between the two killings. And it looks like the killer wants us to be sure of the linkage.' He looked up at Marie Donovan, as if he was about to say something to her. But then he turned back to Milton. 'Step

141

by step, though. First thing is for us to find someone who can identify Granger's body. Any luck with that, Joe?'

'I spoke to Robbie Fletcher. They're putting this on a formal footing now and are going to get their SIO to liaise with us. It looks like there are no close relatives. Parents are both dead. No siblings. They're seeing who else they can track down.'

'If we can't get a relative,' Murrain said, 'we'll need to get a colleague or neighbour to identify the body.' He picked up his mobile from the table between them. 'Looks like I've just missed a fourth call from the Head of Comms. She's having kittens, understandably. We've got to do this absolutely by the book now. It's going to be front-page news.'

'Easiest thing would be to get Granger's boss to come down. He's police staff so can't really refuse.'

Murrain looked at his watch. 'Can you set the wheels in motion, Joe?'

'Will do, boss.'

Murrain turned towards Warwick. 'Any more observations, Pete?'

'Only what I've told you. Cause of death is pretty much identical to the first killing. Same apparent degree of savagery. The only real difference is that the time of death was much more recent. Probably only two or three hours before the body was found. But that may not be what the killer intended.'

'No. Probably planned to string things out a bit further. Buy themselves more time before we got involved. Let's hope that's a miscalculation that works in our favour.' He didn't sound optimistic. 'I feel as if we're going backward. For one glorious minute, I thought we'd identified the Stockport victim and were finally starting to get somewhere. What the hell brought Kathy Granger over to this place, and who the hell's the victim in Stockport?'

'It's not possible that Granger was brought here forcibly?' Donovan said. '

'Doesn't seem likely. Receptionist remembers her checking in last night. All a bit vague because it was late afternoon and they had a queue of business types arriving at the same time. But she was by herself and there was nothing odd about her appearance or manner.'

'CCTV coverage?' Milton asked. 'So we can double-check that?'

'Not of reception, apparently. There are cameras covering the car-park and various of the exits, so we can check those. But it doesn't stack up.'

'None of it stacks up,' Milton said, morosely. 'I'll go and chase up Lancs Police. At least we can push some of the crap in their direction.'

'Not his usual cheery self,' Warwick observed as Milton retreated to a far corner of lobby, thumbing his mobile phone as he went.

'None of us is,' Murrain said. 'We're getting nowhere. The ACC, the Head of Comms, and by now no doubt the Chief himself, are climbing the walls. Young Ms Donovan here must wonder what the hell she's got herself into.'

Donovan smiled dutifully. 'At least I'm doing something here.' She gestured towards the interior of the hotel. 'Speaking of which, I feel like I should be starting to get involved. Do you want me taking statements?'

'Jesus, woman, you're going to get me into even deeper shit with HR,' Murrain said. 'You don't officially start with us till tomorrow. And even that was over HR's collective dead bodies.' He glanced at Warwick. 'Which, admittedly, was an added incentive.'

'I won't tell if you don't,' Donovan said. 'I don't just want to sit here.'

'Go and have a chat with Joe. He won't be short of things for you to do. And thanks.'

He watched as she walked over to join Milton and then turned back to Warwick. 'She's going to be good, that one. Bright, keen—'

'And what vibe did you get from her, Kenny?' Warwick asked.

'How'd you mean?'

Warwick shook his head. 'You're not talking to a newbie now, Kenny. You're talking to Dr Warwick, who knows you better than any other bugger on the force. Eloise obviously excepted. You invited

Donovan along tonight to see what effect she had on those bloody feelings of yours, didn't you?'

'If you say so, Pete.'

'And?'

'Christ knows, Pete. Christ alone knows.'

The feeling had been there as he'd driven up the winding lanes from Macclesfield to this place. He could sense it as he approached, almost taste it in the bitter wind over the moorland. He expected that, of course. He'd expected nothing else. What had surprised him was the strength of the sensation. More powerful even than he'd experienced at the Stockport hotel. At one point, halfway up the narrow road that trailed steeply through a sequence of tiny, close-packed villages, he'd had to pull into a lay-by to allow himself to relax. He'd sat in the car, some half-familiar song playing on the radio, feeling the waves of emotion rippling over him. The visions were there, too, incoherent behind his eyes, rippling and waxing like the northern lights. And the sound. The same sound he'd heard that last Sunday morning. That distant, almost inaudible screaming.

Why here? Why was the sensation so strong here? When he'd finally reached the hotel it had been almost unbearable. Like a soundless shrieking in his ears. As if the dead, all the dead, were trying to tell him what they knew. It had calmed, but it was still there, a murmuring clamour that refused to quieten.

When Marie Donovan had entered with Joe Milton, the volume had risen again. Voices just out of earshot. He didn't know what they were trying to tell him, except that somehow she was a part of this.

He saw that Warwick was watching him with a mix of curiosity and concern. 'Don't worry, Pete. I'm not going doolally. Well, no more than usual. I'm just trying to make some sense of it all.'

'As far as I can see, none of this makes any sense.'

'That's what I'm beginning to realise. Someone's playing games. Yanking our chain.'

'You think?'

'There's some point being made. Some message being sent. You don't do this sort of stuff without a reason. However irrational that reason might be.'

'Sounds right up your street,' Warwick said. 'With respect.'

Murrain laughed. 'Yeah, maybe you're right, Pete. Maybe I've been chosen for this. Maybe it's someone playing games with me.'

Warwick leaned back in his armchair and gazed at Murrain thoughtfully. After a moment, he said: 'You're not joking, are you, Kenny? You're really not bloody joking.'

Murrain sat in a corner of the hotel lobby, eyes closed, head resting in his hands. Anyone passing might have thought he was asleep or nursing a headache. But, after another moment, he opened his eyes and stared around him, relieved that no-one had been there to witness his actions.

Sometimes it worked. Sometimes, if he could find a moment of solitude, he was able to tune back into it. It felt like a letting go, a release of his conscious mind, until suddenly he was back in the frequency. Tonight, it felt like trying to tune a radio to some distant overseas station with only the faintest trace of a signal through a hiss of static. Something there, but nothing he could grasp.

It took him a moment to realise that the rhythmic buzzing was a physical sound rather than an after-effect of his momentary trance. He pulled out his phone and glanced at the screen. The ACC, for the third time that evening.

'How's everything going, Kenny?'

Murrain looked around at the deserted reception area. 'We're just about done here. Finished collecting statements. SOCOs and the doc gone ages ago. Done a thorough check of the room. Collected all the CCTV footage that's available. Just tidying up now.' He knew that Milton and a couple of others were still through in the hotel lounge ensuring all the paperwork was collated properly. He'd sent the rest home. They'd all be back bright and early in the morning.

'At least you've an ID now.'

'Subject to confirmation, yes. And we've got that in hand for the morning. That'll give us some clearer lines of enquiry at least. Including her police colleagues who were at the wedding.'

'That was one reason I was calling, Kenny. We'll need to tread carefully there. I've got a call in to my oppo up north to make sure we secure their co-operation. And maybe get a bit of extra resource if we can. Every little helps.'

The ACC had a tendency to sound like a supermarket advertisement. Murrain didn't particularly mind. That was what senior management was there for and at least the ACC, unlike some of his colleagues, recognised that his role was to make his subordinates' lives easier rather than harder. 'That would be helpful. Thanks. And I will tread carefully.'

'I know you will, Kenny. It's a tricky one, though, isn't it? The tabloids will be out in force now. Serial killer in crazed knife attack stuff. If you get approached by any journos, make sure you route it through Jan.' The Head of Communications, that was, as if Murrain needed telling.

'I'm very practised with the 'no comments',' Murrain said. 'I've no desire to talk to any journalist, if I can help it.' He paused. 'She's done a good job so far, Jan. Struck the right tone. Said enough so it doesn't sound as if we're holding stuff back but not given them anything of any real substance.' Murrain didn't often find himself offering compliments to the Communications Department—which usually seemed to bely its name—but credit where it was due. It never did any harm to keep them sweet.

'I'll tell her you said so, Kenny. She's good, though. The right person to have on your side in a case like this. Reckon the tabloids will be camping out up there by the morning.'

'Rather them than me,' Murrain said, watching the rain hammering against the glass. He could see Milton, Sparrow and Marie Donovan coming out of the hotel lounge, heading in his direction. Sparrow was carrying a hefty pile of folders, Milton holding what looked like several evidence bags. 'Anything else you need from me tonight, sir?'

'Not that I can think of. You'll give me a brief first thing, won't you?'

And every hour on the hour, Murrain added to himself. 'Yes, of course. Night.' He ended the call, and looked up as Milton lowered himself into the seat opposite.

Milton gestured to the phone. 'Imagine the top brass are getting the jitters about this one?'

'You imagine right. That was the ACC. Had the Chief earlier. How's it going?'

'I think we've done just about everything we can. Got all the paperwork sorted now.'

'You three should get yourselves off, then. Get some sleep and then we can all be bright-eyed and bushy-tailed in the morning.'

'Suppose,' Milton said, sounding as if it was the last thing he wanted.

'Big day tomorrow,' Murrain said. 'The day we put a name to at least one of our bodies, I hope. Who's picking up this guy Cartwright from the station?'

Sparrow raised a hand. 'I volunteered. Always wanted to hold up one of those notices. He's getting in around ten. Shall I take him straight to Stepping Hill?' The Stockport hospital where the bodies were being stored.

'Might as well,' Murrain said. 'We can buy him a thank-you coffee once he's done what he's coming for.' With Robbie Fletcher's help, Milton had managed to pull strings to get Keith Cartwright, Kathy Granger's boss, contacted out of hours. Milton had been apologetic about having drag Cartwright in at short notice to identify the body. But the man had seemed happy enough. Milton almost had the impression that the excitement Cartwright felt at being involved in a real-life police investigation might outweigh his grief at the loss of a valued colleague.

'OK, then. Shall we call it a night?'

Milton hesitated, exchanging a glance with Donovan. 'There's one other thing, boss.'

Murrain felt it then, a sudden surge, as if that far-off radio station had suddenly boosted its power. 'Go on.'

'We finished clearing up the room where the body was found. Bagged everything up as evidence. Did a check through all Granger's belongings. She had a credit card holder.' He held up one of the evidence bags containing a leather wallet. 'There wasn't much in it. A debit card. A credit card, which matches the one used to settle-up at the Stockport hotel and check in here. A couple of membership cards—National Trust, that sort of thing. Supermarket loyalty card. And this.'

He held up another bag. Murrain leaned forward to squint at the contents. A business card. 'What is it?'

'It's a National Crime Agency Card. So no details other than name and office address. Guy called Jack Brennan.'

'So what?' Murrain said, though he could feel the tingling growing stronger. He looked up at Marie Donovan. 'Maybe Granger knew him. Worth following up as background, I suppose.'

Donovan was looking straight back at him. 'The thing is,' she said, 'I know Brennan too.'

He could feel the connection now, loud and strong, though as indecipherable as ever. 'You think he's worth talking to?'

'I think so,' she said, after a pause. 'I don't know what his connection with this might be. But, yes, from what I know of Brennan, I really do think so.'

By the time Donovan arrived home, it was nearly eleven. She knew all the parking spaces near her house would be taken so she drove up further and parked at the shadowier end of the road, by the railway line that curved past the Edwardian terraces. The rain had lessened but there was still a steady drizzle, dripping down her neck as she hurried to collect her bag and lock up the car.

As she straightened, she was struck by a sudden sense that someone was watching. She paused and looked around. There was nothing but the lines of parked cars, the orange streetlight on the rain-washed street, the buzz of traffic on the main road. Behind her, beyond the high metal fence, the dark emptiness of the railway.

She hurried down the street, head bent against the rain, trying not to let her anxiety show. She'd had enough bad experiences not to disregard her instincts, though she couldn't imagine why anyone would be out here on a night like this. As she reached her gate she looked back as she fumbled for her keys. Nothing. No-one.

She relaxed only when she'd double-locked the door and then, after another moment's thought, slid the two bolts across. She hadn't had chance to change the locks since Brennan's visit. Brennan, she thought, whose business card had been found in their latest victim's possessions.

Holly was in the living room, wearing pyjamas and a dressing-gown, a half-empty glass of red wine in front of her. She was watching the BBC News channel. 'You've made the national news,' she said as Donovan slumped down beside her.

'What are they saying?'

'Not much. Reported both murders. Police not necessarily assuming the crimes are linked but pursuing a number of avenues. Thought we might see your new boss giving a statement.'

'I get the impression he tries to avoid all that. Any of that wine going?'

'In the kitchen,' Holly said. She pushed herself up from the sofa. 'I'll get you one. You must be knackered.'

'Just a bit.' Donovan settled herself back and watched the news while Holly fetched the drink. They'd moved on to some political story, a Government Minister providing an earnest-faced response to the presenter's probing. At the foot of the screen, she could still read the breaking news that police were investigating a suspected double-murder in the Greater Manchester area. A suspected double-murder. So much for the Communications Department's bland press release.

Holly reappeared and handed over a brimming glass of wine. 'Thought you might need a large one.'

'Thanks.' Donovan laughed. 'Mind you, I'll have another early start in the morning.'

'Not regretting the move already?'

'Not at all. Craving the excitement, to be honest.'

'How's it going?'

Donovan hesitated, conscious of the need to maintain confidentiality. But Holly was a special case. She'd been vetted to the same level and was subject to the same regulations. Until today, they'd been part of the same organisation and would have traded work anecdotes without a second thought. 'Not brilliantly,' she said. 'We still don't have an identity for the first victim. We've just got to hope that the second one starts to produce some leads.'

'It must do, surely,' Holly said. 'At least you know who she is.'

'The whole thing's just so bizarre.' She paused again, wondering what it was appropriate to say. 'We've got one—well, not lead exactly, but something. I'm not sure what it means.'

'Go on.'

'When Jack Brennan was here—'

She could see Holly's body tense. 'What about him?'

'Look, it's none of my business, obviously, but I had the impression that there was some history between you and him. It's just that his name's come up in the investigation.'

Holly sat in silence for a minute, then said: 'You've got your own history with him. What do you think of him?'

'I think he's slick, charming, persuasive. And I wouldn't trust him an inch.' Donovan shrugged. 'I've got nothing substantive to go on, but I just felt he was using me. And, even as a cop, there's something about him that's not quite right.'

Holly allowed herself a smile. 'He's got something in common with you, of course. A whistleblower.'

'Don't think that had passed me by,' Donovan said. 'But, from what I understood, his motives weren't necessarily as pure as mine. Exposed his own Chief Super for taking back-handers, but was supposedly screwing the Super's wife.'

'Yeah, there were those who reckoned his motives weren't exactly altruistic. But there were always rumours about Jack. Back in the day, when I was in the force, the word was that he was the one taking back-handers. And that was how he got the gen on the Chief Super. Christ knows. But I do know he's a bastard.' She rubbed her hands through her hair as if trying to cleanse herself.

Donovan took a sip of her wine, avoiding Holly's eye. 'Like I say, none of my business.'

'You said his name had come up in the investigation. In what way?'

'We found one of his business cards in Granger's possession. That's all. Could be nothing. Maybe she'd just come across him at work.'

'Maybe,' Holly said. 'Probably a sick question now but was she decent looking, this Kathy Granger?'

'I'd have said so. Thirty-something. Brunette. You know?'

'A bit like you?' Holly said. 'And me, for that matter. Jack's type.'

'I suppose.'

'Mind you, some would say that anyone in a skirt is Jack's type. My guess would be that, if she had Jack's card, it was because he tried it on with her, somewhere, somehow.'

'Maybe at the wedding, you mean? It's possible, I suppose. I'd have noticed if he was staying at the hotel or on the guest list for the reception, but it doesn't necessarily mean he wasn't there.'

'I think you need to check him out,' Holly said. She dropped her head into her hands, her fingers moving through her hair in the same

152

cleansing gesture as before. 'Look, it was a few years ago. I was at some conference in Hendon. Jack Brennan was there too, doing some training course. He hit on me one night in the bar. I was thrown at first. I mean, he'd been an old friend of Ben's. Was never really sure what Ben thought of him, but they'd joined the force at the same time. Went through training together. Worked together for a while on some hush-hush stuff apparently, which was a bit of a bonding experience. That's what Ben told me.' She took a deep breath, as if short of oxygen. 'Anyway, he hit on me. This was not long after Ben had left me. I was probably still reeling, really. Anyway, he tried it on—no, that's not right. I could have been OK with that, if he'd just chanced his arm and left it there. I made it clear I wasn't interested. I wasn't ready for anything new. But he was persistent. Became pushy, almost aggressive. In the end, I told him to fuck off.'

'And did he?'

'He did in the bar. There were other people around including some of my friends who'd begun to notice what was going on. I thought he'd got the message. But when I went upstairs to go to bed, he followed me. Caught up with me just as I'd unlocked the bedroom door.' She picked up her glass and swallowed the last mouthful of her wine. 'Didn't say anything. Just grabbed me and pushed me inside. Dragged me to the bed—'

'Jesus,' Donovan said. 'You're not saying—?'

'In the end, not quite. But only because, as he pushed me back on to the bed, I grabbed the phone from the bedside table. He was trying to hold me down, but I managed to dial zero for reception and then—well, I just screamed.' She laughed, through there was an edge of hysteria in her voice. 'It took him a second to realise what was happening, and luckily someone had answered almost immediately. He panicked, because he thought they'd come up to check what was happening. No-one did, actually—they probably just thought it was someone pissing about. But it was enough to make Brennan bugger off smartish.'

'But you think he would have—well, gone through with it?'

'I'm certain of it.'

'And if he'd do it to you—'

'If he'd do that to me, why wouldn't he do it to anyone?' She'd brought the wine-bottle in with Donovan's glass, and now she poured the last inch into her own. 'Before he buggered off, he threatened me. Said if I exposed him, he'd destroy me.' She ran her hands through her hair again. 'But I reported it in the end. There was an investigation and I suppose I at least had the satisfaction of make his life uncomfortable for a while. But I couldn't really prove anything and you know how cops close ranks.'

'Yeah,' Donovan said, 'I know.'

'From what I heard, I suspect I wasn't the first or the last. But the bastard always got away with it.'

Donovan took a deep swallow of her own wine. Christ, she thought, she'd had a relationship with Brennan. Short-lived, going nowhere, but a relationship all the same. Even the thought of it made her feel soiled. 'Sounds like we need to talk to him.'

'I think you do.'

'You think he'd be capable of something like this?'

'Christ knows. I wouldn't have believed he was capable of doing what he tried to do to me. After that, all bets are off.'

Donovan involuntarily glanced up at the uncurtained window. Brennan had keys to this house. She'd bolted the front door and there was no external access to the rear. Even so, she suddenly felt vulnerable. 'I think,' she said, finally, 'that I need to disturb my new boss's beauty sleep.'

'Always a great way to kick off a new job.' Holly smiled, but there was no sign of humour in her eyes. 'But, yes, you're probably right.'

Murrain was already in bed and half-asleep when the mobile rang. Eloise groaned, swore and rolled away from him, pulling the duvet over her head. 'Go on.'

He'd been in the house for little more than an hour. Eloise had offered to cook something ready for his return but he'd told her not to bother. By the time he got in, especially after a night like tonight, the last thing he'd want was to eat. He hadn't imagined he'd be in much of a mood to sleep either but the tiredness had hit him as soon as he'd walked in the door. He'd watched the coverage of the case on the local news, noting with no surprise that the media were already drawing their own conclusions about the links between the two killings. Then he'd made his way upstairs to join Eloise who was already in bed, ploughing her way through the latest Booker winner.

He'd hoped for more than fifteen minutes' rest before being disturbed, but there was no hint of irritation in his voice as he answered. When Marie Donovan began by offering profuse apologies, he politely cut her short. 'Don't worry, Marie. That's what the job is. If you've something to tell me, I don't care what time it is. Especially on this case.'

'I don't know if I have, really. Maybe I'm being stupid.'

She wasn't, he knew already. He could feel it in her voice, down the line between them. Something real. 'Go on.'

She recounted the conversation with Holly, concluding by telling him how she'd found Brennan waiting for her in the house the previous night. 'I never saw that side of him,' Donovan said. 'But there was definitely something that didn't feel right. Even so, it's a long way from that stuff to what we're talking about here.'

'It is,' Murrain agreed, 'but he wouldn't have been the first to make the journey.' Beside him, he could sense Eloise listening, pretending to be asleep. 'You're right, we need to bring him in. I don't think there's enough to make it formal. But it's something. And, frankly, even if he's nothing to do with this, it won't do any harm to rattle his cage.'

'Raises more questions than it answers, though, doesn't it?' she said. 'We've got two killings, at least one of which looks premeditated. I can buy Brennan as a violent rapist. Maybe even as a murderous rapist, in the wrong circumstances. But I'm not sure I can see him as a cold-blooded killer.'

Murrain closed his eyes, feeling the sensation again. 'We can start doing some checks tomorrow. Brennan wasn't booked into the hotel, and I don't recall his name on the list of wedding guests, but that doesn't prove much. I imagine Brennan's the type not to worry too much about receiving an invite, and the wedding night party was a pretty informal affair. It might be time for us to interrupt Mr and Mrs Barton's honeymoon, sadly. Would be interesting to know if DIs Barton and Brennan are acquainted with one another.'

'I hope this isn't a wild goose chase,' she said. 'Wouldn't be the best start to my secondment, would it?'

He laughed, glancing across at Eloise who was managing to convey impatience through her perfectly motionless body. 'I don't know what it means. But it's not a wild goose chase.'

'I'll let you get back to sleep,' she said. 'I'm sorry. This could all have waited till the morning. I just got jittery.'

'You're sure you're OK, though?'

He could sense the hesitation. 'I'll be fine.'

'You don't want me to get the uniforms to keep an eye?'

'I've disturbed you enough. No-one can get into this place tonight. Brennan might still have a front-door key, but he can't undo the bolts.'

'If you're sure.'

'I'm sure.'

'OK,' he said, 'and, Marie—thanks for calling. You did the right thing.'

'Well, thanks for saying so.'

After he ended the call, he lay back staring at the ceiling. Beside him, Eloise rolled over. 'That sounded like it was something,' she said.

'Yeah, it was something. I'm not sure what. But something.'

She peered from under the bedclothes. He had the lost look she knew so well, the expression of a child who'd woken to find himself in an unfamiliar place, far from home. 'You might as well get up,' she said. 'You're not going to sleep tonight. And I'm bloody sure I want to.'

'Sympathetic as ever,' he said, knowing she was right.

She sighed and disappeared under the duvet. After a moment, he rose and made his way downstairs, switching off the light as he left the room.

WEDNESDAY

CHAPTER EIGHTEEN

As it turned out, Eloise was only partly right. Murrain had sat up till the small hours, making desultory attempts to flick through the previous day's newspaper or watch some nonsense on the television, while his mind ran endlessly through the handful of substantive facts they had about the killings, a rat chasing its own tail.

Eventually—he didn't know exactly when—he'd fallen asleep on the sofa, wrapped in a duvet he'd borrowed from the spare room. He woke two or three hours later, his body aching and chilled, and squinted at the clock on the mantelpiece. Just gone five-thirty. His mind was still fogged by fragments of a dream in which he'd been pursuing the killer through the corridors of a hotel, checking room after room, always arriving after the killer had moved on to the next room, the next victim...

He tramped into the kitchen, running the cold tap to splash water on his face and then to fill the kettle. It was still dark. Their neat four-bedroomed detached sat at the edge of the town, with a view out over the Pennines, one reason they were still living there, rattling round like peas in a drum. The kitchen faced south-east, and at this time of the year, he enjoyed standing here, watching the first sun rise over the curve of the hills. He was too early for that today, though, and he knew there was no prospect of sleeping further.

After he'd downed a strong coffee and spent five minutes under the hottest shower he could manage, he felt more human and as if his mind was at least partly engaged. He dressed and bent over to give Eloise a farewell kiss on the forehead—which she batted away with the air of one swatting a fly—and headed out to the car. The first taste of winter was in the air. The rain had passed, and the clear sky was full of stars.

He was in the office in twenty minutes, still barely six-fifteen, but was unsurprised to see Milton there ahead of him. What was more surprising was that Marie Donovan was there, too, sharing a coffee with Milton while they talked through what she'd discovered about Jack Brennan. Maybe she'd felt more uneasy at home than she'd let on.

158

'You two trying to make me look bad?' He looked at Milton: 'I'm assuming you have actually been home?'

'For a few hours,' Milton said. 'Couldn't sleep.'

'Tell me about it. Marie been filling you in about Jack Brennan?'

'Pretty much.' Milton looked sceptical. 'You think there's something in it?'

'Something, yes. What, I don't know.'

'All seems a bit thin in the cold light of day,' Donovan said.

'It's not as if we're knee-deep in leads. If nothing else, this confirms we need to devote more attention to the wedding. From what I hear of DI Andy Barton, it wouldn't surprise me if he was acquainted with Mr Brennan.'

'I've double-checked,' Milton said. 'Brennan wasn't on the guest list for the wedding or the reception. But the disco wasn't necessarily an invitation-only affair, so it's possible he was there.'

'We need to get Brennan in for a few questions,' Murrain said. 'But ideally I'd like to know a bit more before we meet him. Joe, can we find some way to set up an interview with DI Andy Barton and his good lady wife? It'll be a shame to interrupt their honeymoon, but I'm guessing by now it won't be entirely a surprise. Maybe get someone in International Liaison to contact the authorities out there, set up a telephone or Skype interview. I'd like the see the whites of his eyes when we talk to him. I'll clear things with Lancs so they don't think we're treading on their toes.'

While he'd been talking, he'd started booting up his PC—always a frustratingly slow process in this distant corner of the Force network. When it finally finished chugging through the endless start-up procedures, he was greeted by a succession of new e-mails, all but two of which he immediately consigned to the trash.

The first, inevitably, was yet another request for an update from the ACC, who'd clearly managed to beat them all into the office. Not ignorable, but not his first priority. The second, though, was sending a charge through Murrain's body even before he'd opened it.

It was an overnight bulletin sent from the Control Room, who'd picked up on a name flagged by Murrain's team on the HOLMES2 system as potentially pertinent to their case.

'You remember Mrs Berenek?' he said to Milton. 'The receptionist from the Stockport place.'

'I remember. You had some suspicions about the son? What about her?'

The sensation was strong, buzzing behind Murrain's eyes. 'Not her. Funnily enough, it's the son. Found dead. Last night in Stockport. Apparent hit and run.'

Murrain disliked mortuaries. It wasn't the squeamishness that affected some of his colleagues. He had no problem with death, or even with the dead, whatever the circumstances. But he was uncomfortable in those cold gleaming rooms, where the bodies lay stacked in their stainless steel drawers. Walking in there felt like walking into a storm of electrical static. He could almost hear the cacophony of voices hissing in his ears, a distant mob trying to make themselves heard. He could feel their presence, clustered around him as if tugging at his clothes, desperate for his attention.

He'd persuaded Milton to delay as long as possible before heading over there. They sat in the visitors' cafe in the hospital entrance sipping coffees until Sparrow walked through the doors at 9.55. He was followed by a short, nervous-looking man who looked around, blinking, as if he'd never been in a hospital before.

Murrain rose to intercept them. 'Mr Cartwright? DCI Murrain. Many thanks for taking the trouble to help us.'

Cartwright looked as if he'd rather have been anywhere else. 'It's the least I could do. I mean, if it really is—' He trailed off.

'Well, that's what we'd like you to help us with, if you're able.' Murrain gestured behind him. 'My colleague, DI Milton. You've met DC Sparrow. Can we get you a coffee before we go down?'

Cartwright looked longingly towards the cafe. 'I'd rather get it over with, if you don't mind.'

'Perhaps afterwards, then.'

Warwick had been asked to meet them at around ten, and when they arrived he was waiting with one of the mortuary assistants. Murrain took a breath as he entered the room, trying to ignore the cloud of voices pressing at his ears as he introduced Cartwright.

'We won't keep you, Mr Cartwright,' Warwick said. 'We just need a formal identification.'

Cartwright nodded morosely, and followed Warwick across to the rack of storage drawers. 'The body—?' he asked uneasily. 'Is it—well—?'

'We'll just ask you to look at the face, Mr Cartwright. There's nothing untoward.' He was all too familiar with handling these situations. 'Though you may find the features initially look a little unfamiliar. Death can have that effect, I'm afraid.' He pulled open the drawer, managing to avoid any suggestion of a dramatic flourish. He uncovered the face and stood back.

'Take your time, Mr Cartwright,' Murrain said. 'We want you to be certain.'

Cartwright peered into the drawer with the air of one carrying out a particularly challenging intellectual task. He blinked again, then peered more closely. After a long minute, he looked up bewilderedly. 'I'm sorry,' he said, in a voice that sounded close to tears. 'I don't think it's her.'

Murrain looked up, startled. 'Not her?' he said. 'Are you sure?' It sounded an idiotic question.

'Well,' Cartwright looked to Warwick for support, 'you said the face might look unfamiliar. So at first I thought maybe—' He stopped. 'But it's not her. The face and hair are a bit similar. But it's not Kathy.'

It wasn't possible, Murrain thought. The woman had been dressed in Granger's clothes, had been surrounded by Granger's possessions, had left Granger's car parked outside the moorland hotel. How could this *not* be Kathy Granger? What sort of game was being played here?

'I'm sorry to have wasted your time, Mr Cartwright,' he said. 'This wasn't the outcome we expected. But that's the nature of our work.'

'No, of course. And if that's not Kathy—well, that's got to be good news, hasn't it?'

Murrain was having difficulty persuading himself of that, but he nodded. 'Yes, of course.' He gestured to Warwick, who closed the drawer with a shrug. Murrain stopped, suddenly conscious of the voices again, the voices of the dead, gossiping behind his head, tugging at his coat-tails. One voice louder than the rest.

He turned to face Cartwright. 'I'm sorry, Mr Cartwright. If it's not too much trouble, would you be able to do one more thing for us?'

The bewildered look was back. 'Well, if I can—'

Murrain looked across at Warwick. 'We have another body. Our killer's first victim. We don't know what, if any, the connection might be between them, but there's a chance that the body might be familiar to you. We've not yet succeeded in identifying her either. But we do know there were various Lancs police employees in the hotel.'

Cartwright was clearly regretting that he'd missed his chance to escape. 'Well, the force is very large, you know—'

'I appreciate that, but there's no harm in checking,' Murrain said. 'Can you do the honours, Pete?'

Warwick gestured to the assistant to unlock one of the drawers further along the rack. 'Let's see,' he said.

Cartwright stepped reluctantly forward and peered into the open drawer. He took another step closer and then looked up at Murrain. He'd seemed bewildered before. Now he looked utterly lost. 'I don't understand,' he said.

'What is it?'

Cartwright was looking from Murrain to Warwick, as if one or other had been playing some grotesque joke. 'This is her. Kathy. Not that one.' He gestured towards the first, still half-open drawer. 'My God.' He uttered the final words as if the reality had only then hit him.

Murrain exchanged a baffled look with Milton. 'I know this is an absurd question, but you're absolutely sure?'

'Of course. I knew her straightaway.' He looked accusingly at Warwick, as if the doctor had deliberately misled him. 'But how—? I mean, has there been some kind of mix-up?'

'No mix-up,' Warwick said, firmly.

'As I said, Mr Cartwright, this hasn't quite turned out the way we expected.' You can bloody well say that again, Murrain added to himself. 'There were circumstantial reasons for us to believe the first body to be that of Ms Granger. Thankfully, you've saved us from wasting any time. It's really much appreciated.' Any more of this, he thought, and he'd be qualified for a job in Comms. But the last thing he wanted was for Cartwright to go running to the media with some excitable story. 'Now, we really do owe you that coffee.' He took Cartwright's elbow and smoothly led him towards the door, Milton following in their wake. 'Thanks, Pete,' he called back to Warwick. 'We'll be in touch later.'

Warwick stood watching as the door swung shut behind them. 'I hope so, Kenny, old chum,' he murmured to himself. 'I'm really looking forward to hearing your views on this one.'

'I think the apposite phrase is: what the fuck?' Milton said, slumping back at his desk. He'd left Murrain plying Cartwright with coffee and pastries in some upmarket coffee shop in the town centre, no doubt pumping him discreetly for background on Kathy Granger. Cartwright probably thought they were all insane. He was beginning to think so himself.

'It usually is,' Marie Donovan agreed, looking up from where she'd been annotating witness statements. 'What specifically in this case?'

'It turns out,' Milton said slowly, 'that victim number two wasn't Kathy Granger at all.'

'Shit. Does that mean we're back at square one?'

'Not exactly. Because, against all the odds, it turns out that Granger was, in fact, victim number one.'

It took her a moment to process what he'd said. 'You're kidding?'

'Do I look a bundle of laughs? Nope. That's where we are.'

'But—' She was still working through this. 'No, I'm lost. How does that work? Victim number two was dressed in Granger's clothes—'

163

'With Granger's possessions all around her, and Granger's car in the hotel car-park. Good, isn't it?'

She sat back, rubbing her hands across her face. 'So that means—?'

'That means our killer forced or persuaded Granger to remove her clothes before she was killed, as we knew. But it means he then took all her possessions, including her car, away from the Stockport hotel and, ultimately, brought them all up to the moorland place.' He paused, as if he preferred not to contemplate the next part. 'And then somehow persuaded or forced victim number two to undress and put on Granger's clothes   so that he could lead us to the conclusion that she was Granger.'

'It's not even that, though, is it?' she said, thinking through the implications. 'The second victim checked into the hotel as Granger last night. Why the hell would she do that?'

'Christ, you're right,' he said. 'I'd forgotten that. The killer must have somehow forced her to do that.'

'But how? And why? Why go to that much trouble? That much risk?'

'Well, the short answer would be because we're dealing with a madman. Can you imagine what it must have been like for her? To be forced to undress and then dress in someone else's clothes, not knowing what this lunatic's got in store for you. Jesus.' He shook his head. 'It's like he's playing some sort of game, like he's teasing us. Giving us the semblance of a lead then plunging us back into darkness again. And none of this feels like the major breakthrough we need. Even now, we just got a few more leads to pursue. Any sightings of Granger's car leaving the Stockport hotel or arriving at the other place, for example. More interviews with the receptionists who checked Granger out of the Stockport place and into the moorland one.' He paused. 'It's not much. At least we now know for sure that the first victim was part of the wedding party. Let's hope the interviews with Andy Barton and Jack Brennan throw up something. You really think Brennan might be in the frame?'

'If I'm honest, I can't see it. I won't say much in Brennan's favour, but I still can't see him as the kind of person who'd do this.'

'He's the only link with Granger we've got, though.' Milton turned to boot up his computer. 'And that's the real question, isn't it? Just what sort of person would do this.'

Cartwright was sitting with a large caffe latte in front of him, contemplating an incongruously ornate Danish pastry. He was still white-faced but his appetite seemed to be returning.

'It's awful,' he said, taking a bite into the pastry. 'Who'd do a thing like that?' He shook his head, scattering pastry crumbs. 'It's unbelievable.'

'It is,' Murrain agreed, thinking that Cartwright didn't know the half of it. 'Did you know Ms Granger well?'

'Depends what you mean. I knew her well as a colleague. But not outside work, if you know what I mean.' He sounded as if this had been a source of some regret.

'Did she have family? We couldn't track down anyone, which is why we approached you for the identification.'

'I don't think there are any close relatives. I never heard her mention anyone, and I know her parents had both passed on.'

'Relationships? Boyfriends?'

Cartwright eyed Murrain uneasily, as if he'd taken the conversation into inappropriate territory. 'I'm not sure I should—'

Murrain held up his hand. 'I'm sorry,' he said. 'I was being insensitive. But you'll appreciate the more we know about Ms Granger, the more we have to work on.'

'You can't think that this was done by someone she *knew*?' Cartwright coped with his shock by taking another large bite of the pastry.

'We have to explore all avenues. Most murders are committed by someone known to the victim. This looks like some random act of savagery, especially now we have two victims, but we can't take that for granted.'

'I suppose.' Cartwright looked mollified. 'The answer's no, though.'

'No relationships?'

'Not currently, I'm sure of that. There'd been something serious in the past—well, Kathy had thought it was serious—which had ended badly. I think that had rather put her off men.' He shook his head wistfully.

'This relationship,' Murrain said. 'Do you know how it ended? The circumstances, I mean.'

'Not really. She never wanted to talk about it. I think she'd been dumped, pretty unceremoniously. Or two-timed. Or both.'

'You don't know who this man was?'

'She didn't give much away. She got on well enough with the others in the office, but I never really had the impression she had any close friends outside.' He stopped, thinking. 'Before she joined us, she worked for you lot in North Manchester, I think. She was a bit closer to real policing in those days. Worked on case file admin or some such.'

'We'll look into that. By the way, does the name DI Andy Barton mean anything to you?'

Cartwright frowned. 'Yes, I know DI Barton. Well, I've had dealings with him.'

'Sounds like you may not be a fan.'

'Let's just say he's a regular customer. Always complaining we've made some error on his payslip, or that we've underpaid one of his team's overtime or some such.' He shrugged. 'Goes with the territory. Barton's almost always wrong, but he never apologises. You know the type.'

Murrain had a horrible feeling he might *be* the type. 'Bit of a bully?'

Cartwright looked as if he was about to agree, then checked himself, conscious of talking out of school. 'Well, I wouldn't go that far. Why are you interested in Barton anyway?'

Murrain was intrigued that Cartwright had to ask the question. 'It was his wedding,' he said. 'In Stockport. That Kathy Granger was attending.'

Cartwright looked up, surprised. 'Really? I didn't know that.' For a moment, he had the air of a betrayed lover. 'Andy Barton?'

'You don't know how Kathy knew him?'

'I didn't even know she did.'

'Maybe she knew the bride. Woman called Julie Welling. Also with Lancs, we understand. Works in Intelligence?'

'I know the name,' Cartwright said.

'But she didn't tell you anything about the wedding?'

'Not really. Just said it was some old friends from way back.'

'Did she seem to be looking forward to the wedding?'

'She talked about it as a bit of a chore. You know, a duty she felt obliged to carry out.'

'We've all been there,' Murrain said.

'I'm not sure that was the whole story, though,' Cartwright went on. 'Truth was, I don't think Kathy got out much. I used to try to invite her for a drink, sometimes. But she'd never come. Reckoned she preferred her own company. I think she was a bit lonely. Probably couldn't resist the opportunity for a social occasion.' He stopped. 'And it ended like this.'

Murrain swallowed the last of his coffee. 'It's no consolation. But we'll get whoever was responsible. It's only a matter of time.' He hoped that he sounded more confident than he felt. 'This has been very useful, Mr Cartwright. We'll be in touch if we've any more questions as the case develops. But I hope we don't need to bother you.'

'No, that's fine. Anything I can do. I mean, you don't expect this sort of thing, do you?'

'No,' Murrain said, as he watched Cartwright systematically finishing off the last half of his Danish pastry. 'You certainly don't.'

CHAPTER NINETEEN

'Hit and run,' DI Warren said, pushing the file in Murrain's direction.

Murrain had called in on his way from dropping Cartwright at the railway station. He'd intended to call Warren earlier when they'd first picked up the reference on HOLMES2, but there hadn't been time. Heading back up to his own office, Murrain had stopped at the first floor and found Warren at his desk, engrossed in football reports on the BBC web-site.

'Anything suspicious?'

Warren shrugged. 'It was Karl Berenek. Everything's suspicious.'

'Like that, is it? Hear he was working for Patrick Henessey.'

'Suitably charming company.' Warren took back the file and turned it towards him. 'What's the interest? Thought you lot had bigger things to worry about.'

'It's just that we stumbled across Berenek just the other day.' Murrain smiled. 'You know me, Louis. Always intrigued by coincidence.'

'I know you, Kenny. Where'd you stumble across him? Not the first time he's been caught lurking in the undergrowth.'

'It's probably nothing. His mother works at the hotel. We interviewed her at home as a witness and encountered Berenek. He was as welcoming as you'd expect to a couple of plods turning up on his doorstep so that made me do some digging. Then I saw he'd been killed. Like I say, just intrigued.'

'Can't see there's likely to be any connection,' Warren said. 'Berenek was a toe-rag but a fairly straightforward one. Ducking and diving merchant. Thought he was tough and smart, but usually fucked up one way or another. If he was killed, it was most likely just because he inserted himself up the wrong person's nose.'

'You think he might have been killed?'

'It's possible,' Warren said, cautiously. 'It was pouring with rain. He was crossing the road in some Stockport back-street. Car must have come out of nowhere. Who knows? You get some lunatics joy-riding round those streets, especially after a few pints. Wouldn't be surprising if some tosser took the corner too fast. Wouldn't be that surprising if they panicked and didn't stop.' He paused. 'But, then, wouldn't be that surprising if someone decided to take Berenek out. He didn't have many friends.'

'He seems close to Henessey.'

'The son he never had? Maybe a bit of that. But Henessey was using him. Got him to do the deals with the folks up in town, without Henessey getting his hands dirty. Might have been one of them had him bumped off, if they took against him. You know what it's like.'

'What do the collision analysts reckon?'

'Inconclusive. From the tyre marks, the car was exceeding the speed-limit at the point of impact. It came round the corner before hitting Berenek, and there's a possibility it might have deviated slightly from its original path—you know, as if aiming for him. But nothing definitive. And Berenek managed to pick a spot where there's no CCTV coverage nearby—'

'Or his killer did,' Murrain pointed out.

'Either way, there doesn't seem to be sufficient evidence for us to treat it as suspicious. Though the case is still open as a hit and run, obviously. We've spoken to Henessey. He claims to know of no reason why someone would want to take out one of his employees but then he would say that, wouldn't it? Might be even that Henessey's behind it, if Berenek was two-timing him in some way. Who knows?'

Or cares, Murrain thought. Karl Berenek was hardly a major loss to society. If he had been murdered, it would just be the result of some internecine squabble between low-lifes. No-one would say it in so many words, but the police had insufficient resources to worry their heads too much about a case like this.

'You've spoken to his mother?' he asked, wanting to remind Warren that Berenek had still been a human being.

'Can't say that she seemed devastated by her loss. Had the impression that Berenek had been an embarrassment to her.'

'I got that sense too, when we interviewed her. But—well, she is his mother.' Murrain was staring into the middle distance, as if thinking about something else entirely. He blinked and looked back at Warren. 'Impossible to make sense of other people's relationships, isn't it?'

'I don't even try. Anything else you need on Berenek?' The tone was one of dismissal. Warren had match-reports to read.

'No. Like you say, however he died, I can't see that there's likely to be a connection with our killings.'

Warren looked thoughtful for a second. Finally, he said: 'Mind you, the crime-scenes are interesting.'

'Oh yes?' Murrain could sense that Warren was itching to share something. Warren usually played things close to his chest, on the basis that knowledge was power. But he tended to shoot his mouth off when he was looking to impress.

'The two hotels,' Warren said.

'Go on. They're both respectable places, as far as we're aware.'

'*Respectable*,' Warren echoed, in a tone that implied a word of dubious provenance. 'Up to a point.'

'I wasn't aware either place was on our radar, particularly.'

'Well, they're not like some dives we deal with, certainly.' Warren paused, clearly preparing for the big reveal. 'You know our friend Henessey has shares in both, don't you?'

'Henessey?'

'Funny that, isn't it? Thought it might intrigue you, what with your liking for coincidences and everything.'

'Hadn't occurred to us to look at the hotel ownership. How come Henessey's involved?'

'Fingers in a lot of pies, has old Patrick. He's been investing in the leisure industry for years. Started on the Lancs coast. But getting more ambitious. He might be right. Have you seen the number of hotels springing up around Manchester? Christ knows who stays in them but it looks like a growth industry. Henessey's always had a knack of buying cheap and making a decent profit. When the recession hit in 2008, the word is that he was sitting on a pile of ill-gotten cash and looking for something to do with it.'

'Money laundering as much as investment, I'm guessing?'

170

'No doubt. Anyway, there were countless businesses going through hard times. Your Stockport place was one. Had been a decent family business. Son took over and didn't have a clue. They'd over-extended building that new extension. Then the credit crunch hit and business dropped away. Suddenly they were looking at big debts and the bank threatening to foreclose.'

'And Henessey came along as their white knight?'

'Bought a majority share in the business on the cheap, but enough to bail them out and get the bank off their backs.'

'Son reckoned he was the owner when we spoke to him.' Murrain was kicking himself for not checking this out although there'd been no reason to think it was pertinent to the case. There still wasn't but the coincidences were mounting.

'I think you'll find that was a little white lie,' Warren said. 'The family has a sizeable share, but I'm pretty sure Henessey has control.'

'What about the other place? The Wentworth place up on the moors? You're saying Henessey's got a stake in that too?'

'So I understand. Place has changed hands loads of times over the years. Everyone thinks it should be a goldmine. Decent building, brilliant location. But it's just a bit too remote to really make a killing. Another place that went through a hard time in the recession. It was owned by some conglomerate of local business-types. Some of them wanted out, and Henessey bought his way in. Not the same shareholding as the Stockport place—maybe 20%—but not insignificant.'

'You've been making a study of this,' Murrain observed. 'You'll be doing the business news next.'

'It's where we are, isn't it?' Warren said. 'Must be a delight for you working on straightforward murder cases. Most of the serious stuff these days is bloody financial and cyber crime. They don't need coppers. They need accountants and geeks. Our days are numbered, Kenny old son.'

'I don't doubt that. So you're mugging up on the FT and The Economist, are you?'

'With the likes of Henessey it pays to know what he's up to. These days you can find out as much from Companies' House as you can from some snout down the pub. He's a wheeler and a dealer, or likes to think he is. Makes his money where he can and channels it into legit businesses. Maybe one day he won't need the dodgy stuff. That's the theory.'

'So he's got shares in both these hotels. Just these two, is it?'

'Not at all. He's got—what's the term?—a portfolio of investments dotted round the north-west.'

'And these are legit businesses? Apart from Henessey's money, I mean.'

'Depends what you mean,' Warren said. 'Some are more so than others. Your Wentworth place up on the moors, for example. I'd say that's straight enough. Some dodgy money in there from various sources but the hotel washes its own face. Your Stockport place, on the other hand—'

'Go on.'

'Well, a bit of a mixed bag. Still respectable enough on the outside just as it was before Henessey took over. Decent clientele. Business types, visitors, weddings, all that. But the word is that it's been straying into more dubious territory. Not quite a knocking shop, but—you know, escorts, massages, that sort of thing. The more refined end of the skin trade, let's say.'

'They won't keep the respectable clientele if they start dabbling in those areas,' Murrain said.

'No, well, that's where Henessey can be short-sighted,' Warren said. 'Sees the chance for a quick buck now and doesn't realise he's kiboshing the future. Any of this relevant to your case, you reckon?'

'I don't know,' Murrain said, slowly. 'Of all the hotels in all of Greater Manchester, why did the murders happen in two owned by Patrick Henessey? It's difficult to see a direct connection.'

'Some business rival looking to damage his reputation?' Warren offered, already turning back to his PC.

'Fairly extreme way of doing that.' Murrain shook his head. 'Can't see it. Can't really see how Henessey's likely to be relevant.'

'So what brought you here today, then, Kenny?' Warren asked. 'What made you start asking about Karl Berenek? You got one of your feelings, is that it?'

Murrain smiled and pushed himself to his feet. When Louis Warren started taking the piss, it was time to leave. 'You know me, Louis. Always one for the feelings.'

Warren's attention was already fixed on the computer screen. 'If you've any feelings about where United's season's likely to end up,' he said, 'I'll be only too glad to hear them.'

'We've only got twenty minutes,' Wanstead said, recommencing his narrow circuit of the room. 'We're going to look prize tossers if we can't get this to work.'

'Relax, Paul. Maggie's sorting it, aren't you, Maggie?'

'Doing my best,' the voice said from under the table. 'Some joker's been messing with the cabling. It's a dog's breakfast under here.'

Wanstead's expression suggested he might have had a hand in that. When IT support wasn't available—often the case, despite Maggie Robinson's prompt attendance this morning—Wanstead was known to improvise with the available equipment. He finally stopped pacing and sat down heavily next to Milton. 'I pulled a lot of strings to set this up,' he said, plaintively.

'I can see that,' Milton said. 'We can't usually get IT to turn up.' He waited while, inevitably, Maggie Robinson stuck her head above the table to glare at him. 'You're doing a terrific job, Maggie,' he said. They were old friends.

'I'm doing my *best*,' she said. 'Which, in all modesty, is bloody good. I'll have it set up in a second despite Serious Crime's best efforts.'

'I didn't mean here,' Wanstead went on, keen to ensure his contribution wasn't overlooked. 'I meant at the other end. Getting them to play ball.'

Milton was conscious that, having made initial contact with the Maldives Police Service, he'd left Wanstead to organise the logistics. It was Wanstead's strength, but it would have been a challenge. 'Tough, was it?'

'Less than you might think. They were very professional, actually.' He spoke with an edge of surprise. Wanstead believed, often in the face of the available evidence, that the British police were not only the best in the world but in a different league from their overseas counterparts. 'They made the contact with the Bartons, got them to agree to be interviewed and set up all the video-conferencing stuff at their end. Impressive, really.' He spoke in the tone of one amazed to discover that electricity was widely available overseas.

'But we need to be on-line at two?' Milton said. According to the clock over the meeting-room door they had another fifteen minutes.

'That's when we agreed to dial in. They were picking up the Bartons from their hotel and bringing them into the nearest Station. It's early evening their time.'

'And Barton's been co-operative, has he?' Barton wouldn't have had much choice in the circumstances but that didn't always stop people digging their heels in.

'Got the impression he'd rather have kept his new wife out of it but otherwise he's not been difficult.'

'Probably worried we'll ask him things he'd rather his bride didn't know about,' Milton observed. 'Speaking of which, I was hoping that Kenny would be back to handle the questioning. He'll make a better job of it than I would.'

'Must have got waylaid after dropping your Cartwright chap off,' Wanstead said. 'But he knows what time we're on. And, knowing Kenny's tendencies, I've told various people downstairs to make sure he gets his backside up here as soon as he appears.'

'All we can do,' Milton agreed, flicking again through his notes. He'd half-resigned himself to having to lead this.

But, as if summoned by the mention of his name, Murrain chose that moment to make his entrance, just as the large television screen finally flickered into life. Maggie Robinson appeared from below the table, looking triumphant.

174

'All here then, are we?' Murrain said. 'I see Maggie's worked her magic with the technology. So just about ready to go.' He slid himself into the seat next to Milton, facing the camera. 'Sorry I've been so long. Got caught up with Louis Warren downstairs. One or two interesting insights. I'll fill you in when we're done. Expecting to see Mr and Mrs Barton together, are we?'

'Assuming that's what you want.'

'Harder for them to lie if they're both there.'

'You reckon they might have something to hide.'

'Andy Barton strikes me as the sort who'd always have something to hide. Whether it's anything pertinent to our case is another question.'

Maggie Robinson was busy dialling into the specified Skype address. They were a couple of minutes early but after a moment the connection was made and the image of a brightly lit room appeared on the screen. A man in police uniform was standing nervously in front of the camera. Behind him a man and a woman were sitting behind a table, the woman sipping repeatedly from a glass of water. It took a few seconds for the speakers to crackle into life, and there was a slight but disconcerting time-lag between the lip movements on screen and the sounds emanating from the television. 'Hello?' the police-officer enquired, uneasily. 'Can you hear me?'

'Very clearly,' Murrain said. 'Can you hear us?'

The officer looked relieved. 'Loud and clear. Loud and clear.'

'Many thanks to you and your colleagues for setting this up.'

'No problem,' the officer said with a grin. 'Always pleased to do our bit for the old Empire.' His tongue, Murrain assumed, was firmly in his cheek. 'I will hand you over to Mr and Mrs Barton.' The officer stepped back, looking pleased to be out of the limelight.

'Many thanks again,' Murrain said. 'Mr Barton—DI Barton. Mrs Barton. Thank you also for talking to us at short notice. We appreciate this isn't the most convenient time—'

'You can say that again,' Barton said. 'You do know we're on honeymoon? Well, obviously you do.' He was a thick-set man with close-cropped grey hair, only a year or two younger than Murrain. He looked the kind of officer who'd originally been recruited for the size of his boots rather than his brain.

'We appreciate that, DI Barton,' Murrain said, seeing no harm in reminding Barton of their respective ranks. 'And we're grateful to you. You'll appreciate we're dealing with a serious case—'

'And not making much progress from what I hear. Which is presumably why you need to bother us.' Barton was clearly not a man looking to ingratiate himself.

'We need to talk to all potentially material witnesses,' Murrain said. 'I'm afraid that includes yourselves. Particularly now we've confirmed that the victim was, unfortunately, one of your wedding guests.'

Even though they'd formally confirmed Granger's identity only that morning, Murrain had wondered whether someone might have already tipped off Barton. But he looked authentically shocked. 'One of *our* guests?'

'A woman called Kathy—Kathryn—Granger. I understand she worked in Lancs Intelligence.' That well-known oxymoron, he added silently to himself, keeping his face deadpan.

There was silence at the other end of the line. It was Julie Barton who spoke first. 'Kathy? My God.'

Barton leaned over to take her hand, in a gesture that looked awkwardly staged. If nothing else, Murrain thought, it had allowed Barton to turn his face away from the camera. It was impossible to tell how he'd reacted to the news. 'This is a bit of a shock,' Barton said, finally. 'I don't know what to say.'

'I can understand that it's distressing for you both. Was Ms Granger a close friend?'

Barton hesitated. 'Well, not close, exactly. An old friend, let's say. Of Julie's, that is.'

'Ah, I see.' Murrain left the comment hanging in the air, hoping that Julie Barton would feel obliged to break the silence. Barton himself had probably carried out enough interrogations to recognise the technique.

'We worked together,' Julie Barton said after a moment. 'Years ago. Both did case admin stuff in North Manchester.' She looked white-faced but not unduly distressed. 'God, it's awful. We only invited her out of politeness, really, and then it comes to this.' Her voice trailed off.

Murrain had registered what she'd said. 'You hadn't seen a lot of Ms Granger in recent years?'

'Well, no. We'd been quite close in the old days. We were the only young women working on the team so it threw us together, you know? We used to go for a drink after hours, sometimes went out together. But it was mainly a work thing.' She paused, thinking about the relationship. 'You know how it is. You don't have a lot in common, but you've more in common than the others you're working with, so you cling together.'

'You didn't see a lot of her outside work? Even in those days?'

'Not really. I was the clubbing type—' She cast a glance towards her husband, as if seeking his approval. 'Kathy was more of a home-bird. I mean, decent enough company, but a bit solitary. Compared with me, anyway.' She laughed, self-consciously.

'We understand she wasn't currently in a relationship?'

'I wouldn't know. That's not exactly surprising news, though.'

Murrain shifted the papers in front of him as if checking his notes. 'We believe there was a serious relationship in the past. Would you know anything about that?'

He could see her exchange another glance with Barton. 'I think there was someone. But she was always secretive about it.' Murrain could sense the hesitation. 'Don't know what the story was. At the time, I wondered whether he was married or something.'

'But you never had an inkling who he might be?'

'Not really.'

Not really. Which means yes, Murrain thought. He felt the familiar electrical buzz in his head, the echo of an image. 'Could it have been a colleague? Someone in the force, I mean?'

This time the pause was longer and it was Andy Barton who broke it. 'Julie's said she doesn't know. Is this going anywhere? I

177

thought we were here to give you information about the wedding, not making guesses about something that happened ten years ago.'

'In the circumstances any personal history relating to Ms Granger is potentially relevant.'

'Are you suggesting she was knifed by some ancient ex-boyfriend? Who'd traipsed all the way to Stockport to do the deed?'

If said boyfriend happened to be another of your guests, Murrain thought, then, yes, that might be exactly what I'm suggesting. Out loud, he said: 'We have to investigate every possibility.' But he knew when he'd hit a brick wall. 'Did you get chance to spend much time with Ms Granger at the reception?'

Julie Barton looked relieved the interview had moved on. 'You know how it is at weddings—' She laughed. 'Well, at your own wedding, anyway. We chatted when she first arrived, but, you know, there was a queue of people waiting to congratulate us. I said I'd catch up with her later, but I never really did. All a bit too hectic.'

'Would she have known many other people at the reception?'

'Probably not, really. To be honest, I was surprised she came. I only invited her because—well, I ran into her when we were first organising the wedding. Our paths hardly ever crossed at work but I'd had to go up to payroll to sort out some cock-up. I didn't even know that's where she was working. And I started to talk about getting married and the wedding and everything.' Her voice faded. 'Well, from the way she responded I realised I'd been a bit tactless. I got the impression she'd got stuck in a bit of a rut. Lonely. I was feeling bad about it, so I over-compensated and started saying she should come to the wedding.'

'You didn't expect her to accept?'

'Not really. We were hardly bosom buddies. I'd told her we'd be holding it down in Stockport. I thought she'd be pleased by the offer, but wouldn't actually come.' She stopped, and this time appeared genuinely upset. 'I feel awful. If I hadn't invited her—'

'Is this going to take much longer?' Andy Barton intervened. 'We've got dinner booked. I'm not sure we can help any further.'

'Just a couple more questions,' Murrain said, to demonstrate that Barton wasn't calling the shots. 'Did either of you see her again at the reception? After that first meeting?'

That same exchange of glances, slightly more furtive this time, Murrain thought.

'I don't know,' Julie Barton said. 'I didn't speak to her again, but I saw her a couple of times across the room. She was in the bar mainly though I didn't get the impression she was drinking a lot.'

'Did you see anybody with her? Anyone talking to her.'

It was Andy Barton who answered. 'We'd both have been too tied up to notice, really. It was a pretty frantic evening. We didn't manage to catch up properly even with our close friends. Neither of us spent the evening looking out for Kathy Granger.'

The image was almost there, coalescing and growing more solid behind Murrain's eyes but still indecipherable. 'Of course.' He paused, and flicked again through the file in front of him, as if double-checking he'd covered everything. 'One more thing. I don't suppose either of you knows a Jack Brennan?'

The silence was almost palpable. After a moment, Andy Barton said: 'I know him a little. We worked together for a while when we were with you lot.' He laughed. 'Another name from the old days. Memory lane tonight. Ended up as a DI with you, I think, so you probably know more about him than I do. Why bring him up?'

'You hadn't invited him to the reception?'

This time Barton didn't allow the silence to build. 'I think you've seen the invite list. He wasn't on there.'

'No, of course.' Murrain noted that Barton hadn't answered his question.

'I don't see where this is heading,' Barton said. 'None of my business, but you seem to be clutching at straws. Are we done now?'

'I think that'll do us for this evening. Thank you, DI Barton. And thank you, Mrs Barton. We appreciate you've had to interrupt your honeymoon, and we're very grateful. That's been most informative. I hope you enjoy the rest of your honeymoon. We'll try not to disturb you again.'

'I should bloody well hope not,' Barton said.

'At least until your return,' Murrain added. 'And please thank your hosts there for helping organise this. We're really very grateful.' As he spoke, the local officer appeared on screen again, waving a goodnight, before the call was cut.

Murrain's gaze was still fixed on the now blank screen. 'Well, that was interesting.'

'He was lying, wasn't he?' Milton said from behind.

'Thought I was the one with the second-sight,' Murrain said.

'I'm just stuck with a copper's gut,' Milton said, 'but I reckon he was lying about Brennan. And maybe about seeing Granger talking to someone else later in the evening. He jumped in too quickly there.'

'That's a good gut you've got there,' Murrain said. 'That was my feeling too. Weird, though, isn't it? Why the hell would they lie about any of that?'

CHAPTER TWENTY

Bastards. They were all bastards, the lot of them. A shower of fucking bastards.

It was the same every day, every morning when Robin turned up here. They'd stand there, smoking their fucking cigarettes out by the bins, and as he walked up here from the bus-stop, they'd all start to take the fucking piss.

He always wished he'd prepared some smart retort to throw back at them. But he wanted to put it out of his mind until he was actually walking up here from the main road. Then he'd see the three of them, and he'd know he was going to have to go through it all again, and he still didn't know what to say.

It wasn't like they were better than him. They were stuck in this dump, too, even if they thought the kitchen was a step up from cleaning the bogs. They all reckoned they had their reasons for ending up here. Ged was supposed to be a student, though Christ knew what he was studying. He kept saying he'd be off soon to start his course, but he'd been saying that for six months. The other guy, Darren, had been inside, apparently. Theft or some such, but enough for him to make out that he was a hard-case. A hard-case who couldn't get a job anywhere else. As for Martin—well, there was no guessing why Martin was here. He just seemed to be a creep, eyeing up any female guest unlucky enough to find herself in the hotel. The other two took the piss out of Martin too, reckoned he'd drilled a hole in some of the bedroom walls to get his jollies as a peeping tom. It probably wasn't true but Martin didn't like them saying it. Though that didn't stop the three of them ganging up as soon as Robin appeared.

It was all the more galling because the four of them were about the only ones who even spoke fucking English around here, apart from Mo himself. Most working in this dump were immigrants, half of them illegals, who'd ended up here from Christ knew where. All the colours under the sun, speaking languages like nothing Robin had ever heard. Mo didn't care who he took on. Robin knew that, given half a chance, he'd have got rid of the four of them, because he had to pay them minimum wage and through the books. But he needed a few people who could string an English sentence together, even if it was touch and go in Darren's case.

Anyway. Mo had to keep enough legit so the Revenue didn't come sniffing round. You couldn't run a place like this with no wages going through the books at all. But a lot of the rest were cash in hand. No tax, no NI, most of them just glad to get whatever they were given. Some of them were only here for a week or two, then off elsewhere. Keeping moving before the police or Immigration caught up. Mo didn't care. He'd take anyone on to keep the place ticking over.

Robin knew he was brighter than the other three put together, though that wasn't saying a lot. But he struggled with anything outside his routine. He liked to be sure where he was, what he was supposed to be doing. He liked to keep things simple. He could do better than this and one day he would. But, for the moment, he just needed something straightforward and close to home, so he could look after his mother. There were other jobs that would pay more or offer a better place to work. There were certainly jobs that wouldn't involve him having to deal with those three clowns. But that would require effort, and he couldn't deal with that. Not at the moment.

They'd been there again this morning, jeering at him from their usual spot. He'd tramped on past, waiting for them to throw rubbish at his back. That was one of their favourite tricks. They generally missed their target by some distance, but he'd occasionally had to arrive at reception with rotting vegetation dripping down his jacket. Mo found that hilarious.

This morning, they'd been satisfied with a few hurled insults, comments about his manhood or brains or both. He'd tried not to listen, though he could feel his body tensing as he walked past. Bastards. Stupid childish bastards.

Mo was at reception when he arrived. Mo liked to cover the desk himself, not trusting anyone else to deal with customers and certainly not with their money. Robin didn't know whether Mo actually owned the hotel or was just the manager. He liked to give the impression it was his personal fiefdom, but every month or two he had a visit from a couple of older men who took Mo into his office for protracted discussions. Share holders, Mo had once told him. And maybe they were. But, unlike Mo, they really did look like they might own the place.

None of Robin's business, anyway, and he was happy to keep it like that. He just wanted to turn up, do his job, get away. Mostly, he was on cleaning duties—in the kitchen after breakfast, the lavatories in the public areas, the small bar area, especially if there'd been a heavy-drinking crowd in the night before. They got that on Saturday nights in particular, when there were groups of lads up for the football or for a stag do. They ended up back here in the small hours, and Mo usually kept the bar open to sell them over-priced beers and shorts. Robin had to give Mo his due. The place was a dump, right enough, but Mo somehow managed to keep the occupancy up, even when times were hard. You got what you paid for, and he'd managed to undercut most other places on the outskirts. The rooms were shabby, but clean and comfortable enough for the people likely to stay here. Occasionally, you'd see couples turn up, expecting something better, who would turn around and leave. But most people thought it was okay for the price.

And Mo was accommodating. He could get you what you wanted—from alcohol to drugs to sex, if the price was right. They had more than a few regulars who knew that. A quiet word, a few quid in his direction, and he'd see you right. Keeping the bar open till sparrow-fart was only a small part of it but it all brought in the paying guests.

Mo didn't generally use Robin on the rooms. They had an ever-changing team of women of varying ages, nationalities and backgrounds who handled the room cleaning, while Robin did the heavy-duty stuff. But they were short-handed today—'two of the bloody tarts did a fucking runner last night', was how Mo phrased it—so Mo asked Robin to look after some of the upstairs rooms. Mo was slouched behind the desk finishing a greasy-looking bacon sandwich he'd filched from the breakfast buffet. 'We was busy last night,' he said, in the accent that Robin assumed was Cockney. 'Had quite a few in for the match.' City had played some mid-week European match, though that sort of thing passed Robin by. 'You need to give the bar a good seeing-to, as well.'

Another day, then. Robin dealt with the bar first, as there was no point in starting on the bedrooms until guests had begun checking out. If the football fans had been drinking late, most of them wouldn't be surfacing till they were forced to by the 11am check-out time.

The bar wasn't in too bad a state. Dirty glasses scattered around, empty beer bottles lined up on the tables, sticky residue from the odd spillage. But nothing like as bad as Robin had sometimes seen it. People were more restrained on a weekday night, even if they didn't have to be up early the next morning. Robin set to work with his mop and bucket, losing himself, as he liked to do, in the rhythm of his sweeping.

It was nearly eleven before he'd dealt with all the public areas, following his usual schedule. Mo had asked him to deal with the bedrooms on the second and third floors and given him a printout of the rooms that had been occupied. There were more than he'd expected, so it looked like a long afternoon ahead. But that was good. It would save him from being given any jobs that might force him into contact with those bastards.

He enjoyed cleaning bedrooms. It was easier work than the stuff he normally ended up with, and he could approach it methodically. There was a routine for each room, the same every time. Mo intended it to be fairly superficial, not much more than a lick and a polish. But Robin liked to put some effort into it, do a job he could be proud of, even if Mo didn't give a bugger.

He started at the far end, as he usually did, and worked his way back towards the central lifts. Virtually all the guests had checked out now, so he could work uninterrupted. Most of the rooms had been left in a reasonable state, so the work wasn't arduous—cleaning the tiny bathroom, replacing the thin bedding and towels, running the vacuum cleaner over the floor. There were plenty of rooms to be cleaned, though, so it was early afternoon before he reached the rooms at the opposite end of the corridor.

The final room, Room 316, had a Do Not Disturb notice on the door. Robin hesitated. He was pretty sure that, according to Mo's list, no-one on this floor was booked in for a second night. Apart from a few contractors on a local building project, who were all staying on the first floor, not many guests stayed multiple nights. So either someone had slept in beyond the check-out time or, more likely, the occupant had forgotten to remove the sign on departing.

Either way, he couldn't leave it. He knew Mo wasn't best pleased if a room was overlooked, whatever the reason. It had happened once or twice, through forgetfulness or because someone had just buggered off without finishing the job, and Mo had hit the roof.

Robin fumbled with his keys and pushed open the door.

The smell struck him straightaway. What the hell was that? Rich and unpleasant, like the worse things he encountered cleaning the lavatories downstairs. He couldn't imagine what was causing it. He took another step and found himself gagging. Jesus. He couldn't deal with this.

He wanted to get out, shut the door, and go and tell Mo he'd have to deal with this himself. But he couldn't just do that. If it turned out there was nothing seriously wrong in here, Mo would take the piss forever. Worse still, he'd tell the other bastards, and Robin would never bloody hear the last of it. If it was difficult to face whatever was causing that smell, it would be even harder to face those bastards if he made a pillock of himself for no good reason.

He held his breath and took another step into the room. The closed curtains were thin enough, but the sun didn't reach this side of the hotel and the room was almost in darkness. He fumbled behind him for the light-switch, blinked as the light came on, and then froze.

Christ. Christ almighty. He'd never seen anything like it. There was blood everywhere. Thick black pools of blood on the shabby carpet. Showers on blood around the peeling wallpaper. Blood still dripping from the crimson-soaked bedding.

And in the centre, spread-eagled on the bed at that heart of that endless blood, was the body. A lifeless, naked female body, drenched red from head to toe, a blank face staring up as if, even in death, she could see her killer bearing down towards her.

CHAPTER TWENTY ONE

'The good news,' Milton said, perching on the corner of Murrain's desk, 'is that Brennan's prepared to play ball without our having to go down the formal route.'

Murrain looked up. 'Not sure he has a lot of choice. He could call our bluff, but that could end badly if it looks like he's being difficult.'

'No, but he seems willing to be co-operative. Even happy to see us up here. He'd just arrived at their Manchester office when I spoke to him. Reckons he's spending half his life up here anyway.'

'Does he? Well, that's interesting in itself. You said that was the good news?'

'Yes, well. The good news is that he's willing to be co-operative. The bad news is he doesn't see this as his immediate priority.'

'You did point out to him that we're dealing with a high-profile double murder?'

'Yeah. I mentioned that. Fairly forcibly.'

'And he wasn't impressed?'

'Apparently they've got some serious flap on over there. Something to do with an undercover officer who's gone AWOL.'

'Say that again.'

'I know. Bloody brass neck, isn't it, in the circumstances—'

'No, I mean: say it again. What you said.'

This time, finally, Murrain had seen the image. Clearly, if for the briefest of moments. A room. A small, badly-lit room. A terrified naked figure. The relentless slashing of a knife. Up and down, over and over again. And blood everywhere. Endless streams of blood that seemed almost to be filling the room.

'What? An undercover cop who's gone AWOL?'

But the image was gone. Murrain had been unable to discern anything about the figure wielding the knife. Except, perhaps, that it somehow looked wrong. Wrong for the setting. Out of place. Out of context. He closed his eyes, trying to recapture that instant.

'Kenny? You OK?'

Murrain could still feel the sensation pulsing through his veins. 'We need to talk to Brennan. Now. Urgently. Do whatever it takes to get him to take this seriously. Arrest the bugger if you have to. But get him here.'

'You're saying—?'

'It's like always. I don't know what I'm saying. Did he tell you anything about this undercover officer? Male? Female?'

'He didn't say much.' Milton concentrated, recognising the urgency in Murrain's tone. 'I think he said 'she'. He's her—what do they call it?—her contact, minder, you know. She sent him some unintelligible message last night, which got him worried, and she's not responded to his calls. They'd checked, and she hadn't come back to her flat last night, and they couldn't get hold of her. She'd been due to check in but hadn't. I thought it was just some bullshit he was using as a delaying tactic.' Milton was watching Murrain's expression. 'You think she might be another one?'

'Get Brennan over here. Tell him we might have something on his missing officer. I don't mind looking a complete tit if I've got it wrong. At worst, he'll just think we've pulled a fast one to get him in.'

'I'll see what I can do,' Milton paused as he spotted Wanstead heading across the room. 'Looks like we might have a development. Paul's looking agitated.'

'Kenny?' Wanstead sounded as if he might have run up from the floor below, but even a brisk trot along the corridor could have that effect on him.

'All OK, Paul?'

Wanstead gave himself a second to recover his breath. 'Call from the control room. Looks like we've another one.'

Murrain exchanged a glance with Milton. 'Where?'

'Budget hotel out Gorton way. Body found in one of the bedrooms.'

'Does it sound like the same MO as our first two?' Milton asked.

Wanstead took another deep breath. 'From what the FCR said, the answer's yes. There's not much doubt it's another one.' He leaned on the edge of Murrain's desk and allowed his voice to steady. It wasn't just that Wanstead was out of condition, Murrain realised. He looked genuinely spooked.

'But also no,' Wanstead went on, finally. 'This one doesn't sound like the others. This one sounds worse. Much much worse.'

The rain had set in again by the time they reached the hotel. The sky was heavy with cloud and the day felt already over, though it was only late afternoon.

Murrain wasn't sure he'd want to see the hotel in bright sunlight anyway. It would reveal too much about what was wrong with the place, from the unwashed windows and grubby curtains to the incomplete signage over the entrance.

Outside, there was the familiar gathering of the blue-light clans. Two squad cars, an ambulance, the SOCO van, several unmarked vehicles. Two uniforms standing guard by the entrance. A line of hotel staff, in overalls or stained kitchen whites, smoking and watching incuriously from a makeshift shelter by the large kitchen bins. Murrain wondered how many staff would have made themselves scarce once they'd heard the police were on their way.

Warwick was by the entrance, looking as if he might have been glad of a cigarette himself, though Murrain had never seen him smoke.

'Afternoon, Kenny.'

'How's tricks?'

'Tricks is not great,' Warwick said. 'Always glad of the business, Kenny, as you know. But this is getting ridiculous.'

'Tell me about it. I'm running out of things to say to the ACC and the Chief. Had calls from both already.'

'You making any progress catching this bastard?'

'Not as much as he is in ratcheting up the headcount. How's this one? More of the same?'

'Depends what you mean. I've not much doubt it's the same guy. Same combination of savagery and attention to detail as in the first two. You'll obviously have to get a view from Neil Ferbrache, but my impression is the crime scene's been cleaned up in the same way. Though maybe 'cleaned up' isn't quite the right phrase here.'

'How'd you mean?' Murrain could recall the image briefly imprinted on his mind's eye. Those torrents of blood.

'My impression's that, on this occasion, the killer went out of his way to release as much blood as possible. Gone for the main arteries first, while the victim would still have been alive—briefly anyway. Literally sprayed the room with blood.'

'You think the killer did that on *purpose*?'

'With the first two killings, the stabbing looked random, essentially. As if the killer had just stabbed and stabbed, without really caring where or how the blade went in. That's why it looked so frenzied. You had the sense the killer couldn't—or chose not to—control his actions.'

'And this looks different?'

'It's just as savage—more savage in terms of its effects. But it looks more deliberate, as if the killer's picked out where the blade should enter the body each time. The stabbing itself looks just as frenzied—no holds barred once the blade actually enters the flesh—but the targeting of the wounds is much more conscious.'

'Would that require any particular medical knowledge?'

'Not really. Nothing you couldn't get from Wikipedia. Butchery, not surgery, and not even craft butchery.'

'So why would the killer do it differently?'

'That, as I always say, is your territory. Maybe wanted to make even more of an impact? Leave you in no doubt what you're dealing with?'

'With three corpses and rising, we're not in much doubt about that. What's the time of death, you reckon?'

'Last night. Not too late. I'll be more circumspect in my formal report, but if you pushed me I'd say eight, nine last night.'

'How are things going upstairs?'

'Neil and his team will be a while yet. We didn't get here much before you did. I did my bit then came out for a breath of air. You'll need it if you spend too much time at the crime scene.'

'I'll go and see what I can find out.'

Milton was already clustered with Marie Donovan, Will Sparrow and Bert Wallace, discussing tactics and getting ready to take statements, gather evidence, carry out searches, whatever was needed. Murrain left them to it and made his way through the main entrance, nodding to the uniforms as he passed.

The interior of the hotel looked as shabby as the exterior. The floor-tiles were cracked and badly polished. The wallpaper was grubby and peeling behind the radiator that lined the outer wall of the reception. The reception desk was a chipped formica affair that looked as if it had seen better days several decades before.

A youngish-looking man, apparently of Indian or Pakistani extraction, was sitting behind the desk. He looked untroubled by the events unfolding around him.

'You the manager?'

'Suppose,' the man said. He held out his hand for shaking. 'Mo Uddin.'

Murrain shook the hand, trying not to focus on the dirt under Uddin's fingernails. 'DCI Murrain,' he said. 'Officer in charge.'

'Murder, is it?'

'That's our assumption.'

'Never had a murder before,' Uddin waved his hand in a gesture that included the whole reception. 'Though that might surprise you.' He obviously had few illusions about the place he was managing.

'Room 316,' Murrain said. 'Who was the occupant?'

'Hang on.' Uddin tapped at his PC, waiting until a new screen opened up. 'Thing's so bloody slow.' He scrolled down the screen and then stopped. 'Room 316. Elizabeth Monk. One-night stay.'

'Any address?'

'Fairly local, actually. Glossop. I remember registering it when she checked in, and wondering why she was bothering to stay over. But people usually have their reasons.'

'You were on the desk when she checked in?'

'I'm usually on the desk, man. Don't trust those other scrotes to handle it.' He gestured as if his comment encompassed the population at large. 'Morning till night, that's me.'

'You remember her checking in?'

'She was a decent-looking woman, you know. We don't get many of those coming through here. Not solo, anyway. So I tend to remember them.'

'Anything strike you about her? Anything unusual?'

'Apart from that she was an attractive woman in this place? Can't think of anything. She didn't say a lot. Kept her head down. Said something about being up here on business, but I didn't really take it in. People always think we want to know what they're up to. Most times, this place, I'd rather not know.'

'She didn't seem nervous? Under duress? Anything like that?'

'She seemed pretty normal to me. More normal than most people we get through here.'

'Paid by card?'

'We ask for payment up front. Had too many doing a runner.'

'Anything else strike you about her?'

'Not really. She was wearing a big anorak thing. Dripping wet, because it was pissing down outside.' He paused, still thinking. 'She must have gone out for a bit. I didn't see her go—I must've gone to the bog or something—but I saw her come back. Went straight past me to the lift. Didn't even say good night.'

'You're sure it was her?'

'Like I say, man, we don't get many decent-looking women in here. She wasn't exactly hot—bit old for me—but I wouldn't kick her out of bed, know what I mean? She was wearing different clothes— different coat, I think. But must've been her.'

'You didn't see anyone leaving later in the evening? Time of death was probably eight or nine o'clock last night. You didn't see anyone leaving after that time?'

'The killer, you mean? Like someone dripping blood?'

'Our killer seems pretty good at cleaning up after himself, unfortunately. But anyone suspicious?'

'Can't say I did. It was busy last night, with the football and all that. I was covering the bar as well as reception so I was in there mostly, apart from a couple of late check-ins.'

Murrain looked up and around the room. 'No CCTV?'

'Keep telling the boss we should get some, but he's too tight-fisted. Don't even have them in the car park. Guests sometimes complain about that.'

'Thanks for your help, Mr Uddin. We'll need a formal statement from you later.'

Uddin looked anxious for the first time since Murrain had started talking to him. 'I don't like to get too involved with the police, man. You sure I need to do that?'

'It's a murder enquiry, Mr Uddin. You're probably the last person to see the victim alive, other than the killer. So, yes, you do need to give us a statement.'

'OK, man. If you say so. I'd better let the boss know.'

'I think you should. We'll want to take statements from all the staff. Your boss might want to prepare himself for that.'

Uddin looked indignant. 'They're all legit, man. Well, mostly.'

'Who is the boss, anyway? Who owns this place?'

'My boss is a guy called Mick Reynolds. Tough old bastard. Keeps me on my fucking toes, pardon the French. Company owns various dives around town. Call themselves fucking Paradise. Not my idea of fucking paradise.' Uddin laughed.

'That the company, is it? Paradise?'

'Makes me fucking laugh every time I hear it.'

'Name Patrick Henessey mean anything to you?'

Murrain could see the wariness in Uddin's eyes. 'Should it?'

'Local businessman. Has a company called Paradise Holdings. Wondered if it might be the same.'

'Might be. I just deal with Mick. He's the—what you call it? General Manager.'

Uddin was probably lying, but they could check on the ownership of the hotel easily enough. 'I'll get one of the team to come and take a formal statement from you.' Murrain was already heading to the lifts. 'And, if you run into Mr Henessey, do send him my regards.'

Ferbrache, still dressed in the full white suit, was in the corridor, helmet off, taking a breather. Murrain ducked under the police tape. 'Shirking on the job, Neil?'

'Delegation, Kenny. You must have heard of it?'

'You want a job doing properly, get some other bugger to do it? My philosophy in life, too. How's it going?'

'Not a pretty one.'

'Pete gave me that impression. 'I am in blood stepped in so far—'
'

'—'That should I wade no more, Returning were as tedious as go o'er',' Ferbrache finished, surprisingly. 'I did Macbeth for GCSE as well. Funny how those things stick in your head. Mind you, that quote's the story of my professional life.'

'You and me both, Neil. How's it look in there?'

'Well, as Pete must've told you, our killer's done his best to redecorate the room. Apart from that, same old story. Room's been thoroughly gone over to remove any traces of the killer.'

'But you'd expect the killer to be heavily blood-stained?'

'Looks to me like they might have used some kind of protective clothing. Another part of the pattern.'

'Room was booked under the name Elizabeth Monk. That tie in with what you've found?'

'Yeah, this was like the second killing. The victim was left naked. But there were clothes hanging up, a handbag on the dressing table. All belonging to Elizabeth Monk.'

'Which doesn't, of course, confirm that the victim here *is* Ms Monk.'

Ferbrache nodded. 'I heard about the interesting outcome of your identification session. We are dealing with a nutter here, aren't we?'

'Looks like it. Whatever, I don't think we can make any assumptions. Any clues about Monk in the stuff you've got in there?'

'Not been through the handbag in any detail yet. Apart from her phone, the most promising thing looked to be a diary. Want to have a look?'

'Might give us something to get started on. When you've done with the phone, we can get the tech people on to that.'

'I'll make sure the lads and lasses have done the business with the diary, so it's ready to be bagged up. Then you can have a quick shufty.'

'Thanks, Neil.'

Ferbrache replaced his helmet and stepped back into the bedroom. Murrain peered through the door after him. There were three suited SOCOs, all somehow avoiding getting in each other's way. Murrain could see only the bottom of the bed, but even from here the mess looked dramatic. The blood had dried from red to black, and caked the bed and carpet. Whoever owned this hotel, Paradise had never seemed so far away.

Ferbrache reappeared holding an evidence bag containing a small leather-backed diary. He handed Murrain the bag and a pair of disposable protective gloves. 'Here you go.'

Murrain pulled on the gloves and, tipping the diary into his palm, flicked through the first few pages. An address in Glossop, confirming what Uddin had said. A section for contact addresses at the back, left blank. Like most people, she probably recorded that stuff on her computer or phone these days. He flicked back through the pages. It didn't look as if she'd used the diary much. There were a scattering of entries—times of appointments with names of individuals or companies. Jane, 10.30, Costa. The Sparkle Agency, 2pm. Morrigan's, 3.30. Murrain wondered what Ms Monk's line of business had been. Something freelance, he guessed.

He turned to the current week. There was only one entry. Two days earlier. Two words.

'Wentworth Moortop.'

So now he had a good idea which of their victims was Elizabeth Monk. And before those words, she had written two more. A name.

Jack Brennan.

CHAPTER TWENTY TWO

'This better be good,' Brennan said. 'We've got a full scale fucking crisis on.'

'So I understand. It's possible that, unfortunately, we may be able to help you on that front.'

Brennan looked up, taken by surprise. 'What the hell do you mean by that?'

Murrain and Milton had debated how best to handle the interview. Milton had been in favour of arresting Brennan and making the whole thing formal.

'I don't think we've enough to do that,' Murrain had said. 'Not yet.'

'But his name's turned up on two of the victims. And the third could well be one of his colleagues. How much more do we need?'

'We've got a killer who goes to extraordinary lengths to remove any trace of himself from the crime-scene. And he then leaves Brennan's name sitting there?'

'So what are you suggesting? Someone's trying to frame Brennan?'

'I don't know what I'm suggesting. But I don't think I'm quite ready to arrest Mr Brennan yet.'

'Interview under caution?'

Murrain had hesitated. His own preference would have been to keep the interview informal. Let Brennan talk and hear what he had to say. But the diary entry in particular had given them reasonable grounds to suspect his involvement. The caution was needed to protect Brennan's interests as well as their own. 'That's probably right. If this does prove fruitful, we've got to make sure we've done everything by the book.'

'Under fucking *caution*?' Brennan hadn't quite seen things the same way. 'Why the hell would you want to interview me under caution?'

'We've some potentially difficult questions to ask you, Mr Brennan. We thought it better to do so under caution for your own protection.'

'For your protection, you mean. Given you're about to make complete arses of yourselves.'

'If you say so, Mr Brennan.' Milton knew from experience that Murrain's politeness was generally in inverse correlation to his level of irritation with the interviewee. They had offered Brennan the opportunity to obtain legal representation but he'd declined, saying that he just wanted to get it over with.

Murrain turned a laptop screen towards Brennan. 'This isn't the ideal way to handle this but we have no real alternative. For the tape, I'm showing Mr Brennan a photograph on the laptop. Do you recognise the individual in the photograph, Mr Brennan?'

Brennan stared at the screen. Then, his face drained of colour, he turned to Murrain. 'What the fuck is this?'

'Do you recognise the person in the photograph?'

'Shit. Yes, I do. I know who it is. Christ almighty.'

'Can you confirm the identity?'

Brennan shook his head. 'I think I need to clear what I'm able to tell you.'

'OK. We'll try to sort that. But am I right in assuming this is the officer you were concerned about? We don't need a name or details just yet. Just a confirmation of the identity.' He knew Brennan was simply buying himself some time to think but there was no point in pushing it yet.

Brennan nodded, and Murrain noticed that there were tears in the corners of his eyes. He suddenly looked a different man from the individual who'd entered the interview room just minutes before. 'Yeah. You're right in assuming that. This one of your victims, then? Your mad knife man?'

'She's the third victim,' Murrain said, gently. There was something more personal in Brennan's response than simply the loss of a colleague. But there'd be time to explore that later. He was happy to go along with Brennan's request for more senior clearance from within the NCA before they took that enquiry any further. He was well aware of the potential sensitivities here. Another reason to ensure they did everything by the book. 'We found the body this afternoon.'

'Where was she?'

Murrain gave him the name of the hotel. 'Any reason why she should have been there?'

'Never heard of the place. We have—' He stopped. 'We used to have liaison meetings in various places round the city, but never there.'

'And you were her—what's the term? Contact?'

'Look, I really need—'

'Yes, of course. You need clearance. Can we sort that, Joe?'

Murrain formally adjourned the interview while Milton left the room. He returned after just a few minutes. 'I've set Paul on to it,' he said. 'He'll let us know when he's got hold of someone.'

'So can we stop this until we've got that sorted?' Brennan said. He was still looking beaten-down but had regained a little of his former confidence.

'We've a few more questions we'd like to ask you,' Murrain said. 'Not connected with this victim.'

'Oh, for Christ's sake,' Brennan said. 'What's this got to do with me?'

'That's what we need to clarify. Your name seems to have come up in relation to each of our three victims.'

'How the hell can that be?'

'That's the question. Do you recognise this item? For the tape, I'm handing Mr Brennan an evidence bag.'

Brennan peered at the transparent bag. 'What the fuck—?'

'Do you recognise it?'

'It's my bloody business card. What's it doing here?'

'That was our question to you,' Murrain said. 'It was found on our first victim. A Ms Kathryn Granger. Works in HR for Lancs Police, apparently. Any acquaintance of yours?'

'Never heard of her. Why would I know someone who works in HR? For Lancs or anyone else.'

'We all keep dubious company from time to time. Were you at the Grange Hotel in Stockport last Saturday evening?'

There was a definite hesitation in Brennan's response to the unexpectedly direct question. Murrain could almost read the calculation in Brennan's eyes. A moment too late, he said: 'Yes, I was there. Just for a short while on Saturday evening.' He took a deep breath, as if he'd already incriminated himself.

'Not one of your usual haunts?'

'I was there for the wedding reception. I assume you're aware of that. DI Andy Barton. Andy and I go back a way.'

Murrain scribbled on his pad as if taking a note. 'When we spoke to DI Barton, he reckoned you weren't on the invite list.'

It took Brennan a moment to realise he'd been suckered. 'Well, he's right about that. I wasn't on the list.'

'But you and Barton are old friends?'

Brennan shrugged. 'Weddings aren't really my thing. I wouldn't have gone to the wedding or main reception anyway. But Andy knew I was working up here a lot and was keen I should drop in for the after-show party for old times' sake. Disco and a few drinks, you know. I almost didn't bother, but—well, he's a mate.'

'Barton said he hadn't seen you there.' Milton this time, apparently flicking back through his own notes. 'Didn't even give the impression he was particularly expecting you.'

Brennan looked only momentarily disconcerted. 'You know what those kinds of dos are like. Everybody's half-pissed. I was pretty sure I'd wished the happy couple all the best but maybe they didn't register me. Or maybe Andy was too ratted to remember. I don't know. We didn't stay that long. We buggered off after an hour or so.'

'We?' Murrain said. 'You weren't on your own?'

Another brief but discernible hesitation. 'I had a friend with me. Another reason for leaving early.' Brennan took another breath. 'Look, I could get a real bollocking for this. The thing is—I was with Josie. Josie Martin.' He swallowed hard, though his precise emotions were impossible to read. 'Your third victim.'

'Ah.' This time it was Murrain who'd been taken by surprise. 'So she went with you to the wedding of a police officer on the patch where she's operating undercover? With respect, wasn't that just a little risky?'

'Probably. Maybe bloody stupid in hindsight.' He trailed off, as if thinking through the implications of what he'd just said.

'Do you think it's possible that she was murdered because someone at the hotel recognised her?'

'That's ridiculous.' Brennan paused again, as if gathering his confidence. He sounded like a man who realised that, however this panned out, he was already in big trouble. 'Josie never worked for GMP or Lancs. She started out in the Met before she joined the NCA. Nobody there would have recognised her. It was just a wedding.'

'Where one of the guests ended up dead. With two more deaths to follow. Quite a wedding.' Murrain was getting the measure of Brennan. A risk-taker, someone constantly pushing things to the limit. And sometimes, it seemed, beyond the limit. 'So why did you take her?'

'Seemed like a good idea at the time. We'd been for dinner in Manchester, knocked back a few glasses of wine. I kept saying I ought to go to the wedding, that I'd said I was going to go and Andy was expecting me. To be honest, I was doing it partly just to wind her up. That's—that was the kind of relationship we had. And I did feel I ought to go and I wasn't that keen to go by myself. So—you know. We just thought no-one would ever know about Josie. Why would they?'

'Why would they?' Murrain repeated. 'You said you didn't know Kathryn Granger. Do you have any ideas how or why she might have had your business card in her purse?'

'I think it's possible I met her at the hotel. At the wedding do.'

'You think it's possible?'

'Yeah. I—well, Josie had gone off to the little girls' room. I went to the bar to get another drink. I think I met her there. Started chatting to her.'

'You gave her your business card,' Milton said. 'You were chatting her up. Your girlfriend was in the ladies and you were chatting up another woman?' His tone was one almost of disbelief.

'It wasn't that sort of relationship with Josie,' he said. 'She wasn't my *girlfriend*. We didn't own one another. I was just chatting to an attractive woman. There's no law against it.'

'Not chatting, no,' Murrain agreed.

'Anyway,' Brennan went on, 'I knew her. Sort of.'

Murrain looked up. 'I'm getting confused, Mr Brennan.'

'Well, not knew her. Recognised her, I mean. I didn't know her name. I can't even remember if she told me on the night. If so, I didn't take it in.' He paused, thinking. 'She didn't say she worked in HR. She said she worked in Intelligence. If we're talking about the same woman.'

Murrain gestured towards Milton, who tapped on his laptop and turned it round for Brennan to see the screen. 'I'm showing Mr Brennan a picture of the first murder victim,' he said, for the benefit of the tape. 'Is that her?'

'Yeah, that's her.' He laughed. 'Intelligence, eh? I fell for it. It made sense. Trying to make herself sound more interesting, I guess.'

'But you recognised her?' Murrain said. 'From where?'

'From years ago,' Brennan said. 'Well, maybe ten. She worked for GMP then, in the north of the city. Filing clerk, worked alongside Andy Barton's new wife. She didn't know me but I recognised her. At the time, we were all more interested in Julie Welling. But she always had the hots for Andy. He fended her off for years, but she was still there when he wanted to settle down.'

'And Kathryn Granger?'

'She was just another girl in the office. Not a bad looker, I suppose, but not exactly the life and soul of the party. I'd forgotten about her, name and everything, till I saw her standing at the bar.'

'You didn't reminisce about the old days?'

'Christ, no. I didn't let on I remembered her. I'd have ended up stuck talking to her all night. Didn't get the impression she was fighting off admirers. Looked a bit lonely.'

'But you chatted her up?'

'Not seriously. It's just habit. You find yourself chatting to an attractive woman, you flirt a bit, don't you?'

'You gave her your card?'

'I didn't ask for her phone number or anything. I wasn't seriously expecting anything to come of it. But, like I say, she looked a bit lonely. I thought she might actually be the type who'd pick up the phone and call me. You never know your luck.'

'And that was the last you saw of her? In the bar?'

'I saw Josie coming back so thought I'd better make myself scarce. We didn't stay long after that.'

'And can I ask you what you did after that?'

'We got a cab back up into Manchester. Went for a few drinks in the Northern Quarter. Then Josie came back to my hotel and stayed over. I usually stay in one of the budget places up there when I'm in town.'

'Any witnesses to that?'

'I don't know. There were people in the pub but the place was packed so I don't imagine anyone noticed us particularly. And you know what those budget hotels are like. I don't think there was anyone on the desk when we went up.'

'And the next morning?'

'We surfaced quite late. Josie wanted to get back to her flat. We tried not to spend too much time together—you know, in the circumstances. I was staying over till Monday, and I'd arranged to meet some mates for a lunchtime beer. They can vouch for me from lunchtime on, but before that—'

'The only alibi you had would have been from Ms Martin. Who unfortunately is no longer in a position to provide one.' Milton finally looked up and stared, unblinking, at Brennan.

'Look, for Christ's sake—'

'And on the Saturday night you met Ms Martin when?'

'About six-thirty. We went for dinner at an Italian place in town. The people there will remember.'

Murrain scribbled something down on his notepad. 'But before that?'

'I was on my own all day,' Brennan said. 'Got up latish. Just grabbed a sandwich for lunch. Did some shopping in the afternoon. That was it, really.'

'So no witnesses, other than for your dinner with Ms Martin?'

'No, but—'

'Does the name Elizabeth Monk mean anything to you?'

Brennan looked surprised by the non sequitur. 'Elizabeth Monk? Why?'

'Our second victim.' Murrain gestured to Milton, who slid another evidence bag across the table. 'We found this among her possessions.'

'What is it?'

'It's a diary,' Murrain said. 'We've left it open at the day of her death. You should be able to read the entry through the plastic.'

Brennan raised the bag to peer at the open pages. 'What the fuck is this?'

'A note of an appointment with you, apparently. Do you have any explanation for that?'

CHAPTER TWENTY THREE

'Can I call you Paddy?'

Henessey spun on his toes, unexpectedly agile for a heavily-built man. 'Who the fuck are you?' He peered into the shadows, trying to make out the other man's face. The voice sounded odd, with an accent he couldn't place. Someone disguising their voice, he thought. It had been a shit week, and now suddenly it seemed it was getting a hell of a lot worse.

'You don't know me, Paddy. Or do you prefer Patrick? Conjures up such a stereotype, the name Paddy, don't you reckon? Or do you like people to think of you as a thick Irishman?'

'If you're trying to wind me up, you got the wrong fucking man,' Henessey said, motionless. ' 'Cause if I get fucking wound up, I'll break every bone in your fucking body. Who the fuck are you, smartarse?'

'You're a tough guy, aren't you, Paddy? I'm maybe not so tough, though I wouldn't advise you to test it. And anyway I've got this.' The figure lifted his arm just enough to allow the firearm to catch the light from the setting sun. 'And I'm a ruthless fucking bastard.'

Up to that point, Henessey's face had given nothing away. Now, he gave a momentary glance towards the closed fire escape door, wondering about his options for escape or summoning help. It was a serviced-office block, only about a quarter occupied. As far as he knew, there was no-one else on this floor at all. Henessey had invested considerable time and money in establishing the profile of a big company, but really, now that Berenek was gone, it was just him, a part-time secretary, and a bunch of people he mostly paid cash-in-hand. After what had happened this week, he should have known to be more careful. 'What the fuck's this all about?'

'What are these things always about, Paddy? It's about what you owe me.'

'And, once more, who the fuck are you?' He hadn't expected that. A fucking debt collector.

'Someone you owe who's not scared of your bluster, Paddy. I've come to collect.'

'I don't owe you fucking anything.' Henessey couldn't know that this was true. He owed serious money to all kinds of people. Usually, though, they didn't have the balls to try to collect before he was ready to pay.

'I've let it go for a long time, Paddy. Now it's time to pay up.'

'What are you talking about?' Henessey had remained motionless, weighing up his options. They were standing on the dimly-lit stone staircase at the rear of the converted mill. It was intended only for use as a fire escape, but Henessey came out here for a cigarette whenever he could, having confirmed the sensitivity of the internal smoke alarms several times since he'd started renting an office here.

He'd come out here today feeling pissed-off because that toe-rag Jack Brennan hadn't turned up for the meeting. It was Brennan who'd requested it, after all, no doubt because he was after another bit of business, another back-hander. Thought he was God's gift since he'd moved to the NCA, even though he was still the same devious gobshite he'd always been.

Normally, when he came out here, Henessey made sure the heavy metal door was propped open behind him—generally by one of the fire-extinguishers—but today he'd heard an ominous click just after he'd lit up. He'd assumed the door had shut accidentally and resigned himself to a trek to the ground floor. Then the voice had spoken from the shadows.

Another flash of light on the gun. 'Me and my friend here are getting impatient.'

'I don't know what the fuck you're talking about. You've got the wrong fucking man, mate.'

'It's you who've got the wrong man. I'm not someone you should be fucking around, Paddy. You should be crawling on your hands and knees to get me what I'm owed.'

'OK.' Henessey took a breath. If this guy was serious, there was no obvious way out. The fire door was shut and locked behind him, and the gun was between Henessey and the stairwell. The question was whether he really was serious, or just another loser with more balls than most. It would be a hell of a risk to start shooting in a confined space like this, with stone walls on all sides and potential witnesses in the building. 'If you think I owe you something, why don't we go back to my office and sort it out like civilised human beings.'

'It doesn't work like that with me, Paddy. It works like it did with Karl Berenek.'

'Karl—' Henessey stopped. 'What the fuck's this all about?' Henessey suddenly felt as if the temperature in the stairway had dropped several degrees. Maybe not just some fucking street-bailiff, then. Maybe something more serious.

'You can bullshit everyone else, Paddy. You can't bullshit me. I know what you did. What you had done.'

Henessey took a step forward. 'You know fuck all. Who the hell are you?'

'Like I say, Paddy, someone you owe. A life for a life, and all that.'

Henessey realised he still wasn't fully getting this, still hadn't worked out what was going on here. 'What the fuck are you talking about?'

'Time to pay up, Paddy.'

'Fuck it,' Henessey said. 'I'm not taking this shit from you, whoever the fuck you are.' He took a step forward. 'Simple as this, you poor fucker. I'm leaving now. I'm heading downstairs and leaving you here. I don't know who you are or who you're working for or what you want, but if you know what's good for you, you'll bugger off out of here and disappear without a fucking trace. Because if you try to hurt me, you might as well just stick that gun to your own fucking head.' Trying hard to keep his voice steady, he took another step towards the stairs.

'Time to pay up, Paddy.' Behind him, the figure raised the gun and, as Henessey tried to push past, made as if to fire. Henessey ducked, waiting for the gun-fire, and then realised that, with perfect timing, he had simply been pushed, backwards, down the stairwell. There was a moment when nothing seemed to happen before Henessey fell, his hands clawing wildly for the metal stair-rail. But it was already too late and Henessey's own substantial weight sent him tumbling down the flight of stone steps.

The sound of the skull hitting the stone floor was soft but unbearably awful. Henessey twitched for a moment and lay still. In the gloomy light, a dark pool began to spread across the stone beneath his head.

The figure stood for a moment in the shadows, almost as motionless as the supine figure below. Then, with no obvious hurry, the figure began to make its way down the stairs, out into the gathering darkness.

Marie Donovan finished typing and saved the file. Her back aching from sitting crouched at this unsuitable table, she finally looked up and gazed around her. Had she really thought this was going to be more fun than whatever semi-job they'd have foisted on her back in the NCA? She'd forgotten what a balls-aching slog this stuff could be.

But she knew that this case, however frustrating it might be, was as real as it gets. Three murders in three days. There was a growing sense that they were racing against time. That this might be a killer with no reason to stop killing.

Was it really possible that Jack Brennan was behind this? Whatever her feelings about Brennan, she still couldn't see it. She couldn't see how Brennan would have fitted into the scenarios that had apparently played out. But equally—even with an intuition much less finely honed than Murrain's—she was left feeling that somehow he was very much a part of it.

She'd find out soon enough how the interview with Brennan had gone. In the meantime, she, Sparrow and Wallace had been left taking statements at the hotel where the third body had been found. It had been hard work. The hotel staff seemed reluctant to talk to the police, for reasons that had more to do with their employment and immigration status than the case at hand. Many barely spoke English, and the interviews were reduced to the simplest of questions supported by gestures and drawings. Wallace had produced a picture-code communications guide developed by her colleagues dealing with migrant worker communities, and that had helped progress the basic questioning. If necessary, they could have secured interpreters in most of the relevant languages, but, other than the stuttering young man who'd found the body, no-one here had anything of substance to tell them. No-one had seen the victim around the hotel. No-one had seen, or admitted to having seen, anyone who might have been the killer. No-one else had been near the room in question.

It was a necessary part of the process but it would produce nothing of value. There was other work continuing in parallel. They were combing the surrounding areas for CCTV footage to compensate for the absence of any recordings in the hotel itself. They were checking the nearest Automatic Numberplate Recognition cameras for vehicles that might have entered or left the area at the relevant times. But even that felt like going through the motions.

Donovan yawned and stretched. She was sitting in one of the hotel rooms that had been cordoned off for use as an interview suite. The room was depressing enough in itself, with its cheap bedding, thin curtains and worn decor. But worse still, as she sat here alone in the fading afternoon, was the room's resemblance to the murder scene. It was the mirror image of the room where the body had been found, but otherwise identical—the same colour curtains, carpet and bedding, the same outdated wallpaper, the same shabby furniture. It was difficult for her to tear her mind away from what had happened to another solitary woman in the same surroundings just a few hundred yards from here.

She was startled by the sound of her phone buzzing on the table. Laughing at her own unease, she thumbed the phone to take the call. Holly.

'Hi, Hon,' Holly said. 'How you doing in your new working life?'

'Knackered. Just finished a string of pointless interviews. Sitting in a deeply crappy hotel room. Needing a drink.'

'Then you're in luck. I've a treat in store.'

'Don't tell me. Rioja and a selection of your favourite DVDs.'

'Even better. I've got us a night of pampering.'

'You're ordering a takeaway as well?'

'Even better than that. We had some charity raffle in the office last week, and I won. Well, third prize. A visit to one of those spa hotel places out in Cheshire. Free use of the spa facilities and all that, for two people.'

'Wouldn't it be better to use it at the weekend?'

'Places like that are always packed at the weekend. In any case, I had a thought. I've been wanting to do something to thank you for taking me in after—well, you know—'

'You don't have to thank me for that. You're a paying guest. I'm glad of the help with the mortgage.'

'Even so,' Holly said. 'That's not why you did it, and you know it. It helped me out of a hole and I'm grateful. And I thought we should celebrate your new job as well. You know me, any excuse. So I was thinking, we could both head over there straight after work. I could pick you up from the office. Use all the spa stuff for an hour or two. Then we could have dinner on me, and I could even book us a twin room for the night so we can safely have a drink or two.'

'Holly, I couldn't—'

'Oh, come off it, Marie. It's not like I'm short of cash. Still got all the house-sale money. When I've needed a shoulder to lean—not to mention cry—on over the last year, you've been there. It's the least I can do.' She laughed. 'Anyway, I get a discount on the dinner and the room booking if we use this voucher I've won, so it's no big deal. I'll need to pop home first so I can grab an overnight bag for both of us. Come on, we could both do with a little treat.'

Marie Donovan looked around the dreary hotel room, and the pile of hand-written notes she'd been dutifully transcribing into the system. It was difficult to disagree with Holly's last statement. She needed something other than this.

'OK,' she said. 'You've talked me into it. I'll head back to the office to drop stuff off. What time shall I see you?'

209

'You're sure you still don't want legal representation, Mr Brennan? You are entitled to it.'

'I know what I'm entitled to,' Brennan snapped. 'I've sat on your side of the desk often enough.' He paused, obviously thinking about the question. 'No, I don't want you bastards thinking I've anything to hide. I can speak for myself.'

'Your choice,' Murrain said. 'So what about Elizabeth Monk?'

'The thing is,' Brennan said, 'I did know her. Beth Monk. She was a graphic designer. Not my usual type at all. Can't even remember exactly where I met her. In the pub or something.'

'That does seem to be your modus operandi,' Milton observed. 'Approaching unattended women in public bars.'

'It's the way you get into relationships with ladies,' Brennan retorted. 'You'll find out when you grow up.'

'Mr Brennan,' Murrain intervened. 'Elizabeth Monk. Was this recent?'

'No, that's the point. This was years ago. Three, four years. At least three years since we split up.'

'So you had a serious relationship?'

'Depends what you mean by serious. Thing is, I'd been working undercover at the time. Had a relatively short-term assignment gathering intelligence on a couple of environmental groups in the city. One of those jobs where you wonder why you're doing it, you know? Load of well-intentioned tree-huggers. But some of the energy companies had put a bit of political pressure on, and I'd been sent on a fishing expedition. Get to know them a bit, dig out any dirt or anything we ought to be concerned about. My job not to reason why, obviously, so there I was.'

'And Monk was one of these environmentalists?'

'She had one or two friends in that crowd. Like I say, I think I ran into her in a pub when she was with a bunch of other people. She was an attractive woman. I got chatting to her, asked her out. And Bob's your proverbial.'

'You were working undercover,' Murrain said. 'So did she know you as Jack Brennan?'

Brennan hesitated. 'No,' he admitted, finally. 'No, I couldn't give her that name, obviously. She knew me as John McKendrick.'

'So you lied to her?' Milton again.

'It wasn't like that. I couldn't use my real name. I had no choice.'

'You could have chosen not to enter into a relationship with her,' Murrain said.

'We were encouraged to do that sort of thing. Well, not discouraged. Up to a point. Anyway, it happened.'

'And how serious was it, this relationship?'

'More so for her than for me, maybe,' Brennan said. 'I don't know. She was good company. We had a good time together. I was pretty faithful to her.' He laughed. 'By my standards, anyway.' This last comment seemed directed towards Milton. 'It was all OK, you know?'

'And that was how she saw it? All OK?'

'Like I say, if I'm honest, she saw it as a bit more than that. She thought we were really going somewhere.'

'And you let her think that? Even though you were trading under a false identity?'

'You know how it is. She never spelled anything out, and I was happy to fool myself into believing she was as casual about it as I was. But, yeah, I guess I knew it would be a blow when I left.'

'I'd say she was lucky,' Milton offered.

'Yeah, well, son, on this occasion, I wouldn't necessarily disagree even with you. Some of us aren't built for serious relationships.'

Murrain continued before Milton could offer any response. 'And she'd have described it as a happy relationship, would she, Mr Brennan?'

'Not sure what you're getting at. But, on the whole, I'd have thought so, yes.'

Murrain sat back in his chair and regarded Brennan. So far, he'd been surprised by the absence of any inner sensation, any instinctive response to what Brennan had been saying. He'd been expecting some

211

burst of that familiar electricity. He could still feel something, some distant static echo, but that was more like a residue from other places, other times, than anything triggered by this exchange. 'The thing is, Mr Brennan, we've heard you have something of a reputation for—how shall I put this?—for not treating women well.'

'How'd you mean?'

Murrain flicked through the pad in front of him. 'I mean violence, Mr Brennan. Abuse.'

'Who the fuck's been saying—?' He stopped, conscious of the inappropriateness of his instinctive response. 'Maybe you're right about me needing a lawyer,' he said. 'Or maybe I should just get up and leave. I don't need to sit here listening to this bollocks.'

'Your choice. On both counts,' Murrain said. 'You're not under arrest. Not yet.'

'For Christ's sake—' Brennan took a breath. 'I don't know what this is about or where it's come from. I don't pretend to be Mr Goody Two Shoes like your little friend here. I'm not proud of how I've treated some women I've been involved with. But abuse? That's not my style.'

Murrain had dealt with enough abusers over the years to know that this was the textbook response, even when they'd been caught virtually in the act. Many of them didn't appear even to recognise what they were doing as abuse. In their worlds, it was just the way men treated women. 'There's at least one note on your personal file. A complaint of sexual harassment made but not followed through.'

'And that tells you all you need to know, doesn't it? Not followed through. I know exactly who that was. A woman I'd dumped. I didn't treat her well but there was no abuse. She was just looking to get back at me. The accusations fell apart as soon as she raised them.'

'You're a real charmer, aren't you?' Milton said.

'I am what I am. But I don't use violence against women.' His eyes were fixed on Milton in a way that suggested he might hold different views about violence against men.

'And yet here we are,' Murrain said. 'We have three female victims of a violent killer. The first is found with your business-card, and you admit to having spoken to her shortly before the murder. The second is found with your name in her diary, and you admit to having had a relationship with her, although you claim you've had no recent contact—'

'I've had no contact,' Brennan insisted. 'You can check my phone records, my e-mails, whatever you like.'

'We'll do exactly that, of course,' Murrain went on, 'for what it's worth. And then the third victim is your close colleague, with whom you admit you were having a relationship at the time of her death. All seems oddly coincidental.'

The look in Brennan's eyes had changed, as if he'd finally recognised how serious this was becoming. Murrain had had the impression that the revelation of Elizabeth Monk's identity and the diary-entry had both come as genuine shocks. But then Brennan had been an undercover cop. He was a trained liar.

'Do you have any other alibi for your time this week, Mr Brennan? Your only alibi for Sunday morning was provided by Josie Martin. We know you were in the NCA offices at various points in the daytime. But Tuesday or Wednesday evenings?'

Brennan shook his head. 'I was in my hotel. Grabbed a few beers and a takeaway sandwich from a local supermarket and went back to my room to watch the football. European matches.'

'You didn't watch them in the hotel bar or in a pub?' Milton said, sceptically.

'Had hoped to meet up with a couple of mates. They'll confirm I asked. But they were tied up. Married with kids now, so couldn't get passes out.' As before, he stopped, recognising a moment too late that this wasn't the moment for jokey laddishness. 'So, no, didn't fancy sitting in a bar by myself. Paid for Sky Sports on the hotel TV and watched that. Billy No Mates knocking back the beers by myself.'

'Not looking good, Mr Brennan,' Murrain said.

Brennan looked as if any fight had been knocked out of him. 'Shit,' he said, finally. 'This is just ridiculous. You've nothing on me, have you? Just a series of fucking coincidences. That's why you've not arrested me. There's nothing to link me to the murders, nothing to the crime scenes. But now you've got a prime suspect in the frame. So you'll keep plugging away till you've enough to make a case—'

'I don't know how you work, Mr Brennan,' Murrain said. 'But that's not how we do things round here. We've got a killer out there who's already murdered three women, and may intend to murder more. That's the priority. Not improving our statistics.'

'If you say so.' Brennan's gaze swung from Murrain to Milton. 'Fucking Batman and Robin, eh? You done with me then?'

'For the moment. Are you intending to stay up here for the next few days?'

'That was the plan. Still got some serious police business to carry out up here, you know. And there'll be even more crap to sort out now, given what's happened to Josie Martin. Don't be surprised if my bosses want to take that one back off you, by the way. You'll find me in the office or the hotel, if you need me.' He stumbled to his feet and made his way out of the room. The tone had been defiant, but the body language suggested something closer to defeat.

'What do you reckon?' Milton asked, as soon as the door had slammed behind Brennan.

'Like you say, a real charmer,' Murrain said. 'But I don't know—'

'No spider-sense tingling?'

'Nothing. Or nothing much, anyway. And he may be a bastard, but it's difficult to see why he might suddenly have turned into a murderous bastard. On the other hand, it's all a hell of a coincidence.'

'Gives us some other lines to follow up, anyway. Elizabeth Monk and her environmentalist friends. And we'll have to liaise with the NCA on Martin.'

'He's probably right about that,' Murrain said. 'I can imagine those buggers wanting to treat that as their territory. And they might be right. Anything happens to an undercover officer, and your first thought must be that it's linked to whatever she was working on.'

'But it clearly links to our case,' Milton pointed out. 'She was wearing Monk's clothes.'

'Which might just mean they take over the whole case,' Murrain said, morosely. 'And, anyway, what's that all about? This exchanging of clothes. It's like some sort of message.'

'That the identities don't matter?' Milton offered. 'That the women are interchangeable?'

'That would be a fairly callous message.'

'Too right,' Milton agreed. 'But then we know that, don't we? This is a fairly callous bastard.'

As they emerged from the lift, Marie Donovan grabbed Sparrow by the sleeve and pulled him back along the corridor away from the MIR. She looked around frantically, and then pushed him into the small kitchen area.

'Jesus, you must be desperate for a coffee,' Sparrow said.

She took a breath. 'Not really. But now we're here I'll make you one.'

'So what was that all about?'

'Jack Brennan. I saw him along the corridor coming out of the interview room. Assume they'd just finished. I didn't think it would be helpful for him to run into me here.'

'Ah,' Sparrow said. 'Former colleague of yours, wasn't he?'

'Something like that.' She turned to fill the kettle. 'Anyway, I thought he was best avoided.'

'Be interesting to see what's come out of that interview, anyway.'

'Too right.'

She finished making the coffee, delaying long enough to ensure Brennan would definitely have departed. Then, steaming mugs in hand, they made their way to the MIR. Wanstead was in his usual corner, and Murrain and Milton were at their desks catching up on e-mails. In Murrain's case, that meant yet more e-mails from various senior officers and Comms to accompany the various missed calls on his mobile. More catching up he'd have to do before the day was out. He just wished he had something substantive to tell them. He'd—rightly—dismissed Brennan's suggestion that the investigation's focus would narrow from here on, but more than one of those senior officers would probably have preferred an arrest, however tenuous the grounds.

'Anything much from Brennan?' Donovan asked.

'You know him a bit, Marie,' Murrain said, when he'd run through the main outcomes of the interview. 'How good an actor do you reckon he is?'

'I've worked with him,' she agreed, her tone neutral. 'I'd say he's a good actor. Or, more accurately, a good liar. Wouldn't trust him an inch.'

Murrain looked at her. There was obviously some history between her and Brennan, something beyond the merely professional. He could probably find out easily enough if he asked around. His instincts, the silent voice nagging in his brain, told him it might be important.

'I still can't see him as our killer but there's something there. We need to take up his offer to look at his phone records and e-mails.'

'He wouldn't have made the offer if he thought we'd find anything,' Milton pointed out.

'We can't risk missing something. Put his car reg through the ANPR system, too. See if there's anything that puts him in the frame. And anything that undermines his claim to have spent the evening in his hotel room. We need to find out whatever we can about his history. NCA won't want to help, but we can check his history in the force up here. Is that something you could help us with, Marie?'

'I'm not sure. I only got to know him after he joined the NCA. All I'm aware of is the public-domain stuff about his whistle-blowing. He worked undercover for a while but he kept that side of things close to his chest.'

'I can do some digging,' Wanstead said. 'I know people who'd have known him in North Manchester. My impression is he didn't make himself popular, so there'll be one or two happy to spill the beans.'

'And we need to find out about his relationship with Elizabeth Monk,' Milton said. 'See if any friends remember this 'John

McKendrick', and whether their recollections match what Brennan told us.'

Murrain nodded. 'Plenty to get on with tomorrow. Still feels like clutching at straws, though. Unless any of you has any better ideas?' No-one seemed to have. It was already after six. 'OK, people. I've got phone calls to face. Updating the world and her husband about our lack of progress. Suggest the rest of you push off, chill out as much as you can, and we'll all be back bright and early to kick that off.'

'Are you sure?' Milton said.

'Yes, Joe. Bugger off. You'll all be far more use after a decent night's relaxation than if you sit here all night worrying away at nothing. Besides, I don't want you lot listening in while I'm tugging my forelock to the Chief.'

'Come on, people,' Wanstead said. 'Let's leave the man to his abject crawling. It won't be pretty.'

Murrain laughed and picked up the phone. Milton looked over to Marie Donovan. 'Don't suppose you fancy a quick drink?'

She looked surprised, but not displeased. 'I'd love to, Joe. But I can't tonight.'

'Oh.' He tried, not entirely successfully, to conceal his disappointment. 'Got a date?'

She laughed. 'Not really. Girls' night out. Some spa place out in Cheshire, apparently. My housemate's organised it. She's picking me up. I've just texted her to say I'm ready to go.'

'Well, hope you have a good time.'

'I'll take you up on that offer of a drink some other time, eh?'

'That would be good.'

She watched him as he turned away, busying himself with shutting down his work-station, and wondered what his domestic circumstances might be—married, single, in a relationship? Straight or gay, for that matter? It was all academic, anyway. He was pleasant enough and good company, but probably not really her type. Anyway, all he'd done was ask her out for a post-work drink.

She locked away her papers and, waving goodnight to the others, made her way back out to the lifts. Apart from her colleagues in the

MIR, the place seemed deserted. Most civilian staff worked eight till four, and the other offices were in darkness.

One of the two lifts was out of order, and the other took an age to arrive, the indicator showing that, having been on the floor below, it had travelled down to the ground floor before beginning its slow return. The lift's downwards detour suggested that it wasn't empty, and she half-expected it might continue past her floor to deposit its passenger upstairs. But the lift stopped and the doors opened.

She stepped back to allow the passenger to alight and stopped, frozen to the spot.

Her efforts to avoid him had been in vain. The figure stepping from the lift was the last person she wanted to see at that moment.

'Hi, Marie,' Jack Brennan said. 'Bad penny, eh?'

CHAPTER TWENTY FIVE

As he emerged from the lift, she took an involuntary step back.

'Don't worry, Marie,' he said. 'I'm not looking for you. I saw you avoiding me earlier.' His smile went no further than his mouth. 'Hope life's treating you well over here. Your new boss still around?'

'He's still in the MIR,' she said. 'Are you supposed to be in here? I thought there was security to keep out people like you.'

He held up his visitor's pass. 'I never left. Got to reception and had second thoughts. Some of which I want to share with your boss.' He was still standing in the entrance to the lift, making no move to let her pass. At the last moment, as the doors began to close, he turned and held them open, gesturing for her to enter. 'Be my guest.'

She stepped past him into the lift. He held open the doors for a moment longer than he needed. 'Night, Marie.' She released her breath only when the doors had finally closed.

Downstairs, Holly's little Japanese sports car was already waiting in the pick-up bay by the main entrance. Donovan waved a goodnight to the bored-looking security man, and stepped out into the chilly night. Forget Jack Brennan, she thought. She had no idea what the future might hold, but the present was looking pretty bearable. She pulled open the passenger door and climbed in, taking the necessary moment to acclimatise her ears to the boom of the R'n'B that was a constant presence in Holly's car.

'Hi, hon,' Holly said. 'Ready for some fun?'

'Jesus, Holly,' she said. 'You really don't know how much I'm ready.'

'Mr Brennan. This is a surprise.' Murrain's tone couldn't have been described as welcoming. 'How can we help you?'

Without waiting to be invited, Brennan lowered himself into the chair opposite Murrain's desk. 'It's more a question of whether I can help you.'

Milton and Wanstead were still standing by their own desks, as surprised as Murrain by Brennan's unexpected reappearance. 'Is that so?' Murrain waited. He could sense something here.

'I was on my way out,' Brennan said. 'Then I stopped and thought about it.'

'Go on.'

'I meant what I said in there. I'm your only real suspect. I don't care how much *integrity* you and Robin there have.' He spoke the word as if it were an unfamiliar vice. 'I know what it's like. Especially in a high profile case like this. You'll be under pressure to show you're doing something. You'll keep digging and digging to make a case against me stick.'

'You're afraid of what we'll find.' It wasn't a question.

'I've got some skeletons. Show me a policeman who hasn't. Even you.' There was an edge to his voice as he spoke the last two words.

Murrain had only one real skeleton, and it was public knowledge. Even so, some still asked how he'd got off so lightly. Others noted that his wife had subsequently crawled her way up the greasy pole to a very senior rank. Not much more was needed to generate a conspiracy theory. 'So you'd rather we didn't dig too widely.'

'I'd rather you didn't dig at all.'

'So where's this going?'

'It's in my interests as much as yours to get to the bottom of this. I didn't kill those women. Jesus, I'm not exactly Mr Sentimental but I was in a relationship with Josie Martin. I didn't kill her. I want to find the bastard who did as much as you do.'

'So?'

'So I've been asking myself why my name should have cropped up here. I feel I'm being set up. I've got some thoughts.'

Murrain held up his hand. 'Look, Brennan, I've no idea whether you're being sincere or leading us up the garden path. But anything we do here, we do by the book. We've already potentially compromised ourselves by having this informal discussion with you. I don't know whether that was your intention—'

'Oh, for Christ's sake, of course not. Look, if it helps, we can restart the interview. You can read me my rights, all that. I don't want any legal support. I just want to help. Simple as that.'

'You mean now?'

'I'm up for it if you are.'

Murrain looked over his shoulder to Milton. 'Joe?'

'No time like the present.'

'OK,' Murrain said. 'We'll reconvene. Continue the interview at your request. Read you your rights, and you'll formally confirm you're happy to proceed without legal support. And then we're in your hands. Right?'

'One more thing.'

'Go on.'

'I want access to some of the materials you've got. Specifically, I'd like to look at any CCTV footage you've got from the Stockport hotel.'

Milton looked as if he was about to intervene, but Murrain shot him another glance. 'Don't ask for much, do you? OK, at our discretion. If you can give us good reasons.' He could definitely sense something now. A build-up of the energy that had been conspicuously absent during the earlier interview. Why should it be different now? What, other than Brennan's attitude, had changed? 'Can we hook up a laptop to the network in the interview room, Joe?'

Milton looked at Wanstead, who nodded. 'Shouldn't be a problem. Give me a few minutes.'

Murrain smiled at Brennan. 'OK, Brennan. We're in your hands. And, while we're waiting, I'll even go and make us all coffee. Biscuit, anyone?'

In the car, Holly seemed more than usually excited. There were times, Donovan thought, when her housemate could seem like an overgrown teenager. Tonight, she was drumming her hands on the steering wheel in time to some recent hit that meant nothing to Donovan, swearing impatiently every time they hit a traffic queue.

They were past the worst of rush-hour, but the M60 was still crowded and they hit a tailback just before the junction with the M56. 'Come on,' Holly called, apparently to the world in general. 'Come *on*, for Christ's sake!'

'Where is this place, anyway?' Donovan asked, shouting over the thump of the music.

'Just south of Chester. M56, then round Chester on the M53 so shouldn't take us long, as long as the traffic's not like this all the way. Come *on*!'

'Any idea what it's like?'

'One of those big country house places, I think. Want to make sure we get time for a decent pampering before we eat. I'm expecting some big hunky bloke to give me a massage.'

'Rather you than me,' Donovan said. 'I'll be more than happy just to lounge in a hot tub. For that matter, I'll be more than happy just to down a few glasses of wine.'

'You and me both,' Holly said. 'Anyway, the place is supposed to be good. Gets great write-ups.'

'Hope so. I've spent more than enough time in hotels this week. Could do with being in one just for pleasure.'

'I'm sure that can be arranged,' Holly said. 'One more hotel can't hurt, in the circumstances.'

Before Donovan could reply, Holly slammed her foot hard down on the accelerator and pulled out sharply, apparently into the path of a lorry in the next lane. But she was a skilled, if sometimes reckless, driver, and she was across into the outside lane in good time, leaving the lorry-driver with nothing to do but lean angrily on his horn. 'There,' she said. 'Nothing like living dangerously.'

Donovan took a breath. 'You can say that again.'

'Well,' Holly said, manoeuvring the car between two tailgating lorries to exit the junction at the last possible second, 'you have to show the bastards who's boss.'

'So what's this all about?' Murrain said. They were back in the interview room and had gone through all the formalities. Wanstead had successfully connected the laptop to the network, and Milton was waiting for Murrain's word to call up whatever data Brennan might be seeking. 'How do you think you can help us?'

'I was thinking about the three victims,' Brennan said. 'And why my name might have cropped up. They're all different, aren't they?'

'You've been in relationships with two of them,' Milton pointed out.

'But one was current, the other was years ago. She was someone I hadn't even thought about for a couple of years. Someone from a different life. Literally.'

'And yet, if we accept you're not involved, it looks as if the killer might have invited her to a meeting using your name,' Murrain said.

'That's what I'm saying. Why would someone do that, except to set me up?'

'*If* we accept that you're not involved,' Milton emphasised.

Brennan nodded wearily. 'Yeah. I get it. But let's run with that line for the moment, shall we? For argument's sake.'

'So why should the killer use your name to set up the meeting? Do you think Elizabeth Monk would have been unable to resist your company?'

'I doubt it.' Brennan laughed bitterly. 'But she didn't know me as Jack Brennan, did she? If the killer gave her that name, she wouldn't have been expecting *me*.'

'So what would she be expecting?' Milton asked. 'I don't see where this is going.'

'Neither do I, exactly,' Brennan said. 'But if I was the killer, why the hell would I use my own name.'

'That thought had occurred to us. But it doesn't answer the question of why the killer did use it.'

'The one that intrigues me most is the first victim,' Brennan said. 'Granger.'

'Kathryn Granger,' Murrain confirmed. 'What about her?'

'She's the odd one out.'

'Is she?' Murrain could feel the sensations building now. There was something here that had been absent when they'd spoken to Brennan before. Some narrative taking shape.

'In that I've never been in a relationship with her.'

'A small but no doubt select group,' Milton said. 'So what?'

'So if we assume that I'm significant to this, the question is why Kathryn Granger? Where does she fit? I was talking to Granger. Only for a short time, admittedly. But I'm guessing that anyone watching us wouldn't have had much doubt about my intentions.'

'So what are you saying?' Murrain said. 'That Granger was killed because she was unfortunate enough to have you chat her up?'

'Not quite that,' Brennan said. 'But it started me thinking along those lines. And about Granger.'

'And?'

'And I remembered something about her. Like I said, she was a decent looker but one of those 'butter wouldn't melt' types. But, thinking back, there were rumours about her at the time—or, at least, one rumour. That she was having some kind of clandestine affair.'

'We heard something along those lines from Andy Barton,' Murrain said. 'But nobody seems to know the details.'

'From what I remember she played the whole thing very close to her chest. There was gossip around the office that seemed to embarrass her. To be honest, I thought she was maybe just bigging the whole thing up to make herself seem more interesting. Difficult to imagine her in the throes of passion, if you get my gist. But they say it's always the quiet ones.'

'So why do you think this is relevant?'

'Because I suspect one of the office rumours was that the object of her affections was none other than yours truly.'

'But you were unattached, weren't you? Why would you need to keep it a secret?'

'Because I was working undercover at the time, I suppose. Or maybe just because I'd have been embarrassed if anyone discovered I was having it away with the office wallflower? I don't know. But you know what office gossip is like. Doesn't need to be rooted in anything substantial, does it? I had a reputation. One more conquest wouldn't have surprised anyone.'

'Says Sir Galahad,' Milton commented. 'But it wasn't you?'

'Not guilty on that occasion. Hadn't even made any kind of play for her.'

'Do you have any idea who it might have been?' Murrain asked. 'Assuming there was someone.'

'I had an idea,' Brennan said. 'I'll come back to that in a second. It links to another nagging thought I had about Saturday night.'

'I hope this is going somewhere,' Murrain said.

'I'm just thinking this is maybe the link. Two of the victims I've had a relationship with. The third—well, maybe the killer believes that I had a relationship with her.'

'You're suggesting that these women were being punished for having had a relationship with you?' Murrain said.

'As if they hadn't already suffered enough?' Milton added.

Brennan ignored that. 'I'm just following through the logic,' he said. 'I was wondering who might have been there on Saturday who was around back in the day. Who might have believed I'd had a relationship with Granger.'

'The Bartons themselves, presumably?'

'Yeah, obviously. But I'm assuming they have a watertight alibi for the last few days, being several thousand miles away and all.'

'So anyone else?'

'That's the thing. Something's been nagging at me. Someone I saw but didn't register at the time, if you know what I mean. You know how it is at a busy do like that. You see people across the room. Faces you haven't seen for years. You know them from somewhere but you can't really place them. There were a few like that. Some I said hello to, one or two I avoided for various reasons. And there were a couple I just glimpsed in passing across the room and didn't think much about.'

'And?'

'And there was one odd one. There was one person I ran into, in a different context, shortly afterwards. And it suddenly struck me that I might have seen the same person on Saturday night. Just in passing, across the room. At the time I hadn't even registered that I knew them. Maybe just because I hadn't expected to see them there. But I think maybe also because they'd made themselves look different.'

'How do you mean?'

'I'm not sure what I mean. That's why I want to have a look at the CCTV footage. I just have the impression in my mind of someone who didn't want to be recognised. And I'm wondering if I'm right.'

The sensations were growing stronger. Murrain could feel it now, like something coming closer. He looked over at Milton. 'Let's have a look, then, shall we? What do you want to see?'

Milton roused the laptop and tapped at the keyboard.

'Any footage you've got from inside the hotel during the evening,' Brennan said.

'There's not a tremendous amount of internal stuff,' Milton said. 'There was a camera in the reception, and a couple in the function room. Probably in case of any disturbances.' He turned the laptop screen round to Brennan. 'Function room to start?'

'Probably,' Brennan said.

They watched the screen in silence for a few minutes. The image resolution wasn't the best, but they could make out the figures reasonably clearly. Half-drunken people cavorting clumsily on the dance-floor. A spotlight on the happy couple. Jovial relatives raising their glasses. Brennan shook his head. 'Can we have a look at the reception?'

Milton tapped at the keyboard. A new set of images appeared. The reception area was much quieter than the function room had been. There were a couple of children playing, refugees from the melee. A steam of guests heading to the front doors to grab a cigarette. Clusters of guests sipping drinks away from the noise of the dance-floor.

'There,' Brennan said, suddenly. 'Can you rewind that?'

Milton obliged and slowed down the footage that Brennan had indicated. The camera covered the main reception area and the foot of the stairs to the first floor. The footage showed a figure crossing the lobby towards the function suite. 'Pause it there,' Brennan instructed.

The figure was caught in the middle of the screen. A blonde woman, in an evening dress with a shawl pulled closely around her shoulders.

'You know her?' Murrain asked.

'I'm pretty sure so,' Brennan said. 'Holly Finch.'

'Who's she?'

'Works as an analyst for the NCA in the office up here,' Brennan said. 'Someone I've made a point of avoiding when I'm visiting.'

'You have history with her?' Milton asked. 'That's hardly—' He stopped suddenly. 'Boss? You OK?'

Murrain had sat bolt upright, his body quivering as if he were about to have some kind of fit. His eyes were blank, fixed on a spot above Brennan's head, an empty point in the air. He was gripping the edge of the table, knuckles white. After a tense moment, his body relaxed and his eyes refocused. He went on as if nothing had happened, but with a renewed air of urgency: 'Tell us about Holly Finch.'

Brennan stared back at him for a moment. 'Like I say, she's an analyst—'

'Not now. Then,' Murrain interrupted.

'It's a long story. This is—what, ten, eleven years ago. There were three of us in those days, working out of Cheetham. Three undercover officers. It was an experiment to gather intelligence on the main gangs running the north of the city at the time. In the end, it got a bit hairy and they ended up discontinuing it. That was how I ended up buggering about with environmentalists.'

'Holly Finch,' Murrain pressed.

'Like I say, three of us. Three Musketeers we called ourselves— joking and not joking. you know. Thought ourselves a bit special. Me, Andy Barton and Ben Finch.'

'Ben Finch?'

'Husband of Holly. Strange guy, really. Not sure what it was. You might have said on the autistic spectrum. One of those people who doesn't engage with emotions like the rest of us. Don't get me wrong. Day to day, he was pleasant enough. But it was like that was learned behaviour. Everything was a rational calculation for him. If I do this,

227

that happens.' He took a breath. 'It started well, but the whole thing got very messy.'

'The whole thing?'

'The assignment wasn't working the way it should. It looked like there was some compromise.'

'Someone on the take?' Milton said.

Brennan glanced at the tape machine. 'As it turned out. Not for me to speculate on what exactly happened or who was involved, but something was going on. Maybe more than one thing. My suspicion now is that Ben Finch had gone over to the dark side. He should never have been given the job. Undercover work—well, it's a challenge. You're out there behind enemy lines. You're subject to temptations and pressures. You have to keep some kind of moral compass.' He looked at Milton and laughed. 'Yes, son. Even me. But I don't think Ben even had a moral compass. Or if he did south and north meant nothing to him. It was all just a calculation. He weighed up the risks and the potential profits and acted accordingly.'

'Where does Holly fit into this?'

'She was having an awful time. She genuinely loved Ben. But he was more and more difficult to live with, and she knew there was something going on. I was a shoulder to cry on.'

'You had an affair with her?'

'She was at a low ebb and I helped her out. But—well, yes.'

'And Ben found out?'

'I think he knew all the time. The weird thing was that he seemed unfazed. It was the emotionless thing again. Most men would have been angry or despairing or—something. He just took it in his stride and saw it as giving him a licence to do the same.'

'To have an affair?'

'Yeah.'

'With Kathryn Granger?'

'I never knew for sure. But that was my guess at the time. In the event, it didn't matter. A few weeks later, Ben went AWOL for good. That's one reason I didn't think much about Granger after that.'

'Went AWOL?'

'You'll find it all in the files. He went missing on assignment. Vanished from the address he was using while undercover. Never seen again. We investigated as much as we could, though there was always a nervousness about compromising other undercover officers. There were countless theories, as you can imagine. That he'd been taken out. That he'd been exposed and done a runner. Or that he'd gone to work for the other side.'

'And which did you think?'

'My guess is that he was taken out. I think he'd been on the take for a while, but I could see him trying to play both sides against the middle. Trying to find any way he could to maximise his share. It wouldn't take a lot for them to decide he couldn't be trusted.'

'What did this do to Finch?'

'Destroyed her. She had a complete collapse. I'd already split up with her. In her way, she was as much of a loose-cannon as Ben. Maybe that's what attracted them to each other in the first place. She was too much like hard work for me. She blamed me for Ben having an affair. Then blamed me for him disappearing. Everything was my fault.' He paused, thinking. 'Except that I think she blamed herself more. She thought she'd lost Ben because of what she'd done, that she'd let him down. That she deserved to suffer.'

Murrain was trying hard to concentrate. The sensations were as strong as ever, fizzing through his veins but he could no longer recapture the image that, moments before, had leapt into his head. The murder scene in the Stockport hotel. The knife. The figure that had somehow again looked not right, not what he had expected. 'What happened to her?'

'Complete mental collapse. She was a Crime Scene officer up in Lancashire. She'd always been a pretty tough cookie but that can be a stressful job at the best of times, given some of the things you have to witness. From what I heard she just collapsed one day, dealing with the aftermath of some grisly traffic collision. Was off work for months. I didn't go to see her. But I was told she was virtually catatonic. She was invalided out. When she came back—must have been a year or so later—she took on an admin role. She's moved a few times since and ended up in the NCA. As I was delighted to see when I made my first visit up here a few months back.'

'She recognised you then?'

'Oh, yes. I couldn't entirely avoid her, though I did my best. Just one of life's little inconveniences, I thought.'

'Inconveniences,' Murrain repeated. 'And you saw her at the hotel?'

'That's the thing.' He gestured towards the screen. 'You saw her there. That's not how she normally looks. She's wearing a blonde wig. She doesn't normally dress anything like that or wear make-up like that. I glimpsed her across a crowded room. It was one of those unconscious things, you know? I must have registered her without realising it. It was only when I saw her again a day or so later that the memory was triggered. But then I thought maybe I'd just imagined it. Brain playing tricks.'

'There was no reason why she shouldn't have been there, though? She must have known Andy Barton?'

'Andy had told me who was coming from the old days and she wasn't mentioned. I think with everything that had happened, she wasn't necessarily someone they'd want at the wedding. And why was she dressed like that?'

Murrain nodded. 'OK. So when you saw her again, it triggered that memory. Where did you see her? In the office?'

'No, I kept well out of her way there. I ran into her out of the blue. At Marie Donovan's place.'

Murrain looked up, feeling a sudden sharpening of the sensation. 'Marie? Why was Finch there?'

For the first time, Brennan looked confused. 'I thought you knew—' He stopped. 'No reason why you should have, I suppose. Thought it was just me kept in the dark.'

Milton had risen to his feet. 'Knew what?'

'That she shares a house with Marie. Moved in there recently, apparently. Lodger.' He stopped, a thought slowly percolating through his brain. 'Jesus, I've not been joining the dots myself.' The colour had drained from his face. 'Marie Donovan.'

'You're not seriously suggesting—' Milton said, waving his hand towards the screen.

'I think he is,' Murrain said. 'And I think he might just be right. That's why the figure didn't look right. I was expecting a man. Probably a big man. Someone who could have terrorised those women.'

'Christ.' Milton was staring at the blurred static image on the screen.

'Marie Donovan,' Brennan repeated. 'You see, we—'

'Had a relationship,' Murrain finished. 'Of course you did.' The sensation was like a steady pulse now, filling his brain, but he continued calmly. 'Joe, get her on the phone.'

Milton was staring back at him, his face as white as Brennan's. 'I'll try,' he said. 'But she told me before she left—' He stopped and swallowed. 'She was going for a girls' night out tonight. At some spa hotel in Cheshire. With her housemate.'

CHAPTER TWENTY SIX

'Usual rules,' Holly said. 'No calls on the mobile. No texts, messages or e-mails. We just chill.'

Marie Donovan hesitated. They were in the middle of a major case. She already felt like she was goofing off, even if Murrain had told everyone to get a good night's rest. She wasn't sure this was quite what he'd had in mind. She did know he wouldn't be best pleased if he tried to contact her urgently and found her incommunicado. 'Well, I'll try,' she said, finally. 'Might need to check messages later in case anything blows up on this case.'

Holly looked disapproving. 'Well, maybe I'll allow that. But not till later. And not every five minutes.'

'Fair enough.' Donovan's phone was buried in her handbag anyway, and she'd left it on silent after the interviews. 'I want to relax as much as you do.'

They'd made good time down to the hotel. After the brief jam at the M56 junction, the motorways had been clear and it hadn't take them long to reach the junction off the M53.

'Have you been here before?' Donovan asked.

Holly shook her head. 'Had a look at the map before we set off.'

In the early weekday evening, the car-park was relatively quiet. To Donovan's slight surprise, Holly picked a spot away from the main reception near one of the wings of the hotel building. It was an imposing-looking place, an extended Edwardian mansion raised sufficiently above the surrounding countryside to afford an extended view of the vast Cheshire plain, the lights of Chester visible to the north.

Holly pulled two holdalls out of the boot, handing one to Donovan. 'This way,' she said, heading towards the far end of the hotel wing.

'Don't we need to check in first?'

Holly shook her head. 'They do an on-line check in thing. I got us a room at this end of the hotel, so we're nearer the spa.'

'Right.' Donovan followed hesitantly down the gravelled path round the back of the building. 'But the room keys—'

'All sorted.' Holly had already vanished round the corner.

Donovan gazed after her for a moment and then shrugged. She knew from experience that Holly was skilled at short-circuiting bureaucracy. She was one of those people who could get things done without following the usual rules or procedures, either by sweet-talking officialdom or simply by knowing what would work. Christ knew what she'd done this time.

Holly was waiting by a rear entrance that looked like a Fire Exit, but was accessible to guests with the right card-key or access code. However she'd managed it, Holly was holding open the door. 'Come on,' she said. 'I'm still hoping to fit in my hunky man massage.'

Donovan laughed and followed her into the hotel corridor. 'Which is our room?'

'This one.' Holly gestured towards the door nearest the exit. 'Thought if we were up at the end, we wouldn't disturb anyone with our drunken giggling.'

'If you say so,' Donovan said, thinking that. given her need to be back in the office bright and early, the scope for drunken giggling would be limited.

Holly had produced a card-key from somewhere and was opening the door. She dropped her overnight bag inside and stood back to allow Donovan to follow.

Holly caught Donovan's quizzical expression as she ushered her past. 'Yes, I did get a key,' she said. 'I was here earlier, you see. Preparing things.'

Marie Donovan heard the hotel room door close behind her. She dropped her handbag on the bed and looked around the room. Finally, she turned. 'Holly?' she said. 'What the fuck?'

'I should have realised earlier,' Brennan said. 'Josie wouldn't have gone to that dump of a hotel by herself for no reason. Finch had access to the

233

secure lines and codes. Josie probably thought I'd called her to that meeting.'

'Another trail that would have been uncovered in due course, no doubt,' Murrain said. 'Putting you even more in the frame.'

Milton was punching away at his computer keyboard. 'How many bloody spa hotels can there be in Cheshire?'

'Quite a few, I'm guessing,' Murrain said. 'She didn't give you any more clues that than?'

' 'Out in Cheshire' was all she said.'

Murrain peered over his shoulder. 'How about trying to find out which ones Patrick Henessey's got a stake in?'

'There's a name from the past,' Brennan said. 'Paddy Henessey. Where does that old crook fit into this?'

'You've come across Mr Henessey, then?' Murrain said. 'I don't know where he fits in or even if he does. But he has a substantial stake in all three hotels where we've found the murder victims. Another coincidence.'

'More than you think,' Brennan said. He glanced at the now-forgotten interview tape. Murrain took the hint and reached to switch it off. 'I don't know if I'd say this on the record,' Brennan went on. 'Too easy to make enemies. But Henessey was a big presence in the days of the three musketeers. I reckon he was Ben Finch's paymaster. Or one of them, anyway.'

'You think he might have been responsible for Finch's disappearance.'

'I think it's likely,' Brennan said. 'Henessey always wanted to be in control. If he thought someone was two-timing him he could be a ruthless bastard. Christ, this is beginning to feel like a sodding school reunion.'

'I think, in its way, that's exactly what it is,' Murrain said. 'And we all know how much fun those can be, don't we?'

Milton was still drumming away on the keyboard. 'OK, I've got the Companies' House website up. What the hell do I do? Cross-check it with Trip Advisor?'

'The hotel booking sites might not be a bad place to start,' Murrain said. 'Spa hotels in Cheshire. If we can get a short-list, we can see what ownership data's on their websites, try to match those up with Companies' House to find director information. Maybe also look for any owned by a company with 'Paradise' in the name. That seems to be one of Henessey's favourites.'

Milton looked up at the clock. 'It's like looking for a needle in a bloody haystack.'

They'd already put the south and west Manchester neighbourhood teams on alert so they could get officers out to any destination as quickly as possible. Murrain had calls into Cheshire Police for back-up but had heard nothing back. They didn't have the resources to start trawling every country-house hotel in Cheshire.

'It's all we can do,' Murrain said. 'And there's always the possibility—'

'That the old spider sense might start tingling?' Milton said. 'Christ, boss, I've never wanted that more.'

'Keep going, Joe,' Murrain said, ignoring the quizzical look from Brennan. 'It's all we've got at the moment.'

'Too right.' Milton's eyes were fixed on the screen. 'OK. Hotels. Cheshire. Filtered by spa. Here we go.'

'I don't know if I've given you the wrong impression,' Marie Donovan said, slowly. 'But this really isn't my scene, Holly.'

'So what is your scene, Marie? Stealing other women's men?'

Donovan was still gazing slowly round the room. 'I've never—'

'Jack Brennan?'

She turned to face Holly. 'What? Jack and I were scarcely an item. And as far as I'm aware he was unattached. Unless you're telling me different.'

The room was startling. Both single beds had been stripped and covered with plastic sheeting. Similar sheeting was spread across the floor. On the coffee table in the middle of the room, there was a leather bag containing a neat row of metal instruments. Donovan didn't want to think about what the function of those instruments might be. There was another leather case on the dressing table, holding what appeared to be a row of butcher's knives. On one of the single beds, there was an open holdall containing a set of women's clothes.

'And what about betraying your own partner, Marie? Is that something you're into?'

That one hit closer to home. Donovan had had a brief, and ultimately traumatic, affair during her first undercover assignment. There had been extenuating circumstances, she'd tried to tell herself, and her late partner had never known. But it wasn't something she was proud to recall. There was no way Holly could have known, though.

'I don't know what the hell you're talking about, Holly. What the fuck is all this?'

But, really, she already knew what it was. She couldn't bring herself to believe it, but it made some kind of sense. The killer who had entered and left each of those hotels without being noticed. A killer who understood enough about investigating crime scenes to ensure that no identifying trace was left. The odd-looking Mr James who had first checked into the hotel in Stockport. The women who had apparently checked-in voluntarily to the hotels where they met their deaths. The women who had apparently been able to check out even after the victims were already dead. Three victims. Three women who loosely resembled one another. Three women who loosely resembled Holly.

And herself.

Jack Brennan's type.

Donovan took a step back, registering now that Holly had positioned herself in front of the bedroom door. She was holding a large, sharp-looking knife that seemed the match of those in the case. It might be possible to force a way past her, but if Holly was as ruthless as Donovan feared she might be one thrust from that blade would be enough.

Donovan tried to force herself to think calmly. Whatever the odds, she wasn't one of life's natural victims. She wouldn't go down without a fight. 'Look, Holly,' she said. 'I don't have a clue what this is all about.'

Holly shook her head. 'You don't really, do you? I'm sorry it had to be you, Marie. You've been good to me in your way. Better than most. But you're just another one of them, aren't you?' She paused. 'Another one of us.'

'Another one of *what*?' Donovan persisted.

'Another woman who betrays her man. Another woman who causes men to stray.'

'This is bollocks, Holly. You know it is. Men have a choice, too, you know? Especially men like Jack sodding Brennan.'

The expression is Holly's eyes shifted from pain or despair to something like anger. 'You don't know, do you?' she said. 'You really don't understand.'

'No, Holly, I really don't.'

'We're all the same,' Holly said. 'All the same. I betrayed Ben, and he left me. He was right to leave me. But then another of you— another of us—took Jack from me. And continued to take him, year after year, time after time. Jack loved me, but there was always another one to take him away.'

'What prompted all this, Holly? What started it?'

Holly looked as her in surprise, as if the question was unnecessary. 'Seeing Jack again after all these years. Realising that nothing had changed. That I had to stop it. Stop us. Release Jack.'

Donovan shook her head, baffled now by a logic she couldn't begin to comprehend. 'Look, Holly—' She had no idea what she might say next, what magic formula might extricate her from this madness.

Holly was simply smiling back at her, seemingly no different from the woman who, only minutes before, had been talking about wine and massages and pampering.

Now, though, she was raising the bright-bladed knife.

'It's time for you to undress,' Holly said, her voice expressionless. 'We need to prepare you.'

CHAPTER TWENTY SEVEN

'Bingo,' Milton said. 'Here.'

Murrain craned to stare at the screen. The website for a spa hotel near Chester called Belstone Hall. Milton pointed to the small print at the bottom of the home page. 'Registered company: Paradise Leisure. I've cross-checked on the Companies' House site. Sure enough, one of the Directors is Patrick Henessey.' He looked up. 'What do you reckon?'

He was looking for more than simple agreement. Murrain was staring at the screen, his eyes unfocused. 'That's it,' he said, finally. 'That's the one.' He straightened. 'Right. You drive, Joe, and I'll sort back up.'

It took them only another five minutes to reach Milton's car parked under the building. All the way down, Murrain had been on the phone to the control room, organising back up from the GMP neighbourhood teams, briefing the relevant senior officers including the Chief. Then he switched his attention to Cheshire Police, eventually getting himself connected to the Duty Chief Superintendent. He outlined the situation succinctly and asked for an armed response team. 'It may be over-the-top,' he acknowledged, 'but we don't know what we're facing. We already have three brutally murdered victims, and one of our own officers who may have been lured into an ambush.' A pause. 'Yes, of course, I'll take responsibility. But I won't take responsibility for an officer's death if we've not received the necessary support.' Another pause. 'Yes, sir, I appreciate that. I've cleared it up the line with my people, of course. You can speak to the Duty Chief Superintendent here. She'll vouch for me and for what I'm saying. Thank you, sir. It's much appreciated. We can't be too careful.' He ended the call and allowed himself a faint smile of relief.

'Eloise on duty tonight, then?' Milton asked.

'Thank Christ.'

They'd allowed Brennan to accompany them. Murrain had hesitated momentarily about this—it was only an hour or so since they'd been interviewing him as a potential suspect—but decided that

Brennan's presence might be helpful. Now, Brennan sat slumped in the rear seat, shaking his head as if in disbelief at what was happening.

Murrain closed his eyes as Milton pulled out of the car-park. He knew full well that Milton was a trained and experienced high-speed driver, but that didn't provide any immediate reassurance. He opened his eyes only when Milton had skilfully manoeuvred the car into the far lane, heading south out of town.

'Don't take any unnecessary risks,' Murrain warned.

'I won't. May take some necessary ones, though.' Milton's eyes were fixed on the road ahead, half-closed in concentration. They had no blue lights, but Murrain had advised the control room of their intended route. The last thing they needed was to be delayed by some over-zealous traffic officers.

Murrain turned to look at Brennan. 'You really think she might be capable of this stuff?'

'Maybe. Like I say, she was always a loose cannon. She got fixated on me, wanted to see me as the love of her life. As if I'd be the love of anyone's life, let alone hers. She'd got some idealised picture of me in her head, just because I was there when she was going through the hard times with Ben. She'd seen him in the same way at first, then that went pear-shaped so she transferred it to me. To me, it was just a fling. To her, it was—'

'True love?'

'An obsession, I was going to say. I couldn't shake her off. She kept pursuing me. Phone-calls, turning up on my doorstep.'

'She was the one who brought the harassment case against you?' Murrain guessed.

'That's right. Revenge.'

'No substance in it?'

Brennan hesitated a fraction of a second too long, giving Murrain the answer. 'It was something and nothing,' he said, finally. 'She was the one pursuing me. I just tried to turn the tables a bit.'

Murrain made no response. Brennan went on: 'She blamed herself when Ben left her. Because she'd 'betrayed' him. I don't honestly think Ben gave a bugger about that. He left because he got a better offer, quite literally. Then she decided I was the one, and when I went off she blamed—well, me to some extent, but mainly the woman she thought I'd gone off with. Because she'd seduced me away.'

'And it wasn't like that?'

'Christ, no. I finished with Holly because I'd had enough. There were a string of women after that. None of them meant anything. But Holly got wind of one of them and started hassling her. That was out of order. I ran into her at a training thing and—well, I probably got heavy with her. She twisted it and made it sound like I'd tried to assault her. Put me through several months of hell till it got dropped.'

They were out of the town now and on to the motorway, Milton hogging the outside lane and flashing his lights at anyone in their path. Murrain chose not to look at the speedometer.

'They dropped it in the end because they'd recognised what she was like. She was definitely an unreliable witness by that stage.' He paused, thinking. 'A woman I'd been seeing was attacked one night, coming back after we'd been out in town. Vicious assault, right outside her own house. Left her badly bruised and cut. Police thought it was a mugging that had turned nasty, though the attacker fled without taking anything. Never occurred to me at the time, but—' His voice trailed off and he remained staring out of the window. 'Jesus.'

Murrain turned away as his mobile rang. The control room with an update. They were liaising fully with Cheshire now and had three cars heading out to the hotel. The armed team was being mustered, with the Duty Chief Superintendent, one CS McLeish, assigned as gold commander. Murrain had orders to phone him without delay. Moments later, as he'd half-expected, he received a call from Eloise.

'I've just had a Chief Superintendent McLeish on the phone asking about you.'

'Thought you might. What did you tell him?'

'The truth, obviously.'

'Shit. I'd better turn back then.'

'Well, not the whole truth. I'm not an idiot.'

'No, you're definitely not that.' Not even if you made the mistake of marrying me, he added silently to himself. 'So what did you say?'

'I said you were as mad as a box of frogs, but a bloody good copper.' She paused. 'Not in quite so many words.'

'That's good, I suppose.'

'I said that, if you thought this was necessary then he'd be well advised to trust your instincts. And that if he didn't he'd have to take responsibility for that.'

'What did he say?'

'He seemed happy to accept that. He was pretty switched on, actually.'

'That's good to hear, anyway. Did he know that I'm your husband?' Eloise had always used her maiden surname at work.

A pause. 'No, I don't think I got round to mentioning it, since you ask.'

'Well, why would you?'

'No reason. Except that, not for the first time, I'm sticking my neck on the block for you. I just hope you know what the bloody hell you're doing.'

He'd taken that as a gesture of support. 'So do I, El. So do I.'

Eloise's call was followed by another from the Cheshire Chief Superintendent. Murrain updated him as fully as he could.

'And you've no idea what we might be facing?' McLeish asked.

'Not really. It might be nothing. Which would be a relief, even if it would leave me looking like a prize numpty.'

'I'll be content to send your Chief the bill for our time,' McLeish said. 'But you've reason to believe this Holly Finch could be dangerous?'

'Very good reason.'

'OK. We'll tread carefully. Any idea where they're likely to be?'

'She'll have booked a room,' Murrain said. 'That's the track record. But probably not under her own name. You could try Marie Donovan. That's our officer.' He paused. 'Or maybe Josie Martin.'

'Currently plan is to approach the place discreetly. We've already spoken to the management there—tried to prepare them for our arrival without panicking them.'

'We don't want them doing anything that might spook Finch,' Murrain said. 'She's likely to be unstable.'

'Point taken. I'll get someone to speak to them again and find out about the booking. We've a couple of cars approaching there now, so once we've got an idea of where she's likely to be, we can do something to control the situation. How long are you likely to be?'

Murrain looked at the rapidly passing landscape. 'Maybe fifteen minutes.'

'Right. Lead officer on the ground there is a DI Ronson. I'll tell him to wait for you in the hotel lobby unless you hear different. Then you can decide your plan of action. Ronson'll liaise with me.'

'Very good, sir,' Murrain said. 'And thanks for all your help.'

'No problem,' McLeish said, then paused. 'Well, no problem if you're right.'

Swinging the large knife loosely by her side, Holly took a slow step forward.

'What the hell is this, Holly?' Donovan said. 'I'm not undressing. I'm not doing anything for you. This has gone far enough.'

'Nothing like far enough, sadly.' Holly's voice now sounded as if it were tinged with genuine regret. 'I have to carry on until I've dealt with us all. That slut Kathy Granger. Beth Monk. Josie Martin. You. Me. Every one of us.'

'Don't you understand,' Donovan said, 'you won't get any further. They'll catch up with you. Murrain and his team are right behind you. It's only a matter of time now. You need to stop this. Get help.' Donovan realised she was talking just to hear the sound of her own voice, just to try to keep Holly engaged. Trying to buy herself just a few more moments even if she had no idea what she might do with them.

Holly shrugged. 'It doesn't matter. Maybe they'll catch up eventually. Perhaps even very soon. But I'll make sure I'm the last victim. I'm the one that deserves it most.' For the first time she smiled although there was nothing comforting in her eyes. 'But that's not all. I want to punish Jack Brennan for allowing them to do it, again and again.'

'Christ, Holly. We're not the guilty ones,' Donovan said. 'Not even Jack Brennan. Don't you understand. We did nothing wrong. I didn't steal Jack Brennan from you or from anyone. I had a brief—thing with him, that's all. As far as I knew—as far as I know—we were both free agents. No-one deserves to die for that.' Donovan had taken a step back, wondering whether there was any way of getting past Holly. If she could maybe reach the bathroom, lock herself in, snatch enough time to use the phone that was still buried in the handbag she'd dropped on to the corner of the bed in her confusion when they'd first entered the room.

'We all deserve to die,' Holly said. It was, Donovan realised, the voice of a religious zealot. The voice of someone who had handed over her life, her actions, to a truth that only she could comprehend. She was still holding the knife, blade forward, with the air of a priest preparing to perform a sacrifice. 'Jack Brennan most of all. For abandoning me when I needed him. For allowing himself to be seduced, over and over again. He's already implicated in these murders. When they catch up and find my body, it won't look like suicide. I've taken steps to ensure he'll be implicated even more.'

'They won't fall for that.'

'Maybe, maybe not. They'll arrest him and the murders will have stopped. He'll be a convenient scapegoat. Whatever the outcome, they'll make his life hell in the process. Jack Brennan's got enough skeletons locked away not to want anyone investigating him. He'll be destroyed.' It sounded like the purest form of madness.

'None of this make sense, Holly,' Donovan said, searching for another way to engage, another angle. 'Look, you said it yourself this afternoon, I took you in when you needed it. I *helped* you, for Christ's sake.' Though now, of course, it was occurring to her to wonder whether Holly had simply engineered that, had inserted herself unwanted into Donovan's life so that they could end up here tonight. 'I helped you when you needed it.'

Holly shook her head, though it was impossible to read her expression. 'Like I say, Marie, I'm sorry you were part of this. I'm sorry you were one of us. But you are.' She took another step forward, raising the knife higher. 'We need to get started.'

Donovan made as if she were about to begin undressing, as if about to begin the bizarre transformation ritual that Holly had conjured out of her own head as the heart of this sacrifice. But she knew she would have only this one opportunity. As soon as she began to follow Holly's instructions, she would render herself even more vulnerable, even more in Holly's power.

She risked a glance over. If she could somehow manage to scramble across the bed, grab the handbag, reach the temporary safety of the bathroom. It was a huge gamble, with that perfectly-sharpened knife only inches away, but she could see no alternative.

She fingered the buttons on her blouse as if about to unfasten them. Then, trying her best not to telegraph her intentions, she threw herself across the wide kingsize bed, scrabbling for her handbag as she rolled.

At almost the same moment, realising Donovan's intent, Holly lunged forward with the knife, its blade ripping into the thick white duvet. It was too late, Donovan thought. It was already too late.

Holly was looming above her, and now all Donovan could do was clutch the leather bag to her chest in the vain hope of warding off the irresistible blade of the descending knife.

CHAPTER TWENTY EIGHT

As they approached the hotel, Milton had finally slowed, wanting to draw no attention to their arrival. Murrain relaxed back into his seat. 'We seem to be in one piece,' he observed. 'Well done.'

Milton pulled into a space beside a Cheshire marked-car parked discreetly at one end of the car park. Murrain could see an unmarked van and several other occupied cars which he guessed contained local officers. Even an ambulance parked silently at the edge of the car-park. McLeish had lived up to his side of the deal. Plenty of resource but all very quiet and unobtrusive.

Murrain climbed out of the car and made his way to the front entrance, Milton and Brennan following behind. A figure in a dark woollen overcoat was standing outside, finishing a cigarette. 'DCI Murrain?' he said.

'DI Ronson?'

Ronson crushed his cigarette into the bin by the doors and shrugged apologetically. 'Have to take the opportunities where I can these days.' He gestured towards the hotel lobby. 'We've got everything under control as far as we can. We've told the hotel we're investigating reports of a possible incident in one of the rooms. Kept it as low-key and vague as possible, partly so as not to spook anyone and partly to minimise the risk of any word getting back to the room in question.'

'You know which room it is?'

'You were right,' Ronson said. 'Check in was under the name Josie Martin.'

'That at least confirms we're not wasting our time,' Murrain said. 'It's in line with the previous murders.'

'Room 128. Ground floor, far end of that corridor.' He pointed along the length of the lobby. 'It's the room you'd pick if you wanted to be as far away as possible from other guests. Understand from reception that she requested it specifically because she wanted somewhere quiet.' He allowed himself a faint smile. 'She may get a shock on that front.'

'You've an armed team here?'

'On standby, at the moment, if we should need them.'

'Any clues what might be happening in the room?'

'I was hoping you'd be able to enlighten us on that. We've checked from the outside. Curtains tightly drawn. No way of seeing in. The room next door was unoccupied so we've had someone in there with equipment trying to pick up any sounds. But it's solidly-built old place. All we can get is the murmur of voices. Two females. That's what you expected?'

Murrain nodded. 'We believe our officer, Marie Donovan, is in the room with the suspected killer, Holly Finch. Shall we go and see where things stand?'

Ronson led the way inside. 'We've used the 'possible incident' line with the guests as well,' he said, indicating that the corridor in question had been cordoned off. 'We've asked guests in that wing not to return to their rooms for the moment. Most are at dinner anyway, and the rest are in the lounges and bars. Nobody seems agitated just yet.'

'OK. We really don't know what we're dealing with here,' Murrain said. 'All I can tell you is that the previous murders have been extremely brutal, especially the most recent. The killings have all been stabbings, and we've no particular reason to think Finch might have a firearm but she's not someone who seems to have much concern for the sanctity of human life.' He looked behind him. 'I don't think we can afford any risk she might get out into the public areas.'

'Understood. Maybe position a couple of the armed team at this end of the corridor. And a couple outside at the far end. There's a fire escape just beyond the bedroom.'

'If we can get them in there discreetly,' Murrain said. 'I don't want to panic the clientele.'

'We can do that,' Ronson said. 'And then all we have to do is go down there and find out what's going on.'

'And stop it,' Milton added from behind them. 'Before it's too late.' He paused, and looked up at the ornate clock over the reception. 'If it isn't already.'

It took Ronson only a few minutes to organise the back-up team, once he'd cleared the tactics with McLeish back at HQ. Armed officers positioned discreetly in the corridors and outside the fire escape, further back-up in the reception, outside in the car-park and at the rear of the hotel. He'd obtained Kevlar vests for Murrain and Milton as well as for his own officers. Miraculously, Ronson had achieved this without alerting any of the guests to the serious nature of the operation.

'OK,' Murrain said. 'I think it's up to us now.' He'd asked the hotel management to supply them with a duplicate of the card-key for Room 128. Although the room was lockable from the inside, there was no point in battering down the door if a simpler solution was available.

He and Milton made their way along the corridor, with Ronson and two other local officers following behind. Brennan had been left in the reception, Murrain's judgement being that his presence was unlikely to be helpful until they had a better understanding of what they were facing.

Once the double-doors from the lobby had closed behind them, the corridor seemed eerily silent, the heavy pile carpeting swallowing even their own steps. Twenty feet from Room 128, Murrain paused. 'We need to get in there,' he said. 'Quickly but cautiously. I'll try the card-key and hope it works. If it doesn't, we'll have to kick the door in or crowbar it open, which I'm guessing won't be easy in a place like this. That'll give Finch more time, so Christ knows what it might mean, but I don't see an alternative. Let's try the easy route first. Look after yourselves if I manage to throw the door open.'

This was the moment, he thought, when he desperately needed some intuition, some clue as to what the hell was going on in there. But, true to form, the transmitters had shut themselves down just when they were most needed. It was as if, when it all finally became real, all the feelings, the visions, just dissolved away.

He took another step forward, preparing for the instant when he'd slip the card into the locking mechanism, and it would work or it wouldn't. And the moment, beyond that, when they'd find out what was in that room.

It never happened. Or not in that way.

As he took the step forward, they all heard the scream—loud, piercing, agonised. A scream of horror at what was happening or what was being witnessed. A scream of terror at what would happen next.

Then it stopped. It died away into a moan and then into silence.

Murrain didn't hesitate. He jumped forward and thrust the card into the door, hoping against hope that it would work, that they would be in time to do something. 'Police,' he shouted, trying to make his voice heard through the thick panelling.

Inevitably, the card failed on his first attempt, the lock blinking a red light. Desperately, he tried again, trying to calm himself, to slide the card smoothly into the aperture. The light turned green and, finally, the handle gave under his hand and the door opened, a foot or so, before jamming against some object. He pushed it harder, Milton next to him, adding his weight.

Then the door was open and they were able to see into the room.

Pools of crimson blood spreading slowly across the pristine cream carpet. Splashes of blood on the walls and bedding, seeping across now useless protective sheeting, dripping softly and steadily on to the floor. A scene from Hell.

And bodies. Two bodies. One slumped on the floor by the door, still preventing it from opening fully. One spread face down on the bed, blood pouring from beneath it.

Two bodies, both drenched with the ever-flowing blood.

CHAPTER TWENTY NINE

It had seemed to take forever for the ambulances to arrive, although Milton knew it was only minutes. Not, he thought, that it mattered.

Murrain had caught the look in Milton's eyes and suggested he should travel in the ambulance containing Marie Donovan. He and the Cheshire team would stay behind to sort out the aftermath in the hotel and begin the endless paperwork that would inevitably follow from this. Murrain could collect Milton later.

As the ambulance headed into Chester, Milton gazed at the tightly-wrapped body lying beside him. He felt presumptuous and somehow intrusive being here. But he hadn't wanted her to be alone, and, after all, who else was there? Someone, somewhere, presumably, who cared, but he didn't know who.

They were almost at the hospital before her eyes finally flickered open. 'Christ Almighty,' she said.

'Near enough,' he said. 'Joe Milton.' Next to him, one of the paramedics began checking the drip attached to her arm, encouraging her not to get agitated.

She managed a smile at that. 'I'm all right?' she asked, finally.

'You seem to be. A couple of cuts, one of them pretty deep apparently. But Kenny was able to provide some improvised first-aid and you didn't lose much blood. And we had the paramedics standing by so you got treated immediately. But they'll check you out properly once we get to the hospital. You'd collapsed in there but they reckoned it was probably shock as much as anything else.'

Still wrapped in the blankets, she tried to shake her head. 'She did it,' she said. 'She was behind it. She tried to kill me and then—' She stopped.

'What?'

'I don't know. I don't know what happened in there. I was on the bed. She was trying to kill me. I was screaming—'

'That was what brought us in there.'

'That was it,' she went on. 'There was the sound at the door. Someone trying to come in. Then Murrain shouting.'

249

'What happened?'

She paused, trying to make sense of her still chaotic memories. 'I think she knew it was over. That she'd got to the end. She stopped lunging at me and I was able to scramble my way out from underneath her. Then—' She stopped again, her eyes wide. Milton could see that the paramedic was considering sedation, but after a moment she went on, calmly enough: 'She held the knife against her stomach and thrust herself on to it. Like, you know, *hara-kiri*.' She was staring up at Milton. 'She killed herself instead of me. It was—I don't know—as if she was completing the ritual.'

Milton glanced up at the paramedic, who was preparing a sedative in a syringe, and nodded. She needed the rest, he thought. 'But why did she do it?' he asked, more of himself that of her. 'And why all the changes of identify, the changes of the victims' clothes—why all that?'

She gazed back up at him. 'That was part of the ritual. She thought we were all interchangeable. That we were all the same. Her, me, all the other victims. All just the same women, there to lead astray the likes of poor Jack Brennan.' She laughed, for the first time since she'd woken, but it was a bitter laugh. 'Which I suppose isn't far from the way that the likes of Jack see us, anyway.'

Her voiced trailed off, and the paramedic took the opportunity to inject the sedative.

Lying there, Milton thought, she looked incredibly, desperately vulnerable, with her dark eyes and her bleached white skin. He knew it wasn't true but he felt in that moment as if, more than anything, she needed him, she needed his protection.

He told himself it was ridiculous. He was ending up as not much better than a well-intentioned Jack Brennan, seeing her not as the strong woman she was, but just as a target for his dubious affections. In any case, for the moment at least, he was spoken for. He had a partner. Three hundred or so miles away, and maybe not coming back. But still his partner.

He started to move away to let the paramedic get on with his work. But, as he moved, Marie Donovan reached to take his hand. Her eyes were already blurring.

'Still can't do it tonight,' she said, her voice fading. 'But don't forget, Joe. You promised you'd take me for a drink.'

About Alex Walters

Alex has worked in the oil industry, broadcasting and banking and now runs a consultancy working mainly in the criminal justice sector including police, prisons and probation.

As Michael Walters, he has published three crime novels set in modern-day Mongolia. As Alex Walters he has written two books set in and around Manchester and featuring the undercover officer, Marie Donovan, *Trust No-One* and *Nowhere to Hide*. *Late Checkout* is the first in a series featuring, alongside Marie Donovan, the rather distinctive DCI Kenny Murrain. The second book in the series, *Dark Corners*, is scheduled for publication in Autumn 2016.

Alex lives in Manchester with his wife, occasional sons and too many cats.

He can be contacted at: mike@whitmuir.com
Twitter: @mikewalters60
Facebook: www.facebook.com/alexwaltersauthor/
Blog: https://mikewalters.wordpress.com/

Printed in Great Britain
by Amazon

66407610R00145